Bill Daly lives and writes in his native Glasgow where his bestselling DCI Charlie Anderson novels are set. In 2016 he was awarded the Constable Trophy by the Scottish Association of Writers. *Never Proven* is the fourth in the series.

PRAISE FOR THE DCI ANDERSON SERIES

'Daly evokes Glasgow with a masterly touch'
ALEX GRAY

'Impressive … a vivid new voice in Tartan noir'
MAGGIE CRAIG

'A stylish police thriller … includes a beautifully formulated "locked room" mystery … a cracking read'
DAILY MAIL on *Double Mortice*

'Brilliantly gripping and fast-moving … and the characters all have a rich credibility'
EUROCRIME on *Black Mail*

'Daly effortlessly incorporates the seedy underbelly of the city… *Black Mail* can proudly sit alongside books by far more established writers in the Glasgow noir field … A highly enjoyable debut' **crimefict.uk/libraries**

NEVER PROVEN

NEVER PROVEN

Bill Daly

Published in Great Britain in 2018 by Old Street Publishing
c/o Parallel, 8 Hurlingham Business Park, Sulivan Road
London SW6 3DU

www.oldstreetpublishing.co.uk

ISBN 978-1-910400-77-7

The right of Bill Daly to be identified as the author of this work has been asserted by him
in accordance with the Copyright, Designs and Patents Act 1988.

10 9 8 7 6 5 4 3 2 1

A CIP catalogue record for this title is available from the British Library.

Typeset by JaM

Printed and bound in Great Britain.

For Lesley, Dan & Stevie

CHAPTER 1

Saturday 3 September

Jack Mulgrew was whistling tunelessly as he came out of the toilet cubicle, his eyes cast down as his gnarled fingers fumbled with the buckle on his belt. He smiled to himself when he heard the opening bars of *I Will Survive* pulsing down from the karaoke session in the lounge upstairs. Gloria Gaynor was one of his favourites. He stopped whistling and started to sing along. As he glanced up, the words of the song died on his lips when he saw the two men leaning against the far wall. He recognised Jim Colvin straight away; improbably-black, slicked-back hair, trademark sharp suit, blue silk shirt and matching tie. He didn't know the squat figure by Colvin's side; unkempt hair, short-sleeved T-shirt, muscular, tattooed arms, flabby stomach bulging over the waistband of his jeans.

'I wasn't expecting to see you here tonight, Jim,' Mulgrew stammered.

'I'm like the Spanish Inquisition, Mulgrew.' Colvin gave a mirthless smile. 'I turn up when I'm least expected.'

'I'll get it sorted, Jim.'

'I seem to remember that's what you told me last week,' Colvin said, his words echoing from the tiled walls.

'I did, Jim. I know I did.' Beads of sweat started to form on Mulgrew's wrinkled forehead. 'Just give me a break!"

You had your chance – and you blew it,' Colvin interjected as he started walking slowly towards Mulgrew. 'I told you last week that you were on a final warning. You know what's coming now. Sit down on the floor.'

'No, Jim, not that.'

Colvin hooked his foot around Mulgrew's ankles and swept his legs from under him, causing him to crash to the ground. 'I don't like having to repeat myself, Mulgrew. Now sit up straight with your back against the door.'

As Mulgrew was scrambling into a sitting position, Colvin nodded to his companion. 'Okay, let's do this.'

The steel-tipped heels of the enforcer's boots clattered on the floor as he strode across.

Colvin bent down and grabbed Mulgrew's right arm.

'No!' Mulgrew pleaded. 'Not that, Jim! Don't do it!'

Stretching Mulgrew's arm out straight, Colvin held his wrist against the wooden door of the toilet cubicle while the enforcer produced a six-inch nail from the hip pocket of his jeans. Unhooking the claw hammer hanging from his belt, he placed the point of the nail against Mulgrew's closed fist.

'Open your hand,' Colvin demanded.

'For God's sake! No!' Mulgrew yelped.

'I told you to open your fucking hand,' Colvin repeated forcibly.

'I'll have it sorted by Tuesday, Jim. Honest – I will!'

'It's your call,' Colvin said with a dismissive shrug. 'But it'll be a hell of a lot worse for you if the nail has to go through your fingers first.'

His whole body shaking, Mulgrew slowly unclenched his fist and spread his trembling fingers.

Holding the hammer poised, the enforcer made eye contact with Colvin, then, on Colvin's nod, he drove the point of the nail into the palm of Mulgrew's splayed hand.

'One!' Colvin chimed, to the crescendo of: *I've got all my life to live.* 'Two!' The head of the nail was thumped again: *And all my love to give.* 'Three!' Another solid blow from the hammer: *And I'll survive. I will survive!*

To the accompaniment of raucous applause and shouts of approval from the lounge bar upstairs, Mulgrew's eyes glazed over as he passed out in a dead faint, his head falling onto his chest, his bleeding hand pinned to the cubicle door.

CHAPTER 2

That looks like him now – coming out of the gate. I'm watching the entrance to Cottiers' pub garden from behind the large tree on the corner of Partickhill Road. I light a cigarette, then I start to walk slowly up the hill. I stop and bend down to re-tie the laces on my trainers, all the while watching him out of the corner of my eye. He hesitates and looks anxiously up and down the street before heading off down Hyndland Road. When he gets to the nearest street lamp, he takes out his mobile phone and starts tapping at the keypad.

I resume walking. I've only gone a few paces when I hear a gentle ping from the phone in my pocket as his text arrives. When I glance back over my shoulder I see him hurrying away. I wait until he's turned the corner into Lawrence Street before pulling out my phone and clicking onto his message.

"Where are you, Ronnie? This is the third time I've texted you in the past hour. We arranged to meet in Cottiers at eight o'clock. It's after half-past ten now. Do you want it or don't you? What the hell's going on?"

I grin as I read his message. He doesn't even know how to text. He writes in proper sentences, with punctuation, just like a teacher. Hardly surprising, when you come to think of it, considering he used to be one. I delete his message, just as I'd deleted the previous ones, before slipping my phone back into my pocket.

Being dressed in dark clothes is useful, now that darkness has fallen. I'm kitted out in black trainers, grey jeans and a loose-fitting black jacket. I turn on my heel and yank the brim of my navy-blue baseball cap down tight over my eyes as I make my way quickly down the hill. When I get to the corner of Lawrence Street, I see him up ahead, his hands thrust deep into his trouser pockets. I flick my half-smoked cigarette into the middle of the road before tugging my leather gloves from the hip pocket of my jeans and pulling them on. I pick up the pace. He's only a few yards in front of me now. He's swaying from side to side. It looks as if he might be a bit drunk. When I hear a vehicle approaching from behind I slow down, turning my face away from the road. I wait until the car has driven past and turned into Dowanhill Street before checking all around. There's no one in sight. This is looking good. I'll wait till he's half-way between the next two street lamps, level with the parked van. That's where the shadows are deepest.

I move quickly now, the footfall of my trainers making little sound on the damp pavement. He doesn't look round as I close in on him. I unhook the length of rope I have fastened around my waist. It's three feet long and knotted twice in the middle. I'm right behind him and he doesn't even know of my existence. I can hear him whistling a soft, off-key rendition of Flower of Scotland. I mouth the words under my breath. I wait till he gets to the line: "and sent him homeward – to think again".

It's you who should have thought again, pal!

I fling the rope over his head and yank the ends closed behind his neck, twisting them into a tight tourniquet. His legs go from under him. I go down with him, my knee jammed into the small of his back. The side of his face smashes into the rear wheel of the van, dislodging the hub cap, which clatters noisily in the gutter. He pulls his hands from his trouser pockets and desperately tries to prise his fingers between the rope and his neck. No way! I'm too strong for you. The knots in the rope are crushing into his Adam's apple, choking off his air supply and causing his cheeks to swell. His face has turned bright red, his eyes are bulging – they're almost out of their sockets. He's coughing and spluttering – globs of spittle are drooling from the corners of his mouth. His bloated tongue is sticking out of his mouth at a grotesque angle.

I bend down low to make eye contact with him.

4

'Do you know why this is happening to you?' I mouth in front of his face. He tries to respond, but he's incapable of uttering a single word. 'And do you know why it's happening tonight?' His eyes are pleading with me to stop. I move my lips close to his ear. 'I'm doing this for Tommy,' I say in a hoarse whisper. 'You do remember Tommy, don't you? Today is his anniversary. By the way,' I add, 'I like the beard – it suits you.'

Small, squeaking sounds of protest emanate from his puffed-up lips. His arms and legs are twitching involuntarily. I twist his body round and grind his face into the pavement as I give the tourniquet another sharp tweak. His body goes into spasm. I hang onto the rope tightly.

After a couple of minutes his limbs stop trembling and his body goes limp. I check to make sure there's no one in sight, then I give the rope another couple of twists, just to make sure. I pull off one of my gloves and feel for any sign of a pulse in the side of his neck. There's nothing.

Breathing heavily, I scramble to my feet. I put my glove back on quickly before searching through his pockets. When I find his mobile phone I switch it off and slip it into my jacket pocket. I take the thick envelope from his inside pocket and weigh it in my fist. It's tempting. It would be nice – but it's too much of a risk. The notes might be traceable. Some people, you just can't trust. I stuff the envelope back into his pocket before unhooking the rope from his neck and looping it back around my waist.

Without a backward glance, I hurry to the corner and stride out down Dowanhill Street, whistling an up-tempo version of Flower of Scotland as I go. Crossing Dumbarton Road, I make my way down Benalder Street towards the River Kelvin, stopping in the middle of the bridge. Because of the amount of rain we've had recently, the river is in spate. Having checked to make sure I'm not being observed, I take his phone from my pocket and remove the battery and the SIM card before flinging the phone as far as I can into the fast-flowing water. I do the same with my own phone. Snapping both the SIM cards in two, I drop them into the river, then I drop the batteries in after them.

'Best of luck with finding that lot, officer!' I whisper to the night sky as I hear a faint splash when the batteries hit the water. The way mobile phones can be traced these days, I didn't want to have those ones in my possession for a minute longer than necessary. Unhooking the length of rope from around my waist, I drop it into the river.

Everything's gone exactly to plan. I've earned a drink, but not around here. Before long this place will be crawling with cops, stopping all the passers-by to ask them questions and noting down a load of useless information. That's the police for you. That's what they do. They waste their time on pointless activities. Headless chickens spring to mind. They interview people who know bugger all about what happened and write down every meaningless word they say. Just going through the motions – while bastards like that one are allowed to walk the streets.

Where were the police when Tommy needed them? Sat on their collective, useless arses, probably – typing up their irrelevant notes. It took a long time, but Tommy has got his justice at last, only thanks to me.

I tug off my baseball cap and stuff it into my jacket pocket as I head back towards Byres Road. Light rain starts falling as I'm walking up the hill towards the university, so I pick up the pace and hurry down the other side. Half-way along Gibson Street, I go into Stravaigin. It had to be Stravaigin tonight; the pub where I bumped into Murdoch will be the place where I celebrate bumping him off.

The downstairs bar is heaving.

'What can I get you?' the over-worked barman calls out when I eventually manage to catch his eye.

'Captain Morgan's rum, please. Make it a large one. Splash of water – no ice,' I add, placing a twenty pound note on the bar.

The barman slides my drink across the counter and picks up the money. I feel my hand trembling as I raise the glass to my lips – probably some kind of delayed reaction kicking in. I pause to offer a silent toast. 'Justice for you at last, Tommy,' I mouth.

I mime chinking my glass against his before taking a slow, satisfying sip.

6

CHAPTER 3

Charlie Anderson grunted in annoyance when he heard the shrill ring of his phone. Hitting the mute button on the TV remote control, he stretched stiffly across the settee to the coffee table and picked up the handset.

'I'm sorry to disturb you at home, sir.'

Charlie recognised PC McArthur's voice. 'I'm hoping you're calling to give me good news, Lillian,' he said, 'such as our office syndicate has won the rollover jackpot – but I don't think I'll be holding my breath.'

'Good decision, sir.'

'What's the panic?' Charlie asked.

'Looks like we've got a murder on our hands. A body was found this evening in Lawrence Street and – '

'Remind me?' Charlie interjected. 'Where's Lawrence Street?'

'It runs from Hyndland Street to Byres Road.'

'Got it! Was the victim male or female?'

'Male. He appears to be in his late twenties or early thirties, but he's not been ID'd yet. A young couple came across the body lying in the street and they phoned for an ambulance. They told the paramedics they'd been for a drink in Cottiers and they were on their way home when they saw someone lying in the gutter on the other side of the road. They thought the guy might have hurt himself, or maybe he'd fallen down drunk, so they went across to see if he needed any help. As soon as they saw the state he was in they called 999. When the ambulance crew got there, it was a case of DOA. The paramedics sized up the situation and called us out before making any attempt to move the body.'

'When did this happen?'

'The ambulance was called out at ten forty-five. We don't know how long he'd been lying in the gutter.'

'And we're sure it was murder?'

'The way one of the paramedics put it to me, sir, was: "Cases of self-strangulation in the middle of the road are comparatively rare".'

'Too much to hope that there were any witnesses, I suppose?'

'Not as far as I know, sir.'

'Who's handling things?'

'DC Renton's on his way across there right now with a SOC team. The paramedics told the kids who found the body to wait with them until the police arrived. Renton said he'd be bringing them back to Pitt Street to take their statements and he asked me to get in touch with either you, or DI Munro, to let you know what was going on.'

'Who else is around tonight?'

'DS O'Sullivan and DC Freer were in the office earlier on, but they were called out about an hour ago – something to do with an assault in a pub in the Calton.'

'Have you tried to get in touch with Munro?'

'I thought I'd call you first, sir.'

'You're too good to me, Lillian.'

'I was about to call DI Munro, sir, then I remembered he mentioned yesterday that he was taking his wife out to dinner tonight. I think he said something about it being their twenty-fifth wedding anniversary.' Lillian hesitated. 'If you want, I could try calling him on his mobile? I could tell him that I couldn't manage to get hold of you.'

Charlie heaved himself stiffly to his feet. 'Thanks for the offer, Lillian, but it's not worth the hassle. If Hugh's missus ever found out that I'd dumped this on him on their wedding anniversary, she'd have my guts for garters. Give Renton a call and tell him I'll meet him in Pitt Street in half an hour.'

Replacing the handset, Charlie picked up the remote control and switched off the television. 'It was a crappy film anyway,' he muttered to himself as he trudged up the narrow flight of stairs to his bedroom.

'That was Lillian McArthur on the blower, love. I'm afraid I'm needed in the office.'

Kay Anderson closed the paperback she was reading and sat up straight in bed.

'What's the panic?'

'It looks like there's been a murder in the West End.'

'And it has to be you?' Kay said, peering at Charlie over the top of her reading glasses. 'There's no one else who could possibly handle it?'

'O'Sullivan and Freer have been called out to deal with an assault in the Calton, so Renton's more or less holding the fort on his own tonight. Besides, we'll need to get statements from the people who found the body while everything's still fresh in their minds.'

'And Renton couldn't manage to take their statements on his own? Or, if he needed assistance, he couldn't call out somebody else?'

'He suggested to Lillian that she give Hugh Munro a call, but I told her not to bother. It's Hugh's twenty-fifth wedding anniversary today and he's taking his wife out for dinner.'

'If I remember correctly, you ended up working half the night on our twenty-fifth wedding anniversary.'

'Did I?'

'I thought you said that was it, Charlie?' Kay said with an exasperated shake of the head. 'You've only got a few months to go till you retire. I thought you said you'd steer clear of any more murder investigations?'

Charlie's fingers travelled over his bald skull. 'I said I'd *try* to steer clear of any more. And I will. This isn't necessarily going to be my case, just because I'm helping out tonight.'

'Where have I heard that before?'

Charlie plucked his jacket from the chair at the end of the bed. 'I'll be back as soon as I can.'

'Sue and Jamie are coming across to us for lunch tomorrow. Any chance you might make it back by then?'

Charlie managed a weak smile as he shrugged on his jacket. 'Touché!'

DS Tony O'Sullivan could feel his car being buffeted by the strong wind blowing off the Clyde as he drove along the Broomielaw. Light rain started falling as he was passing the King George V bridge. He flicked the windscreen wipers on to a slow wipe.

'Have you been to the Calton before, Tom?' he asked his passenger.

'I don't think so, sir.'

'You won't find it among the top ten places to visit on the Glasgow tourist trail, but you would remember it all right if you'd been there.'

'What's so special about it?'

'Things have improved a lot recently, but for a long time it was the district with the lowest life expectancy – and one of the highest crime rates – of anywhere in Europe.'

'You mean even worse than the Farm?'

'Where's that?'

'Broadwater Farm - in Tottenham. That's where I was brought up. It's hard to imagine anywhere worse than that.'

'If I remember the figures right,' Tony said, 'male life expectancy in the Calton used to be about fifty-four – which was on a par with Kabul when it was in the middle of a war zone.'

'Why were things so bad?'

'Years of poor housing and social deprivation, combined with a high dependency on drugs, alcohol, and tobacco. The life expectancy rate wasn't helped by the fact that the city fathers had decided to move a lot of the sheltered accommodation for the homeless – and most of the rehab clinics for drug addicts – to the Calton.'

'I thought the district was called 'Calton'?' Tom said. 'Why does everyone refer to it as *the* Calton? You don't talk about *the* Govan – or *the* Maryhill?'

'That's a good question, Tom. I've no idea why. It's just one of those things. Glaswegians always call it *the* Calton,' Tony said as he pulled up on the double yellow lines outside The Jacobite Arms.

The rain was heavier now and the street was deserted. Switching off the ignition, Tony twisted round in his seat.

'What does this place remind you of?' he asked.

DC Tom Freer studied the grey masonry and the small, barred windows set high up in the wall. 'My first impression is that it looks a bit like Barlinnie, sir, but not as welcoming.'

'Fair comment,' O'Sullivan said, gripping the door handle 'You stay here while I go into the bear pit and find out what's going on. Your job is to make sure the car still has four wheels by the time I come out.'

'Why do I always get the tricky assignments?'

'Because I'm pulling rank. Besides, you're English. You wouldn't understand a word that was said in there.'

'I know that one grunt means you're in trouble – and two grunts mean you're in deep shit,' Freer said.

'You're starting to get the hang of it, Tom,' O'Sullivan said, turning up his jacket collar as he eased open the car door. 'But this is three-grunt territory.'

CHAPTER 4

As he hurried towards the pub entrance, O'Sullivan glanced up at the faded graffiti sprayed on the wall above the door – a proclamation to the world that the premises he was about to enter were ruled by the Calton Tongs.

As soon as he stepped inside, the buzz of conversation died away and a dozen pairs of curious eyes followed his progress as he made his way up to the bar. The shaven-headed, heavily-tattooed barman glanced up at the wall clock, which showed two minutes to eleven.

'You're pushing your luck, Jimmy. I hope you're a quick drinker.' The barman picked up a half-smoked cigarette from the ashtray on the counter and took a long, slow drag. 'What are you for?'

'Has the law banning smoking in pubs not filtered through to the Calton?' O'Sullivan asked.

The barman narrowed his eyes as he looked O'Sullivan up and down. His gaze switched to the hand-rolled cigarette in his fist. 'There's nae filters around here, pal,' he said,' tapping the ash from his cigarette into the ashtray. 'Filters are for poofters.'

'Are you the landlord?'

'I might be,' he said with a shrug of his shoulders. 'It depends who's asking.'

O'Sullivan cupped his warrant card in the palm of his hand and showed it to him.

'Are you here on your own?' The barman feigned incredulity as he made a production of staring over each of O'Sullivan's shoulders in turn. 'Are you up for some kind of bravery award?'

'It's been a long day,' O'Sullivan said as he pocketed his ID. 'What seems to be the problem?'

'What problem?'

'We got a call from here half an hour ago, to let us know someone had been stabbed in the toilets.'

'It must be a mistake.' The barman shook his head slowly from side to side. 'Nothing like that happened in here tonight. Hey, guys,' he called out, addressing the customers. 'This is the polis.' Muffled groans ran around the room. 'Don't worry, Sammy, he doesn't know that you're dealing coke.' The groans turned to guffaws. 'Did anybody here phone the cops to report someone getting stabbed in the bogs?'

'Tell him he's here a week early,' was shouted from the back of the room. 'That's not going to happen until next Saturday.' More guffaws followed.

The barman drew hard on his cigarette, the aromatic fumes wafting across the bar and drifting into O'Sullivan's face.

'Sorry I'm not able to help you, pal,' he said, exhaling smoke slowly through his clenched, tobacco-stained teeth. 'It looks like someone's been pulling your plonker, though, come to think of it, there is a pub in Dundee called The Jacobite Arms. Maybe you should try there?'

'Right, you lot,' the barman called out. 'Start drinking up. I've got a home to go to, even if you don't.'

As the customers turned their attention back to their drinks, the barman slid a folded piece of paper across the bar towards Tony. 'Take this,' he whispered, 'then fuck off.'

All the eyes followed Tony again as he turned round and made his way out of the pub.

When he got back to the car, Tony unfolded the slip of paper and read the hand-printed note:

'GIVE ME A CALL ME ON THE PUB PHONE AT HALF-PAST ELEVEN'

Apart from a few high, wispy clouds, the night sky was clear when DCI Charlie Anderson merged with the M8 from the Renfrew slip road. He was mulling over what Kay had said. Not long to go now till he retired – nine months, and counting. Understandably, Kay wanted him to get through the next few months with as little hassle as possible, and he'd promised her he'd do that. There was no reason he should have to get involved in this case. He had more than enough on his plate right now, trying to trace the source of the recent influx of crystal meth and cracking down on the dealers. Just help Renton take the witness statements tonight, he thought to himself, then he would delegate everything tomorrow. Hugh Munro wasn't overloaded. He would allocate the SIO role to him.

Charlie checked the time on his car clock. It showed a quarter past eleven. The motorway didn't seem too busy, but by the time he got to the Kingston Bridge there was a fair amount of traffic heading towards the city centre. Having crossed the bridge, he took the exit for Waterloo Street before looping up the steep incline towards the CID headquarters in Pitt Street. At the crest of the hill he turned left, then drove round the block towards the entrance to the underground car park. The officer on duty waved in recognition when he saw Charlie's car approaching. Charlie lowered his window and leaned out.

'How's it going, Frank?'

'Not too bad, sir. I wasn't expecting to see you tonight.'

'I wasn't expecting to be here.'

'Which means bad news, I suppose?'

'It looks like there's been a murder in the West End.'

'At least that makes a change,' Frank said with a grunt as he raised the barrier. 'The last two homicides were both in Govanhill.'

Charlie drove down the steep ramp before reversing slowly into a narrow parking space between two concrete pillars. Getting out of his car, he trudged up the flights of stairs to his office on the second floor where he found DC Colin Renton sitting behind his desk, a young couple seated on the chairs opposite him.

As soon as he saw Charlie enter the room, Renton scrambled to his feet. 'Good evening, sir.'

'Have you offered these good people something to drink?' Charlie asked as he stripped off his jacket and hung it on the hook on the back of the door.

'Not yet, sir.'

'What would you like?' Charlie asked, taking a handful of loose change from his jacket pocket and spilling the coins onto the desk. 'Tea, coffee, juice or water? I'm afraid that's as good as it gets around here.'

The girl made eye contact with her friend, then nodded. 'Coffee would be good for both of us, thanks.'

'I'll go for them,' Renton offered, scooping up the coins. 'How do you take it, miss?'

'Black with no sugar for me,' she said. 'And white with sugar for Kyle.'

'The usual for me, Colin,' Charlie said, settling down on his swivel chair. 'I'm DCI Anderson,' he offered by way of introduction. 'And you are?'

'I'm Gill,' the girl said, 'and this is my partner, Kyle.'

Charlie made small talk to put Gill and Kyle at their ease until Renton arrived back with four coffees balanced on a tray.

'Before we get round to taking your official statements,' Charlie said, picking up his coffee and blowing on the hot liquid, 'tell me what happened this evening.'

'We were, like, walking home from Cottiers – along Lawrence Street,' Gill said.

'We have a flat in Elie Street,' Kyle chipped in.

'As *I* was saying,' Gill continued forcibly, looking askance at Kyle, 'we were walking along Lawrence Street on our way home from the pub. It had started to rain, so we were, like, hurrying. When I looked across the road I saw a pair of legs sticking out from behind the rear wheels of a van. I wasn't at all sure about going across. I thought the guy might've had one too many.'

'But I said,' Kyle interjected, 'what if the poor sod's had a heart attack, or something like that? I think we should, like, go over and check.'

'He was lying face-down on the pavement,' Gill said. 'I tapped him gently on the shoulder, but he didn't stir.'

'I bent down and turned him over,' Kyle said. 'As soon as I saw the state his face was in, I knew straight away he was dead.'

'I called 999 from my mobile,' Gill said. 'We waited with him until the ambulance got there.'

'When the medics arrived, they confirmed that the guy was dead,' Kyle said, 'and they called the police. The ambulance driver told us to wait with them until the cops arrived. It was raining quite hard by this time, so the paramedics let us sit in the back of the ambulance with them. When Constable Renton arrived he asked us to come back here with him to give our statements.'

'Tell Inspector Anderson what you saw earlier in the evening – in the pub,' Renton prompted.

'I'm sure it was the same guy,' Kyle said. 'We were in the garden area, outside at Cottiers, and so was he.'

'Was he with anybody?' Charlie asked.

Kyle shook his head. 'He was sitting by himself at a table near the gate. I noticed him because he seemed to be, like, drinking a lot for someone on his own. He walked past our table three or four times in the space of less than an hour to get another drink. All the time he was sitting at his table he was, like, constantly checking his phone and looking at his watch, as if he was waiting for somebody. Then all of a sudden he got to his feet and hurried off, leaving an almost–full pint.'

'What time would that have been?' Charlie asked.

'I'm not sure,' Kyle said, looking at Gill.

'It was about a quarter of an hour before we left the pub,' Gill said, 'which means it must have been around half-past ten.'

'And the next time we saw him,' Kyle said, swallowing hard, 'he was dead.'

'Did you see anyone else in or around Lawrence Street at that time?' Charlie asked.

Gill and Kyle looked at each other, both of them shaking their heads. 'No one, Inspector,' Gill said. 'Nobody at all.'

'Okay, thanks for that.' Charlie got up from his chair and used both hands to massage the stiffness at the base of his spine. 'When you've finished your coffees, go downstairs with DC Renton. He'll take your statements and get you to sign them. We might need to talk to you again later, once the dead guy's been identified, but that's all we need from you this evening. Thanks for coming in – and sorry about messing up your Saturday night.'

'No need to apologise, Inspector,' Kyle said as he slowly got to his feet. 'Our evening wasn't really messed up, like – not compared with that poor sod's.'

Deciding he might as well do something useful while he was waiting for Renton to come back, Charlie unlocked the top drawer of his desk and lifted out a pile of unanswered correspondence. Unscrewing the top from his fountain pen, he read the first memo and jotted down his response in the margin. He had dealt with three items of mail and was half-way through reading the next one when Renton rapped on his door and walked in. Putting down his pen, Charlie rocked back in his seat and swung his feet up onto the desk.

'What do we know about the dead guy, Colin?'

'Not a lot, sir. No ID on him. One thing we can be sure of is that the motive for the murder wasn't robbery. Apart from forty quid in his wallet, there was an envelope in his inside jacket pocket stuffed with a thousand pounds in tens and twenties.'

'Very interesting. Why do you think he would be carrying money like that around?'

'Have you checked the price of bus fares recently?' Renton asked.

Charlie smiled. 'Assuming for the moment that he wasn't planning to catch a bus, an envelope stuffed with cash smacks of blackmail. Could his killer have been a blackmailer who lured him to Cottiers?'

'In which case, why did he not relieve him of the cash after he strangled him?' Renton asked.

'Good point.'

'There is one other interesting thing, though,' Renton added. 'The kids who found him in the gutter told us the victim had been checking his mobile phone regularly while he was in the pub, but there was no sign of a phone on the body. For some reason, the killer appears to have relieved him of it.'

'Not a random killing, then? Probably somebody who knew him,' Charlie suggested. 'Perhaps someone who was in the contacts' list in his phone?'

'That seems like a distinct possibility.'

'Has the cause of death been established?' Charlie asked.

'It looks odds-on that it was strangulation. We'll have to wait for the post mortem for formal confirmation, but from the abrasions on his neck the paramedics reckoned he'd been choked to death with something like heavy duty twine or rope.'

'Which increases the probability that the murder was premeditated,' Charlie said, swinging his feet down to the floor with a thud. 'Okay, Colin. Let's call it a day. There's not a lot more we can achieve here tonight. Are you on duty tomorrow?'

'Yes, sir.'

'Who else is in?'

'O'Sullivan and Freer.'

'Bring O'Sullivan up to speed with what happened tonight as soon as he gets in. Tell him he's in charge of things until I get here. The usual routine. Check the victim's description against the missing persons' list and organise door-to-door enquiries in Lawrence Street and Hyndland Street.'

Renton raised a quizzical eyebrow.

Charlie let out a world-weary sigh. 'I do realise that tomorrow's Sunday, Colin, but unfortunately the Glasgow criminal fraternity don't take into account the fact that I've got a tight overtime budget to manage. Organise appeals in the newspapers and on television for anyone who was in Cottiers tonight between nine o'clock and eleven o'clock to come forward – and also anyone who was walking or driving in the vicinity of Lawrence Street between ten o'clock and eleven o'clock. And arrange for someone to talk to the bar staff who were on duty in Cottiers tonight,' Charlie added, 'to find out if they know anything about the victim.'

'Will do, sir.'

'Is there anything I've missed?' Charlie asked, stifling a yawn.

'How about an appeal for anyone who committed a murder in Lawrence Street at around half-past ten tonight to come forward?'

'Why didn't I think of that?' Charlie said, snapping his fingers. 'With an incisive brain like that, Colin, you'd be a shoo-in for promotion to sergeant.'

Renton's craggy features broke into a broad grin. 'I've got less time to go till I retire than you have, sir. If it's all the same to you, I don't think I'll bother applying.'

Having looked up the phone number for The Jacobite Arms on his mobile, Tony O'Sullivan waited until half-past eleven before punching it into his phone.

'Is that the landlord?' he asked when the call was taken.

'It is.'

'This is DS O'Sullivan. You asked me to give you a call.'

'I couldn't say anything earlier on, but it was me who phoned the cops about the stabbing in the pub.'

'What happened?'

'One of my regulars, a bloke called Jack Mulgrew, got nailed tonight – literally.'

'What do you mean?'

'One of the customers went downstairs to the bog and he found Mulgrew pinned to the door of one of the cubicles. A rusty, six-inch nail had been hammered through the palm of his hand.'

'Jesus Christ!' O'Sullivan said, wincing.

'There were certain similarities,' the landlord agreed. 'I'll give you that.'

'What did you do?'

'What could I do? I fetched a hammer from my flat upstairs and I thumped the point of the nail back through the door from the other side. It was one hell of a carry on, let me tell you. Mulgrew had passed out, but he came round when I started hammering on the nail and he started squealing like a stuck pig.'

'Where is he now?'

'My brother took him across to A&E.'

'What state was he in?'

'His life's probably not in danger, but I don't think he'll be playing tennis for a while.'

'Does he know who attacked him?'

'He told me it was two complete strangers.'

'Does he know why they picked on him?'

'I asked him that. He said he'd no idea.'

'Do you have any idea who might have done it?'

The landlord hesitated. 'One of Jim Colvin's goons was in the pub earlier on this evening – about seven o'clock. He was asking around if anyone knew where he could find Mulgrew.'

'Jim Colvin? Is he still running his pay-day lending racket?' O'Sullivan asked.

'No one around here has got a job, pal. We call it dole-day lending.'

'Does Mulgrew borrow from Colvin?'

'Aye. And when one of Colvin's heavies is asking about somebody's whereabouts,' he added, 'it's a pound to a pinch of shit that the guy's going to get a doing. Everyone knows the goon works for Colvin, so when word gets out that Mulgrew's been claimed, Colvin's clients all know who was responsible. That way, none of them get any smart-arsed ideas about not paying up on time.'

'You don't normally involve the police in your domestics,' O'Sullivan said. 'Why this time?'

'Colvin's interest rates stink,' the landlord said, 'They make Wonga look like a charitable institution. His guys have been leaning on Mulgrew for the past couple of weeks. In fact, they've been putting the screws on quite a few of my regulars recently – and that scares them off from coming into the pub – which isn't good for business. It's about time your lot sorted Colvin out.'

'If you'd be prepared to take the stand and testify against him, that would be a big help.'

The barman chortled. 'Aye, right!'

The rain had slackened off and the motorway traffic was light as Charlie Anderson was driving home. Leaving the motorway at the exit for Renfrew, he drove a short distance along Paisley Road before turning left into Wright Street, a wide avenue of nineteen-fifties, semi-detached houses. Pulling up in the driveway alongside his pebble-dashed house, he got out of the car. He turned his key in the front door as quietly as he could, then used the downstairs toilet before tip-toeing up the staircase without switching on the light. Changing into his pyjamas in the dark, he slipped under the duvet.

'What time is it?' Kay's sleepy voice asked.

'It's just after one o'clock.'

'Was it a murder?

'It looks like it.'

'Did you manage to delegate everything?'

Charlie hesitated. 'I'll tell you all about it in the morning, love.'

Rolling over onto his side, Charlie closed his eyes. It was another two hours before he managed to drop off to sleep.

CHAPTER 5

Sunday 4 September

Sitting at his kitchen table, Tony O'Sullivan poured himself a second cup of coffee. Having added a splash of milk, he stirred in two lumps of sugar before picking up his mobile phone and clicking onto Sue's number.

'I hope I didn't wake you up?' he said when she took the call.

'Not at all. I'm just out of the shower,' Sue said, towelling her long hair vigorously as she spoke. 'What are you up to?'

'I'm about to go into the office. I was hoping for a quiet day, but I got a text from Colin Renton a couple of minutes ago to let me know there was a murder in the West End last night. It appears that I'm in charge of proceedings until your father gets in.'

'Dad's not working this weekend.'

'He is now. Renton told me he got called out last night.'

'You don't say? Mum will be pleased.'

'Talking of your Mum, I've been keeping this a secret from you for the past couple of weeks, but I think I'd better tell you now before you go and organise something else for next weekend.'

'Tell me what?'

'I've made plans for your birthday.'

'What plans?'

'I've got us tickets.'

'What for?' Sue asked excitedly.

'Guess.'

'I've no idea what's on next weekend, apart from *The Sound of Music* sing-along at the Kings. If it's for that, I'll kill you!'

'Think further afield.'

'Edinburgh?'

'Further than that.'

'Stop teasing me! Where?'

'London.'

'London?'

'I've got us tickets for the Radiohead gig on Saturday night. Best seats in the place. The flights are booked and the hotel's confirmed. We fly down on Friday evening and come back on Sunday afternoon.'

'That's fantastic! I hope Mum will be able to look after Jamie.'

'She will. It's all arranged.'

'You mean – my mother's in on this?'

'I had to tell her to make sure it wouldn't be a problem for her to take care of Jamie while we were away.'

'How long has she known about this?'

'I'm not sure – about a couple of weeks, I think.'

'The sly old so-and-so. She never breathed a word about it to me.'

'She was sworn to secrecy.'

'I'm amazed that Dad managed to keep it quiet.'

'He doesn't know anything about it.'

'Jamie and I are going across to their place for lunch today. I'll give Mum into a row for keeping it a secret from me. But it's just as well you told me today,' Sue added. 'I was thinking about organising a girls' night out on Saturday.'

'If you'd rather do that, I could always ask Kylie, the barmaid in Òran Mór, if she'd like to come with me to London. I happen to know she's a big Radiohead fan.'

'Just you watch it! Any more cracks like that and you'll get more than your head in your hands to play with.'

'I think I get the message.'

'Just as well.'

'What are you doing tonight?'

'I've got school tomorrow, so I'm just going to slob out in front of the telly.'

'Could you handle a bit of company?'

'That depends.'

'On what?'

'If the aforementioned company happened to turn up with a chicken dansak carry-out from Balbir's, there's every chance I might let him in.'

'How about if he brought onion bhajis and naan bread as well?'

'That would probably swing it.'

'What time would you like to eat?'

'Give me time to get Jamie settled down. How about eight o'clock?'

'Eight o'clock it is.'

Charlie Anderson washed down a slice of buttered toast with a slurp of lukewarm tea as he scanned the front page of the Sunday Post, the lead story being about an unidentified body having been found in Lawrence Street at ten-thirty the previous evening. Draining his cup, he got to his feet.

'I just need to go into the office for a couple of hours to make sure everything's organised, love. I'll be back in time for lunch.'

'Jamie's bringing his boots and his ball across and he's expecting you to play football with him this afternoon. Don't disappoint him, Charlie.'

'I won't.' Bending down, Charlie gave Kay a peck on the cheek before lifting his jacket from the back of the chair and shrugging it on. 'What time are we expecting them?' he asked as he picked up his car keys from the kitchen table.

'Sue said they'd be here between half-past twelve and one o'clock.'

'I'll make sure I'm back by then.'

As Charlie was navigating the steep slope down to Pitt Street's underground car park, he noticed Superintendent Nigel Hamilton's silver Mercedes was parked in its usual bay.

'That's all I need this morning,' he muttered to himself as he twisted stiffly round in his seat to reverse into a tight parking space. Switching off the ignition and pulling on the hand brake, he got out of his car.

When Charlie climbed the stairs to the second floor he saw Tony O'Sullivan standing by the vending machines, waiting for his coffee cup to fill.

'Can I get you one of these, sir?' O'Sullivan asked, lifting his plastic cup from the tray and holding it aloft as Charlie approached.

'Thanks.'

O'Sullivan took the appropriate coins from his pocket and dropped them into the slot, punching the button for black coffee with extra sugar.

'Lillian McArthur told me you were called out last night,' Charlie said as he was waiting for his coffee to dribble out. 'She said it was something to do with an assault in a pub in the Calton. What was that all about?'

'Someone literally nailed one of the regulars, a guy called Jack Mulgrew, to a bog door in The Jacobite Arms.'

'Ouch! Do we have any idea who was responsible?'

'When I spoke to the landlord, Jim Colvin's name cropped up in the conversation,' O'Sullivan said, lifting Charlie's cup from the tray and handing it to him.

'Now there's a surprise!' Charlie said, blowing hard on the hot liquid before taking a sip.

'Apparently one of Colvin's heavies was in the pub earlier on in the evening, asking around if anyone knew where he could find Mulgrew,' O'Sullivan said.

'Is Colvin still loan-sharking?'

'So it would appear.'

'It's not like the good citizens of the Calton to involve us in their squabbles,' Charlie said.

'That's what I thought, but apparently Colvin's guys have been scaring the customers away from coming into the pub – and that's not good for the landlord's business.'

'Don't tell me that capitalism has spread its tentacles into the inner sanctum of the Calton?' Charlie said with a shake of the head. 'Jimmy Maxton will be turning in his grave.'

'According to the landlord, Mulgrew was made an example of because he'd got behind with his payments, in order to make sure that the rest of Colvin's clientele don't get any smart-arsed ideas about not paying up on time.'

'Has Colvin been picked up?'

'Not yet – but we've got the word out that we're looking for him.'

'Are you up to speed with what happened in Lawrence Street last night?' Charlie asked.

O'Sullivan nodded. 'Renton filled me in. Which reminds me, sir. Niggle got here half an hour ago. He told me to let you know that he wants to see you as soon as you get in.'

'Well he'll just have to wait until I've had my fix of caffeine,' Charlie said, swallowing a mouthful of hot coffee. 'Find Renton and join me in my office.'

Charlie rocked back in his swivel chair when Renton and O'Sullivan walked in. They took the chairs facing his desk.

'Any joy with identifying the victim, Colin?' Charlie asked.

'Not so far, sir,' Renton said. 'There's no one on the mispers list who remotely fits his description.'

'Did the SOC team come up with anything useful?'

'I've got their initial report,' Renton said, taking a sheet of paper from the folder he was carrying. 'They bagged everything they found within a ten metre radius of the body,' he said, referring to the report. 'Which comprised two buckled lager cans, one lollipop stick, one fish-supper wrapping paper, three fag ends, a wad of chewing gum and a broken syringe.'

'More or less everything you could possibly want for a good Saturday night out in Glasgow,' Charlie said. 'All that's missing from making it a right belter is a used condom.'

'DNA checks are being carried out on everything they found,' Renton said. 'So far, there haven't been any matches with the national data base.'

Renton handed Charlie a photograph of the corpse.

'Hard to tell how old he was from this,' Charlie said. 'Though the beard should help to make him recognisable to anyone who knew him.'

'I'm getting the photo cropped to show only his face,' Renton said, 'and photo-shopped to stick his tongue back into his mouth. I'll take it across to Cottiers as soon as they open this morning and find out if the bar staff know anything about him.'

'Tony,' Charlie said, 'get copies made of that photo and organise door-to-door enquiries in all the properties between Cottiers and where the body was found in Lawrence Street. While you're organising that, I'll go upstairs and try to keep Niggle off our backs.' Charlie glanced at his watch and drained his coffee cup. 'We'll meet back here at twelve o'clock and take a checkpoint. I have to be out of here by quarter-past twelve at the very latest or my life won't be worth living.'

'Has the victim been identified?' Superintendent Nigel Hamilton demanded.

Charlie Anderson was perched on the edge of a leather chair in DS Hamilton's office. 'Not yet.'

'Who's going to be taking charge of the investigation?' Hamilton's high-pitched, sing-song delivery grated on Charlie's ears.

'I'll assign the SIO role to DI Munro,' Charlie said. 'He doesn't have too much on his plate right now.'

Hamilton shook his head firmly. 'I need Munro full time on the task force that's looking into revamping the crime statistics,' his squeaky voice intoned. 'The Chief's biting my arse to get the new reporting system up and running before the end of the year.'

'In that case, I'll give the SIO role to DI Cunningham.'

Hamilton drummed his fingertips rhythmically on his desk as he shook his head again. 'Cunningham's a good officer, but he hasn't been with us long enough to get to know the local scene. Why don't you handle it yourself?'

'I'm up to my neck in trying to track down the source of the recent influx of crystal meth.'

'Hand that investigation over to Cunningham – he's got relevant experience of drug-related crime – and you take charge of the murder inquiry.' Without waiting for Charlie's reaction, Hamilton swivelled round in his chair to face his computer screen. 'Keep me up to date with your progress,' he said without turning round.

CHAPTER 6

Colin Renton was leaning with his back against the wall outside Cottiers when the doors of the pub were thrown open on the stroke of eleven o'clock.

'Have you been waiting long?' the barman asked, eying Renton up and down

'I'm not desperate for a drink, if that's what you're thinking,' Renton said, fishing out his ID and showing it to him.

'Sorry about that, officer,' the barman said with a grin. 'People queuing up outside before we open usually are. What can I do for you?'

'Do you know this guy?' Renton asked, handing him the photograph.

The barman narrowed his eyes as he studied the image. 'I think so,' he said hesitantly. 'It looks like John.'

'John who?'

The barman shrugged his shoulders. 'I only know them by their first names.'

'Who is *them*?'

'Two guys, Kevin and Pete, have been coming here for the past couple of years. Regular as clockwork, they walk through the door at half-past twelve every Sunday – and for the past few months this guy, John,' he said tapping the photo, 'has been joining them from time to time.'

'Do you happen to know if John was here last night?'

'I've no idea. I wasn't working.'

'Will any of the staff who were on last night be working this morning?'

'I don't think so,' he said, handing back the photo.

'Well, if you reckon Kevin and Pete will be here at half-past twelve,' Renton said, glancing at his watch, 'I might as well wait for them.'

The barman led the way up the four steps to the ground floor bar.

'Do you have any CCTV cameras in here?' Renton asked, looking all around.

'I'm afraid not.'

'How about in the pub garden?'

'There's no CCTV outside either.'

'That's not what I wanted to hear.'

'Sorry about that. Can I get you something to drink while you're waiting?' the barman asked.

'Just a tonic water.'

'Ice and lemon?'

'Please.'

Charlie Anderson was sitting at his desk, ploughing his way through his backlog of paperwork, when the phone on his desk rang. He picked up.

'Renton here, sir. I'm over in Cottiers.'

'Did you get anything useful?' Charlie asked.

Renton relayed the information the barman had given him.

'In which case, you might as well wait there and have a word with John's pals when they turn up at twelve-thirty,' Charlie said. 'When you've had a chance to talk to them, let me know what you find out.'

'I thought you said you were heading off at twelve-fifteen at the latest, sir?'

'That was the plan,' Charlie grunted, 'but it looks like I've drawn the short straw.'

Disconnecting the call, Charlie weighed the phone is his fist for a moment before tapping in his home number. 'It's me,' he said when Kay answered.

'Are you on your way, Charlie?'

Charlie hesitated. 'It's bad news, I'm afraid, love. Niggle's lumbered me with the SIO role.'

There was a pause before Kay responded. 'Does that mean you won't be home for lunch?'

'It doesn't look like it.'

'Oh, Charlie! It's not for my sake – or for Sue's. God knows, we're used to it. But you did promise Jamie that you'd play football with him this afternoon.'

'I know I did.' Charlie let out a long, low sigh. 'Explain to Jamie for me, love. Let him know I have to work this afternoon. Tell him I'll give him a call this afternoon and sort out a time soon when we can have a game.'

Colin Renton was half-way through his second tonic water when the barman made eye contact with him, nodding in the direction of one of the booths facing the bar where two men, who looked to be in their early thirties, were about to sit down. Renton made his way across and slid onto the bench seat opposite them.

'Good afternoon,' Renton said.

'Do we know you?' the taller of two men asked.

'I don't think so Kevin – or is it Pete?' Renton asked, showing his warrant card.

He eyed Renton quizzically. 'I'm Kevin.'

'I've got a couple of questions for you guys,' Renton said, placing the photograph on the table in front of them. 'Do you know who this is?'

Kevin picked up the photo and examined it carefully. 'It looks like John Preston,' he said, handing the photo to Pete.

'It's definitely John,' Pete said as he studied the photograph. 'What's up? Is he in some kind of trouble?'

'When did you last see him?'

'On Friday afternoon – at work,' Kevin said.

'Is he a close friend?' Renton asked.

'More a work colleague than a friend,' Kevin said.

'We're meeting him here today,' Pete offered. 'He should be here any time,' he added, glancing at his watch.

'John won't be joining you today,' Renton said.

'Why not?' Pete asked.

'I'm sorry to have to tell you this,' Renton said quietly, 'but I'm afraid John is dead.'

'Dead!' Kevin exclaimed. 'What on earth happened?'

'He was murdered – last night.'

'Jesus wept!' Pete mumbled.

'I'm sorry I had to break it to you like that,' Renton said, taking the photo from Pete's limp fingers and slipping it back into his pocket 'But there isn't any easy way to communicate news like that.' He took out his notebook and pen. 'You said the guy's name was John Preston?'

'That's right,' Kevin nodded.

'How well did you know him?' Renton asked as he jotted down the name.

'Not all that well.' Kevin shrugged. 'He joined our firm about a year ago – and he sometimes came here for a pint with us on Sundays.'

'What kind of work did he do?'

'He was a computer programmer,' Kevin said. 'Pete and I are systems analysts. We work for a consultancy firm that provides cus-tomised software solutions for various companies. We specialise in the retail business.'

'Do you know where Preston worked before he joined your company?'

'I don't,' Kevin said, looking at Pete, who shook his head.

'He was a competent enough programmer,' Pete said, 'but I don't recall him ever mentioning anything about his previous employment.'

'Do you know where he lived?'

'He said something about having a flat near the University,' Kevin said, 'but I don't know the address.'

'Was he in a relationship?'

'I don't think so,' Pete said. 'At least, he never said anything to me about having a partner.'

'What's the name of your firm?' Renton asked.

'Murdoch & Slater, Computer Consultants,' Kevin said. 'Our head office is in Bath Street.'

'Who would be able to give me Preston's address?'

'There won't be anyone in the office on a Sunday,' Pete said. 'But I can give you my manager's home phone number,' he added, taking out his mobile phone and paging through his contacts' list. 'His name's George Slater.'

Renton wrote down the number as Pete read it out. 'Thanks. I'll need your names and addresses as well – and your phone numbers,' Renton added.

Having noted down the information, Renton slid out of the bench seat.

When Kay Anderson answered the ring of her doorbell, Sue stepped across the threshold and wrapped her arms around her mother, giving her a big hug. 'How are you, Mum?'

'I'm fine – but I'm afraid your father's gone and done it to us again,' Kay whispered in Sue's ear as Jamie bounded past them, bouncing his ball along the hall.

'Don't tell me he's working?'

'I'm afraid so. There was a murder in the West End last night and he's just phoned to let me know that Niggle's lumbered him with the SIO role.'

Sue pulled a face. 'Jamie!' she called out. 'Bad news, I'm afraid. Grandad has to work this afternoon.'

Jamie stopped bouncing his ball and spun round. 'But he promised to play football with me today.'

'I know he did, love,' Kay said, walking across and ruffling Jamie's unkempt hair. 'It couldn't be helped. He really wanted to be here, but a man was killed last night and Grandad has to find out who did it. He'll call you this afternoon,' Kay added, 'to sort out a time when he can have a game with you.'

Jamie screwed up his face as he bent down to pick up his ball. 'I'm going outside.'

'I've got a bone to pick with you,' Sue said as Jamie was trudging out of the back door into the garden. 'I have reason to believe you've been keeping a secret from me.'

'Really? Which one have you found out about?' Kay asked with an enigmatic smile.

'You mean there's more than one?'

'There might be,' Kay teased.

'Let's start with the Radiohead concert next weekend.'

'Oh, that! Tony had to let me in on it to make sure I'd be able to look after Jamie while you were away.'

'And can you?'

'I think I might just manage.'

'Thanks a million,' Sue said, planting a kiss on her mother's forehead

'How are you and Tony getting on?' Kay asked.

'It's going well.' Sue's cheeks reddened. 'And he gets on great with Jamie. The two of them talk about football for hours on end.'

'That's good.'

'One thing I really like about him, Mum,' Sue added, 'is that he knows how to make me laugh.'

'That's very important in a relationship, Sue.'

When Colin Renton arrived back in Pitt Street he found Tony O'Sullivan sitting with Charlie in his office.

'Any joy at Cottiers, Colin?' Charlie asked as Renton walked in.

Renton referred to his notebook as he recounted his conversation with Kevin and Pete. 'They told me that Preston had a flat somewhere near the university, but they didn't know the address. They gave me the phone number of one of the partners in the firm where he worked.' Renton handed the slip of paper with the number on it to Charlie. 'His name's George Slater.'

When Charlie dialled the number, Susan Slater answered the call. Charlie introduced himself and asked if he could speak to her husband.

'George is outside, washing the car, Inspector. Hold on and I'll get him for you.'

'This is DCI Anderson, Glasgow CID, Mr Slater,' Charlie said when Slater came to the phone. 'I'm sorry to disturb you on a Sunday afternoon, sir, but I need some information.'

'What can I do for you?'

'I believe your firm has an employee called John Preston?'

'That is correct.'

'I need his address.'

Slater hesitated. 'I'm not trying to be difficult, Inspector, but I can't give out personal details over the phone, especially to someone I don't know. I've no reason to doubt for one minute that you are who you say you are,' he added quickly, 'but I would need confirmation.'

'Of course, sir.'

'Besides, I don't keep personnel data at home. I would have to go into the office to get the information. Is it urgent, or is it something that could wait till the morning?'

'I'm afraid not, sir. I need to have Mr Preston's address as soon as possible.'

'Why? Is there a problem?'

'There was a murder in the West End last night,' Charlie said. 'We have reason to believe that the victim might have been John Preston.'

'Good grief!'

'How long will it take you to get to your office?' Charlie asked.

'If I leave straight away, depending on the traffic, I could be there in twenty minutes. Our office is in Bath Street – in the block between West Campbell Street and Blythswood Street.'

'I'll meet you there,' Charlie said.

'I'll be driving a blue Audi.'

Charlie Anderson found a place to park in Blythswood Square. As he got out of his car he looked all around, his mind going back to his days in uniform when this part of the city had been his patch.

A lot had changed over the years, Charlie reflected. Twenty-five years ago, the square had been one of the most popular hangouts in the city for prostitutes. The girls had always grumbled when Charlie moved them on, telling him that they got a much better class of punter in the city centre. All that had changed when Glasgow was awarded the status of European City of Culture for nineteen ninety. A red-light district in the middle of town wasn't in keeping with the image the city fathers wanted to portray, so a purge had been initiated. The police had been instructed to clamp down hard on prostitution in and around the square. Any girls found soliciting had to be arrested, not just moved on. This had done nothing to reduce the overall level of prostitution in the city. All it had achieved was to force the girls to ply their trade in areas that were much more dangerous for them, such as the housing schemes in Castlemilk, Drumchapel and Easterhouse. The statistics said it all. City centre prostitution was reduced by forty percent while prostitution in the suburbs went up by a lot more than that – and violent assaults on working girls in the housing estates went up by over fifty percent. Charlie recalled that the city council had considered the purge to be a major success. As he made his way down the hill towards Bath Street, he shook his head.

Standing by the kerb, Charlie waved in acknowledgement when he saw the approaching blue Audi slow down. The car pulled up alongside him and George Slater stepped out, a small, dapper, moustachioed man with a ruddy complexion. Charlie showed him his warrant card, then produced a photo from his inside jacket pocket and handed it across.

Slater tugged his reading glasses from his shirt pocket and slipped them on to examine the photograph. 'That's John Preston all right,' he said, handing back the photo before turning round and leading the way to the entrance to his office block, a few yards further along the street. Climbing the stairs to the second floor, he unlocked the heavy, wooden door and ushered Charlie in ahead of him.

Charlie took the chair opposite Slater's desk in the cramped office.

'From memory, John had a flat in Oakfield Avenue,' Slater said as he crossed to his filing cabinet. He riffled through the files in the top drawer and pulled out a manila folder before sitting down behind his desk. Thumbing through the folder, he ran his index finger down one of the pages. 'Here we are,' he said, squinting at Charlie over the top of his spectacles. 'Oakfield Avenue, as I thought,' he said, noting down the address on a slip of paper. 'It's a rented flat, I believe,' he added.

'Do you have his phone number?' Charlie asked.

Slater referred again to the file. 'Just his mobile,' he said, writing the number down under the address and handing the slip of paper to Charlie. 'There's no mention in the file of him having a land line.'

'How long had Preston been working here?' Charlie asked.

'About a year.'

'What can you tell me about his background?'

Slipping off his glasses, Slater stared fixedly at Charlie without offering a reply.

Charlie held his gaze. 'I asked you, sir. What do you know about John Preston's background?'

'This is sensitive, Inspector.' Slater's fingers twitched back and forth across his mouth. Charlie could see the colour rising in his cheeks. 'Extremely sensitive – and highly confidential. I really need to talk to Henry.'

'Who is Henry?'

'Henry Murdoch. He's my partner.'

'Why do you need to talk to him?'

Slater hesitated. 'John Preston is – ' He broke off and dabbed at the beads of perspiration on his brow with the back of his hand. 'John Preston *was* – Henry's son.'

CHAPTER 7

'Let me make sure I've got this straight,' Charlie said, leaning back in his chair. 'What you're telling me is that your partner, Henry Murdoch, is John Preston's father?'

'That's right.'

'How come they don't share the same surname?'

'Up until recently, they did. John Preston's name used to be John Murdoch. Perhaps you remember the case, Inspector? The trial was in the High Court – about a year ago.'

'John Murdoch?' Charlie mused, rubbing reflectively at his chin. 'That name rings a bell. Wait a minute – I've got it!' he said, snapping his fingers. 'The case had something to do with child molesting, if I remember correctly?'

Slater nodded. 'John was a school teacher at the time and he was accused of grooming and sexually assaulting one of his pupils – a boy called Tommy Carter.'

'And if I'm not mistaken,' Charlie offered, 'the verdict was not proven?'

'That is correct. And the day after the trial, Tommy Carter threw himself in front of a train. The story made a big splash in the newspapers at the time. Murdoch was subjected to a deluge of hate mail, as well as several threats to his life on the Internet. He gave up his teaching position, moved flat, and changed his name to John Preston. His father, Henry, my partner, asked me if I would be prepared to let John have a job in our firm so he could make a fresh start. Of course, I agreed. The poor guy had been acquitted, yet the press were hounding him – making his life a living hell by suggesting that he was in some way responsible for Tommy Carter taking his own life.'

'Did anyone else in the firm know about Preston's background?'

Slater shook his head. 'Definitely not, Inspector. Only Henry and I knew anything about John's situation.' He paused. 'Who's going to break the news to Henry and Sarah?' he asked anxiously.

'I'll take care of that, sir,' Charlie said. 'If you could let me have Mr Murdoch's address?'

Slater opened the top drawer of his desk and took out a business card. 'This has Henry's home address and his phone number on it,' he said, handing the card across.

'Do you know if Mr Murdoch is likely to be at home this afternoon?'

'I'm sure he will be. He very rarely goes anywhere at the weekends. His wife had a stroke last year, brought about by the stress of their son's trial. She's completely paralysed down one side of her body. She needs full-time nursing. Henry has someone who comes in to look after her during the week while he's at work, but at the weekends he nearly always stays at home and takes care of her himself.'

'Thank you, sir,' Charlie said. Tucking the business card into the breast pocket of his jacket, he heaved himself to his feet.

When he got back to his car, Charlie pulled his mobile phone from his jacket pocket and clicked onto his home number.

'It's me,' he said when Kay answered.

'How are things?'

'It looks like it could be a long day.'

'Have you had anything to eat?'

'Not yet. I'm not hungry, but I'll try to grab a sandwich.'

'Make sure you do.'

'How is Jamie?'

'Disappointed, of course, but he's putting a brave face on it.'

'Let me talk to him.'

'I'm really sorry about today,' Charlie said when Jamie came to the phone. 'I have to work this afternoon.'

'Grandma told me that.'

'How about I come across to your place tomorrow morning and we can have a game of football before you go to school?'

'That would be great, Grandad!' Jamie said excitedly.

'What time can you be ready?'

'I can get up at half-past seven. Which means we'll be able to play for an hour.'

'Great!' Charlie grimaced. 'Half-past seven it is.'

'Thanks a million!'

'Let me have a word with your Mum, son.'

'I'm sorry about today, Sue,' Charlie said when his daughter came to the phone.

'Mum explained – it couldn't he helped.'

'I've arranged with Jamie to come across to your place at half-past seven tomorrow morning to have a game of football with him before he goes to school. I hope that's all right?'

'Of course it is. Thanks for doing that, Dad.'

Disconnecting, Charlie scanned his contacts' list and clicked onto Colin Renton's mobile number. 'Are you in the office?' he asked when Renton took the call.

'Yes, sir.'

'I've got John Preston's address and his mobile number,' Charlie said. 'Do you have a pen and paper?'

'Sure.'

Charlie read out the information. 'Get Freer to check out the phone number. Tell him to find out who Preston's service provider was and get hold of his phone records. When you've done that, wait for me at main reception. I'll drive by in five minutes and pick you up.'

'Where are we going?'

'To break the news to the victim's parents. I'll fill you in when I see you.'

*

Charlie drew up alongside the kerb outside the CID headquarters in Pitt Street and gave a quick toot on the horn. Having taken Henry Murdoch's business card from his jacket pocket, he was punching the postcode in Giffnock into his sat nav when Renton came out of the main entrance and trotted down the steps.

'Do you remember the John Murdoch trial?' Charlie asked as Renton was clipping on his seat belt. 'It was in the High Court – about a year ago.'

Renton thought for a minute. 'Wasn't he the teacher who was up on a charge of kiddie fiddling?'

'That's the one. It seems that he changed his name from John Murdoch to John Preston after the trial to try to get out of the limelight.'

'With limited success,' Renton suggested, raising an eyebrow.

'So it would appear.' Charlie pulled away from the kerb and followed the sat nav's directions towards the Kingston Bridge. 'His father is a partner in the computer consultancy firm where Preston was working. When his son was forced to pack in teaching because of the witch hunt in the press, he gave him a job in the family firm.'

After crossing the bridge, Charlie filtered onto the M77, the sat nav instructing him to leave the motorway at the junction signposted for Paisley. From there, he drove the length of Rouken Glen Park, arriving a few minutes later in Huntly Avenue, a narrow street lined with two-storey, red sandstone, semi-detached properties.

"You have reached your destination" the high-pitched, female voice chimed out as he pulled up outside Henry Murdoch's residence.

'This is the part of the job I hate most,' Charlie said as he turned off the ignition.

'Even worse than a session with Niggle?' Renton queried.

'It's a close call, Colin – but I reckon so.'

When Charlie rang the door bell, Henry Murdoch, a slight, nervous-looking man, came to answer it. Charlie guessed he was in his mid-fifties. Having introduced himself, he showed Murdoch his warrant card. 'This is my colleague, DC Renton,' Charlie added.

'What can I do for you, gentlemen?'

'Could we come in, please?' Charlie said.

Murdoch stepped aside to allow them to cross the threshold before closing the door behind them. He led the way along the hall to the spacious lounge at the rear of the building where he indicated the settee for Charlie and Renton. They both remained standing.

'I'm afraid we have some very bad news to impart, sir,' Charlie intoned gravely. Murdoch grasped the back of the settee with both hands. 'It concerns your son, John.' The colour drained from Murdoch's face as his grip on the settee tightened. 'Last night, sir, in Lawrence Street – '

'The murder – ?' Murdoch interjected, his voice little more than a whispered croak. 'The murder I read about in the papers this morning?' Charlie gave a curt nod. Murdoch stared vacantly out of the French windows in the direction of the water feature at the far end of the ornate garden. There was a long pause before he spoke. 'I've been dreading this moment, Inspector, each and every day for the past year. One of the Carter brothers killed John. You do know that?' he added in a matter of fact tone.

Renton took Murdoch's arm and guided him down onto a chair. 'Could I get you something to drink, sir?' he asked. 'A glass of water? Perhaps you'd prefer a cup of tea or coffee?'

Murdoch shook his head, his jaw hanging limp. 'You mustn't say anything about this to my wife,' he implored, gripping Renton's forearm tightly. 'The shock would kill her. I'll have to find some way to tell her, of course – but in my own time.'

'We won't say anything to your wife, sir,' Renton reassured him.

'We will need access to your son's flat, Mr Murdoch,' Charlie said. 'To find out if there's anything there that could help us establish who was responsible for his murder.'

'You mean to say – if it was Tommy Carter's father – or his uncle – who killed John? It was one of them, Inspector.'

'We're not ruling anyone in – or anyone out – at this stage, Mr Murdoch.'

'The fact that John was acquitted meant nothing to the Carter family,' Murdoch said. 'They swore they would track him down and kill him.' Murdoch's hands were twitching uncontrollably. 'Do you know how they managed to find John?' he asked.

'We have no information regarding that,' Charlie said. 'Mr Slater gave us your son's mobile phone number. We'll analyse the records of his calls to see if that gives us any indication as to what might have happened to him. Do you know if your son had a computer in his flat?'

'Yes, he did.'

'I'd like to check that out. I could organise a search warrant, but it would get things moving a lot faster if you would give us authorisation to enter the premises.'

'I don't have a problem with that. I can give you John's address, but I'm afraid I don't have a set of keys. You'd have to contact his landlord to get a spare set.'

'Mr Slater has already given us his address, sir. And there were house keys among your son's possessions,' Charlie added. 'Could we have your permission to use them to enter the flat?'

'Of course – and if you require it, you have my authorisation to remove his computer – and anything else you might need. I would go with you – but my wife. I can't leave her alone....' His voice tailed off.

'I understand,' Charlie said.

'But it's not in John's flat that you're going to find out what happened to him,' Murdoch stated grimly. 'For that, you'll have to talk to the Carter brothers.'

'I'm afraid I will have to ask you to come to the mortuary to make a formal identification of your son's body,' Charlie said.

Murdoch nodded his concurrence. 'Would tomorrow be all right for that?'

'Of course.'

'Is it the mortuary in the Saltmarket?'

'Yes.'

'I'll go there first thing in the morning – as soon as the nurse arrives to take care of Sarah.'

Getting slowly to his feet, Murdoch showed them out.

Tony O'Sullivan was sitting in his car, unwrapping the egg mayonnaise sandwich he'd bought for his lunch from Marks and Spencer, when his mobile ringtone sounded.

'Is that you, Mr O'Sullivan?' the caller asked.

He recognised Bert Tollin's voice. 'Yes, Bert. What can I do for you?'

'Word on the street is that you're looking for Jim Colvin.'

'Good news travels fast. De you know where he hangs out?'

'He runs his operations out of the south side. He has an office upstairs in the *Black Seven* snooker hall. But if you'd like to see him straight away, you might want to drop into The Ettrick bar in Dumbarton Road.'

'Are you sure he's there?'

'As sure as if I was standing at the other end of the bar right now, watching him drink a pint of Guinness and guzzle a packet of cheese and onion crisps.'

'Is he on his own?'

'He's with someone I don't know. About five feet six, shoulder-length, greasy hair and a big paunch.'

'That sounds like a fair description of his missus.'

'It could be, Mr O'Sullivan.' Bert chortled. 'It could well be.'

'Is the pub busy?'

'Most of the lunchtime crowd have drifted off. There are only about a dozen diehards left, propping up the bar.'

'I'll be there in about ten minutes.'

'If you don't mind, I won't hang around and wait for you. I don't like to be seen in the vicinity when the cops turn up out of the blue. It's not good for my image.'

'Okay, Bert. I'll settle up with you later.'

'No problem, Mr O'Sullivan. Your credit's good.'

CHAPTER 8

As soon as he got back to his office Charlie checked his address book, then picked up the phone and dialled James Ramsay's number. He recognised the deep, gravelly, heavy-smoker's voice that answered.

'It's Charlie Anderson here, James. My apologies for disturbing you on a Sunday afternoon.'

'That's not a problem, Charlie. Now I'm retired, one day is much the same as any other. What can I do for you?'

'Could I drop in and see you for a chat? I'd like to pick your brains.'

'You're welcome to try – if you can find any. When were you thinking of?'

'How are you fixed today?'

'Fine. Come across any time you like. I'll be at home all afternoon.'

'How about,' Charlie said, checking his watch, 'four o'clock?'

'Four o'clock it is.'

Tony O'Sullivan walked up to the two men standing at the far end of the bar in The Ettrick. Jim Colvin was dressed in an expensive, Italian suit, in stark contrast to his squat companion's grubby T-shirt and frayed jeans. When Colvin saw O'Sullivan approaching, he frowned and broke off from his conversation.

'What the hell are you doing here, O'Sullivan?' he demanded.

'Are you not going to introduce me to your friend?' Tony nodded in the direction of the tubby individual whose stomach was protruding over his leather belt.

Colvin's brow shrivelled. 'Am I supposed to think it's a coincidence that you just happened to drop in here this afternoon?' he asked, eyeing the group of men at the far end of the bar with suspicion.

Ignoring the question, O'Sullivan held out his hand to Colvin's companion. 'I'm Tony O'Sullivan,' he offered. 'And you are?'

'He forgot to mention the "Detective Sergeant" part of his moniker, Andy,' Colvin interjected.

Andy refused O'Sullivan's proffered hand, staring at him in surly silence.

O'Sullivan turned back to Colvin. 'Does Andy have a surname?' he asked.

'How about Pandy?' Colvin suggested.

'You're giving away your age.'

'And as far as you're concerned, that's all I'll be giving away.'

'Does Andy Pandy have a tongue?' O'Sullivan asked.

'He's very particular about who he speaks to,' Colvin said. 'And anyone who's name begins with "Detective" doesn't qualify.'

'Okay, smart arse. It's you I want to talk to – on your own.'

'You can say anything you like in front of Andy. He's my business partner. We don't have any secrets.'

'What kind of "business" would that be?'

'He supplies me with odds and ends.'

'Does that include rusty nails?'

'I've no idea what you're wittering on about, O'Sullivan. I'm a busy man, so get whatever you have to say off your chest, then sod off and leave me in peace.'

'Is Andy the business partner who was in The Jacobite Arms round about seven o'clock last night, asking if anyone knew where he could find Jack Mulgrew?'

'Who told you that?'

'A wee birdie.'

Colvin furrowed his brow. 'Of course!' he said, snapping his fingers. 'I remember now. I'd borrowed a few quid from Mulgrew last month and I wanted to pay him back. He was decent enough to sub me when I was skint, so I asked Andy to make sure – ' Colvin broke off to pick up his pint of Guinness from the counter. He weighed the glass in his fist, then took a long, slow sip, before enunciating carefully. 'I asked Andy to make sure that Mulgrew got what was coming to him.'

'And did he?' O'Sullivan asked. 'Did Mulgrew get what was coming to him?'

'Unfortunately, Andy didn't manage to catch up with him,' Colvin said with a smirk as he placed his glass back down on the bar. 'Is that it, O'Sullivan?'

'For now, yes.'

'In which case, why don't you do us all a favour – and fuck off!'

Charlie Anderson parked outside the imposing, wrought-iron gates of the detached, red sandstone property in Langside. Getting out of his car, he turned his jacket collar up against the light drizzle as he made his way up the tree-lined drive, his shoes scrunching noisily in the thick gravel. When he rang the bell, James Ramsay came to the door. A big man, both in height and in girth.

Smiling, Ramsay made a show of checking his watch. 'Four o'clock on the dot. Bang on time, Charlie, as always.'

'How's retirement treating you, James?' Charlie asked, folding his collar back down as Ramsay led the way to the lounge, the large, bay windows looking out onto the manicured lawn.

'I have to say, life is pretty good.'

'Are you managing to fill your time all right?'

'That's never a problem. I spend most mornings taking care of the garden and pottering about in my greenhouse. If the weather's good I usually play bowls at my club in the afternoon – and if it's not, I quite often have a game on one of the indoor rinks.'

'I hope I haven't messed up your game today?'

'Not at all. I give the club a wide berth on Sundays. It's too busy with the world's workers. Grab a seat while I fix us a drink,' he said, crossing to the well-stocked cocktail cabinet by the window. 'What'll it be?'

Charlie settled down on the leather settee. 'A glass of water would be fine, thanks.'

'Could I not tempt you?' Ramsay said, holding up a decanter. 'It's a rather fine, twenty year-old malt.'

'No thanks.'

'Are you sure? I'm retired now. I won't report you for drinking on duty.'

'It's a bit early for me, James.'

Ramsay shrugged. 'As you wish. You don't mind if I have a snifter?'

'Not at all. Carry on.'

Ramsay tipped a generous measure of Scotch from the decanter into a crystal tumbler, then filled a tall glass from a bottle of Evian water, adding a slice of lemon. Joining Charlie on the settee, he handed him his drink.

'Cheers!' he said, raising his tumbler to eye level. 'It can't be long now until they put you out to pasture, Charlie.'

'Nine months – and counting. But I don't reckon I'll be heading for any pasture, James,' Charlie said with a grimace. 'More likely I'll be given a one-way ticket to the knacker's yard.'

Ramsay picked up a packet of cigarettes from the coffee table. 'You mentioned on the phone that you wanted to pick my brains,' he said as he tapped out a cigarette. 'I'm intrigued. What can I help you with?' he asked, lighting up.

'Do you remember the John Murdoch trial?'

'Of course I do. It was my last day on the bench before I retired, which means it must've been almost exactly a year ago. Hard to believe it's a year already – doesn't time fly?'

'Did you know that Murdoch's dead?'

Ramsay's hand froze with his cigarette half-way to his lips. 'You don't say? What happened to him?'

'He was murdered last night – in the West End – on his way home from the pub.'

Ramsay inhaled deeply. 'I read in the papers this morning that a body had been found in Hyndland,' he said as he exhaled, 'but they didn't give a name.'

'The victim will be identified in the press tomorrow as John Preston. Murdoch had changed his name.'

Ramsay nodded. 'I knew he was planning to do that, but I didn't know he would be calling himself Preston.'

'How did you know that?' Charlie asked.

'The lawyer who acted as Murdoch's defence counsel is a member of my bowling club. We often have a drink together. After the trial, he told me that Murdoch had asked him what he needed to do to change his name by deed poll.'

Charlie smiled. 'Might that not be perceived as creating a conflict of interest?'

'I'm very even-handed, Charlie. I drink with the prosecution lawyers as well.' Ramsay took a sip of whisky before continuing. 'The lawyer explained to Murdoch that the concept of a deed poll doesn't exist in Scottish law, however, he could achieve the same effect by arranging a meeting with a Justice of the Peace and making a statutory declaration of a change of name. Murdoch was worried that the Carter brothers might still be able to find him, but his lawyer reassured him on that score. The statutory declaration process is confidential. There's no way a change of name can be traced through the public records.'

Ramsay put his whisky tumbler down on the glass-topped coffee table and looked enquiringly at Charlie. 'My original question still stands, Charlie. What can I help you with?'

'Yesterday was the third of September – and Murdoch was killed at ten-thirty in the evening. Which happens to be a year to the day, and more or less the same time, as Tommy Carter threw himself in front of a train.'

'So it is,' Ramsay nodded, tapping the ash from his cigarette into an ashtray. 'And you don't think that's a coincidence?'

'Do you?'

Ramsay shook his head slowly from side to side. 'We've both been around long enough to know that the odds against that are a million to one. So you reckon someone caught up with him?'

'It certainly looks like it,' Charlie said. 'Do you have any idea who that might've been?'

Ramsay picked up his glass and swilled the liquid round. 'The Carter brothers have to be prime candidates, I suppose,' he reflected.

'What did you think of the verdict in Murdoch's trial?' Charlie asked.

Ramsay looked quizzical. 'What do you mean by that?'

'I mean – did you think justice had been done?'

'I directed the jury to return a verdict of not proven. My role was to implement the law of the land and, on the evidence presented, there was no other action I could reasonably have taken.'

'What do you think of not proven as a verdict?' Charlie asked.

'What do I think of it?'

'Would we not be better off having just 'guilty' and 'not guilty'? Other countries seem to manage fine with that. Not proven always gives the impression that the court thought the accused was guilty, but there wasn't enough evidence to secure a conviction.'

'That's a common enough interpretation,' Ramsay said. 'When he was the sheriff in Selkirk, Sir Walter Scott referred to not proven as the bastard verdict. There are pros and cons, I'll give you that. But overall I think it's a good thing. Take a rape charge, for example. Quite often there is insufficient corroborating evidence – and the victim's testimony alone doesn't constitute a legal ground for a conviction. If the not proven verdict didn't exist, fewer women would be willing to proceed to trial because, if the accused is found not guilty, the victim would feel stigmatised in the eyes of the public. On the other hand, a not proven verdict doesn't damage the victim's credibility as it indicates that the jury didn't disbelieve her, only that the evidence presented wasn't sufficient to secure a conviction.

'The downside of that, of course, is that the general public considers that not proven means the accused has got off on a technicality and that can incite vigilantes to take the law into their own hands.'

'Off the record, what was your gut feeling in Murdoch's case?'

Ramsay took a pull on his cigarette as he reflected. 'As far as I was concerned, Murdoch was guilty as charged. However, the prosecution case wasn't at all well handled and Murdoch's lawyer was as sharp as a tack. He never missed a trick. The boy, Tommy Carter, wasn't present in court – he gave his evidence via a video link. Under cross-examination, Murdoch's lawyer managed to pick holes in Tommy's story and he homed in on inconsistencies in the boy's version of events with regard to dates and times. I thought the inconsistencies were probably due to the lad's nervousness, but Murdoch's lawyer didn't do anything that could be construed as exploiting Tommy's anxiety – and he didn't apply any undue pressure on him. But what he did manage to achieve was create doubt in the jury's mind with regard to what had actually happened, the result of which was that the only verdicts they could realistically consider were not guilty or not proven. I directed them towards the latter.'

'How did Tommy's family react when the verdict was announced?'

'They were not at all happy. That's putting it mildly. In fact, they were spitting blood. There had been several instances of comments being shouted out from the public gallery while evidence was being presented. On more than one occasion I had to threaten to clear the court if the interruptions didn't cease. When the chairman of the jury delivered the not proven verdict, there was a lot of vitriol being bandied about.'

'Who was being vociferous?'

'I really couldn't say.' Ramsay gazed at his whisky as he swilled the contents round and round in the glass. 'Keeping the prosecution and the defence counsel in line, as well as having to instruct the jury, is a full-time job. You don't have time to pay attention to who's making a nuisance of themselves in the public gallery.'

'Would it be worth my while pulling the transcript of the trial?' Charlie asked. 'Will there be anything in there that would identify who was causing trouble?'

Ramsay got to his feet and crossed to the cocktail cabinet to top up his drink. 'You'll get the official record of what happened from the transcript. However, if you want to know who was causing a stooshie, you could do a lot worse than have a word with Mark Houston.'

'Who is he?' Charlie asked.

'Mark's a court stenographer. He was on duty throughout Murdoch's trial. I worked with him for more than ten years. As well as being one of the best in the business as far as recording accuracy's concerned, Mark always made notes about everything that was going on in court during a trial, including anything that was happening in the public galleries. If you want the lowdown on who was stirring things up, I suggest you have a word with him. He has a photographic memory – and he wouldn't necessarily have included all his observations in the official record. Would you like me to give him a call and set something up?'

'That would be helpful, James.'

Ramsay picked up his address book from the coffee table and flicked through the pages until he found the number he was looking for. When he dialled, the phone was answered on the second ring.

Having explained the situation, Ramsay arranged for Charlie to meet Mark Houston at six-fifteen at Houston's tennis club in Hyndland Road.

'Thanks for arranging that for me, James,' Charlie said.

'Glad to be of assistance,' Ramsay said, folding his cigarette into the ashtray before getting to his feet and taking Charlie's hand in a firm grip. 'If you ever get bored with life in the knacker's yard and fancy a hammering at bowls, give me a bell.'

Charlie reversed into a tight parking place near the top of Hughenden Drive, round the corner from the Western Racquet club. As he walked down the steps towards the clubhouse he checked his watch. It was just after six o'clock. All the tennis courts on both sides of the clubhouse building were in use. Stopping in front of a wooden bench set against the wall, he peered at the faded memorial plaque on the back of the seat. He could just about make out that it was inscribed with the words: "From Stan".

It's a pity that Stan didn't leave enough dosh for a lick of paint, Charlie thought to himself as he dusted off a few loose flakes before sitting down. It was a warm evening and Charlie was starting to nod off to the rhythmic sound of tennis balls being patted back and forth across the net when Mark Houston emerged from the clubhouse.

'Inspector Anderson?' he asked enquiringly as he approached Charlie.

Charlie judged him to be in his late thirties; tall and thick-set, his slicked-back, brown hair still damp from the shower.

'It's good of you to see me at such short notice, Mr Houston,' Charlie said, getting to his feet and proffering his hand. 'How did your game go?'

'It was close, but I lost.' Houston shrugged. 'Would you like to come inside?' he suggested. 'The coffee isn't bad.'

'That sounds like a very good idea. I could do with something to keep me awake – I nearly dropped off while I was waiting for you.'

'How do you take it?' Houston asked.

'Black with two sugars.'

Having ordered the coffees at the counter, Houston carried the cups across to the table by the window where Charlie had installed himself. They were the only customers.

'James Ramsay tells me that you're a stenographer in the High Court,' Charlie said as Houston sat down on the seat facing him.

'That's correct.'

'How long have you been doing that?'

'Ever since I graduated, which means it's more than sixteen years now. But I won't be doing it for very much longer,' he added.

'Why not?'

'It's a dead-end job, Inspector. The word is that the courts are planning to do away with stenographers in the not too distant future and replace us with recording equipment.' Houston let out an indignant snort. 'It's one of the most ridiculous ideas I've ever heard. It's driven by cost-cutting, of course, like so many other things these days. Competent stenographers do a lot more than document the actual court proceedings. As well as identifying who has said what, which is not a straightforward task, let me tell you, especially when things get heated and several people are talking at the same time, they also record when a witness answers a question with a nod or a shake of the head, or when someone is pointed out in court. How is electronic equipment going to handle that?'

'That seems like a fair question.'

'And if you look beyond that,' Houston added, 'filming in court is probably going to be permitted before too long, which will completely wipe out the stenographer's role, so I reckon it makes sense for me to jump ship before I get pushed. Sorry!' Houston broke off with an embarrassed smile. 'I didn't mean to get onto my hobby horse.'

'That's okay.'

'James said you wanted to talk to me about the John Murdoch trial. What can I help you with?'

'I'm looking for any information you can give me about what happened in court throughout the proceedings. Do you remember much about the case?'

'I am blessed – or some people would say, cursed – with an excellent memory. I can recall everything that happened in great detail.'

'I'm told the jury returned a verdict of not proven.'

'That's correct.'

'Did you agree with that verdict?'

'What a strange question.' Houston paused while he stirred sugar into his coffee. 'It's not for me to agree, or disagree, with a jury's verdict.'

'I realise that – but you must have had an opinion.'

'I've sat through a lot of trials in the High Court, Inspector. Human nature dictates that you always form an opinion.'

'And what was your opinion in John Murdoch's case?'

Houston shrugged. 'I empathised with the young boy, Tommy Carter. He wasn't in court – he gave his evidence over a video link. He came across as a truthful lad, but he was muddled and confused with regard to dates and times. Murdoch had been his guidance teacher and Tommy appeared to have built a bond of

54

trust with him. Tommy told the court that he had confided in Murdoch that he was worried about his sexuality. Murdoch had apparently been very sympathetic – taking time out to explain to Tommy that not all boys fancied girls – and that his feelings for other boys were perfectly natural.

'Tommy told the court that he had bumped into Murdoch in Kelvingrove Park on a Friday afternoon – the eighth of July – and that Murdoch had invited him back to his flat. When they got there, Tommy said Murdoch had given him a glass of Irn Bru. After he'd drunk it he said he started to feel woozy and the room started to spin. He said that Murdoch had sat down on the settee beside him and put his hand on his knee. He claimed that Murdoch had told him that the only way he'd ever know for certain whether or not he was homosexual would be to have sex with a man. Tommy said that Murdoch had helped him to his feet and led him through to his bedroom, where intercourse took place.

'Murdoch's version of events was that, on the day before the school broke up for the summer holidays, Tommy had stayed behind when the other pupils had left the classroom. When they were on their own, Tommy had blurted out that he was in love with him and wanted to have sex with him. Murdoch stated that, when he categorically refused, Tommy reacted badly. He said Tommy became agitated and abusive before running out of the room. He claimed that Tommy had made up the story about bumping into him in the park and being accosted in his flat out of spite.'

'Which version of events rang true?' Charlie asked.

'I never had any real doubt that Tommy was telling the truth,' Houston said. 'However, under cross-examination, Tommy claimed that this had happened on the afternoon of Friday the eighth of July. Murdoch's defence lawyer pressed Tommy to confirm that he was absolutely sure about the date, giving him ample opportunity to reconsider. Tommy was adamant about it – but it transpired that Murdoch had a watertight alibi for that date and time. Tommy became flustered – then he changed his story and said it had happened the following day, Saturday, the ninth of July. In his closing address, Murdoch's lawyer delivered an impassioned speech – asking the jury to consider which scenario was more likely. That Tommy had got the date wrong – or that or he had fabricated the story because his advances to his teacher had been spurned. I was convinced that the kid was telling the truth, but there was no way Murdoch could've been convicted on the evidence as presented. I imagine the options the jury would have been considering would have been not guilty or not proven. However, in his summing up, Judge Ramsay directed them towards the latter.'

'James Ramsay told me that there were several instances of disturbances taking place in the public gallery during the proceedings,' Charlie said.

'There was a lot of shouting and swearing going on.'

'Will that be documented in the official transcript?'

'It will be noted that there were disturbances in the public gallery, but the transcript won't give the names of those involved, because no one was formally identified during the trial.'

'Do you know who was causing the trouble?'

'Several members of Tommy's family. As far as I could make out, the main instigator was Tommy's uncle, though his father wasn't far behind. Throughout the hearing the uncle was continually shouting out abuse, mostly directed at Murdoch's defence counsel, accusing him of distorting the facts and deliberately misinterpreting Tommy's account of what had happened. Tommy's mother, Alice Carter, and her new man, Mitch Weir, were also in court. Mrs C. kept her distance from the Carter brothers – as far as I could see they didn't exchange a single word throughout the two days of the hearing – but she wasn't holding back when it came to letting Murdoch know what she thought of him – alternating between calling him a filthy pervert and screaming that hanging was too good for him.

'On more than one occasion I thought Judge Ramsay would have to clear the court. When the verdict was delivered by the chairman of the jury, both the Carter brothers – as well as Mrs C. and Mitch Weir – went ballistic. They were all shouting the odds – yelling and screaming that Murdoch was a paedophile and a liar and threatening him with retribution.'

'Did they specify what kind of retribution they had in mind?'

'If I leave out the expletives, the gist of what they were saying was that, if the court wasn't prepared to deal with Murdoch, they would take matters into their own hands. It was all very highly-charged and emotional.'

'Did you know that Murdoch had changed his name after the trial?'

'I didn't know that, but I'm not in the least surprised. The Carter family didn't leave me with the impression that they were about to let the matter drop after the verdict was announced.'

'Murdoch changed his name to Preston.' Charlie paused. 'And John Preston was murdered last night.'

The coffee spoon froze in Houston's fingers. 'Really?'

'I'm sorry to spring it on you like that,' Charlie said. 'Are you all right?'

'I'm okay. It came as a bit of a shock, that's all. Do you think his death could have been related to what happened in court?'

'Yesterday was a year to the day from when Tommy Carter threw himself in front of a train.'

'Of course it was. Do you think a member of the Carter family was responsible for killing him?'

'I didn't say that. But it's a fair bet that whoever committed the murder had some connection with Tommy Carter.'

Houston took a sip of his coffee. 'Is there anything else I can help you with?'

'Not for now, but I might want to talk to you again later. Could I have your address and phone number?'

'Of course.'

Taking out his notebook, Charlie opened it at a blank page and handed it across, along with his pen. Houston jotted down the information.

When they'd finished their coffees, Charlie walked with Houston as far as his car. As Houston was driving off, Charlie took out his phone and clicked onto Tony O'Sullivan's mobile number.

'Where are you?' Charlie asked when O'Sullivan took the call.

'I'm in Pitt Street, sir.'

'I'm on my way there. Meet me in my office in fifteen minutes. And if Renton's in the building,' Charlie added, 'tell him to be there as well.'

O'Sullivan and Renton were waiting for Charlie in his office when he got back. Having updated them on his discussions with James Ramsay and Mark Houston, Charlie swung his feet up onto his desk.

'Where do we go from here, sir?' O'Sullivan asked.

'When the press get wind of the fact that Preston and Murdoch are one and the same person,' Charlie said, 'and that he was murdered on the anniversary of Tommy Carter's suicide – they're going to have a field day. At the time of the trial the red tops were all up in arms about the not proven verdict, so we can expect the full horror story now: "The Revenge of the Carters" – "Divine Retribution" – "Justice Is Done" – you name it.'

'Should we release the information that John Murdoch and John Preston are the same person?' Renton asked.

'Absolutely!' Charlie said. 'And the sooner we can do that, the better. Get a press release to that effect out as soon as you can. Give them chapter and verse. There's no way we can keep the lid on the fact that the person who was murdered last night was John Murdoch and I want that information to be seen to be coming from us, rather than wait for it to be dug up by some tabloid hack, otherwise we'll be accused of trying to orchestrate a cover-up. When you've organised that, Colin, arrange for someone from forensics to go with you to Preston's flat tomorrow morning. Here's the address,' Charlie added, handing across the slip of paper George Slater had given him. 'You'll be able to pick up a set of keys for his flat from the mortuary. Tell forensics to give the place a thorough going over to see if they can come up with anything useful.'

'Will do.'

'Tony,' Charlie said, turning to O'Sullivan, 'we need to trawl through everything we have regarding Murdoch's trial – the transcript of the court proceedings, the witness statements, any background information, the whole shooting match. Arrange for copies of all the relevant documentation to be sent across here. We also need to check out what we have on file regarding Tommy Carter's father and his uncle.'

'The Social Work department would be a good place to start,' O'Sullivan suggested. 'It's a fair bet they'll have had dealings with the family over the years.'

'Good point,' Charlie said. 'Get on to them first thing in the morning and find out what they've got. We'll meet here at nine o'clock tomorrow and take it from there.'

As O'Sullivan and Renton were filing out of his office, Charlie picked up his phone and called home.

'I'm on my way,' he said when Kay answered. 'I'll be home in about twenty minutes.'

'Did you get something to eat at lunchtime?' Kay asked.

'I grabbed a sandwich,' Charlie lied.

'Sue and I had lasagne. There's a lot left over. Would you like me to re-heat it for you?'

'That would be great.'

It was after eight o'clock by the time Charlie turned the key in his front door.

'It's just me!' he called out as he crossed the threshold, pausing in the hall to inhale the inviting smell of lasagne drifting out from the kitchen.

Kay appeared in the doorway. 'Do you fancy a dram before you eat?'

'Not right now,' Charlie said, stripping off his jacket. 'I'll maybe have one later.'

'I'm prepared to bet it wasn't a big sandwich you had for lunch,' Kay said.

'Not very,' Charlie said, forcing a weak smile.

When he'd finished eating, Charlie put down his fork. 'I really did my best to duck out of it, love, but Niggle wouldn't wear it.'

'That's okay, Charlie.' Kay reached across the kitchen table and took Charlie's hand in hers, gently squeezing his fingers. 'I realise I've been tetchy recently. I was just hoping for your sake that you'd be able to see out the next few months without too much hassle. Would you like some more?' Kay asked, pointing to Charlie's empty plate.

'No thanks,' Charlie said, patting his stomach. 'That was fine.'

'How about some biscuits and cheese? I got a nice bit of Mull cheddar yesterday.'

'You could tempt me with that.'

'Go on through to the lounge and put your feet up. I'll bring it through.'

As Charlie was settling into his favourite armchair by the unlit gas fire, Blakey stirred in his basket. Stretching up on all four paws and arching his back, the cat padded quickly across the room and sprang agilely onto the arm of the chair. Stepping delicately from there onto Charlie's knees, he circled twice before curling himself up on Charlie's lap.

'How was your day, old boy?' Charlie asked, scratching gently at the top of Blakey's bony, jet-black head. The response was a deep, satisfying purr.

'It didn't take his lordship long,' Kay said as she came into the room carrying a tray, which she set down on the coffee table beside Charlie. 'Do you want me to take him?'

'No, leave him. He's fine,' Charlie said, continuing to scratch at Blakey's head as the sound of purring rose in a crescendo.

Charlie eyed the contents of the tray – several oat cakes and a thick slab of Cheddar cheese on a plate, alongside a large glass of malt whisky.

'You think of everything.'

'Do you want to talk about it?' Kay said, settling down on the armchair opposite. 'You know that sometimes helps.'

Charlie cut himself a thick wedge of cheese and munched on it slowly as he recounted the events of the day. 'John Murdoch had changed his name to John Preston,' he concluded, 'but it appears that someone managed to track him down.'

'Do you think one of the dead boy's relatives was responsible for the murder?'

'That has to be a strong possibility, but by no means the only one.'

'Where do you go from here?' Kay asked.

'The usual routine,' Charlie said with a sigh. 'A pile of documents to plough through and a lot of people to interview. Hey, that's enough of my problems.' Charlie broke off to take a sip of whisky. 'Tell me about your day,' he said, doing his best to sound upbeat. 'How were Sue and Jamie?'

'They were both in good form. By the way, Sue and Tony seem to be hitting it off,' Kay added. 'She likes him a lot, Charlie. And it seems that he's getting on very well with Jamie, which is important.'

'Don't read too much into things, Kay. They've only been seeing each other for a few months.'

'I realise that. But never underestimate a mother's intuition.'

'That was great,' Sue said, folding the last of the curry sauce into a piece of naan bread and popping it into her mouth.

'Balbir's best.'

Sue settled down on the settee beside Tony and picked up the bottle of Rioja from the coffee table.

'No more for me,' Tony said, holding his hand over his glass. 'It would put me over the limit.'

'You don't have to drive tonight,' Sue said, nudging Tony's hand aside and tipping a generous measure of wine into his glass.

Tony raised his eyebrows. 'I thought you had school tomorrow?'

'Don't get your hopes up. You're being invited to stay over. Nobody said anything about a night of unbridled passion.'

'Oh, you know how to spoil everything,' Tony said. Putting his wine glass down on the coffee table, he slipped his arm around Sue's shoulders and drew her towards him. Their mouths met in a long, lingering kiss.

'On the other hand,' Sue said as she slowly untangled herself from Tony's arms, 'if you play your cards right, there might be the possibility of a bit of bridled passion.'

'You've got a bridle?' Tony said, feigning surprise. 'I didn't know you were into the kinky stuff?'

'Wouldn't you like to find out what happens when I get the bit between my teeth?' Sue breathed into his ear.

'It all depends on which bit you're talking about,' Tony said with an impish grin as he pulled her back into his arms.

CHAPTER 9

Bumping into Murdoch was a stroke of luck, but, when you come to think of, the West End of Glasgow isn't all that big a place. It was in early March – about six months ago; a Friday night, just after ten o'clock. I'd popped into Stravaigin for a quick drink and I was about to head off when I saw him walk in. It looked like Murdoch, but I wasn't sure at first. It was the beard that threw me. I did a double take, trying to imagine what he'd look like without it. The same height, the same build, the same, slightly-hunched shoulders. I heard him order a pint of lager at the counter – the same, breathy voice. It was him all right. The pub was crowded, so I moved down to the far end of the bar. I saw him carry his drink across to a table that had just been vacated. It looked like he was on his own. He took a paperback from his jacket pocket and started reading it. I ordered another Captain Morgan's and stood at the bar, sipping at my drink, all the time watching him out of the corner of my eye.

When he'd finished his pint, he closed his book, got to his feet and headed out of the door. I threw back the rest of my drink and followed him outside. Light snow had been falling when I went into the pub but now it was coming down steadily in large powdery flakes that were lying. I saw him up ahead, walking along Gibson Street. Keeping a respectable distance, I followed him up the hill. He turned right when he got to Oakfield Avenue. Half-way along the road, he went up the short drive to the entrance of a block of flats. I stopped and bent down to re-tie my shoe lace as he turned his key in the front door. A couple of minutes later I saw a light go on in a window on the second floor. I wandered casually up to the building and scanned the nameplates.

There were only two flats on the second floor, the occupants' names being "Singh" and "Preston".

The following Monday morning I was in position before seven o'clock, far enough away from the entrance to the block of flats so as not to be observed, but close enough to see anyone entering or leaving the building. It was half-past eight before I saw him come out. I followed him as he made his way gingerly along the pavement towards University Avenue, the weekend's snow having turned to ice. He joined half a dozen people in the queue at the bus stop. I turned up my hoodie to hide my face as I waited in line. When a 4A bus arrived he got on board and went upstairs. I stayed down below. I followed him when he got off the bus at the last stop in Sauchiehall Street before the pedestrian precinct. He crossed the road and made his way up to Bath Street, where he went into a building. I waited for a while before going across to check the names of the firms occupying the premises. One name plate leapt out at me. "Murdoch & Slater, Computer Consultants". I took out my mobile and looked up their phone number.

It appeared that he started work at nine o'clock. I waited until the following morning and phoned Murdoch and Slater's number at eight-thirty. A secretary took my call.

'Could I speak to Mr Preston, please?' I asked.

'I'm sorry, sir, John's not in yet. Could anyone else help you?'

'Not really. I was dealing with John. He asked to send him some figures about a potential contract and I seem to have lost his e-mail address. Could you possibly give it to me?'

'Of course.'

I allowed myself a self-satisfied smile as I noted down his address. There was no hurry to do anything else right now.

Vengeance would be at a time of my choosing.

CHAPTER 10

Monday 5 September

Charlie Anderson was already wide awake when he heard the first trill of his alarm clock. Snaking his arm out quickly to silence the bell before it woke Kay, he slid from under the duvet. Having had a quick shower, he shaved and brushed his teeth before dressing and tiptoeing down the stairs. In the kitchen, he tipped a generous helping of cornflakes into a bowl, added a splash of milk, then scoffed his breakfast as quickly as he could.

Charlie was behind the wheel and heading towards the city before seven o'clock. He switched on the car radio, which was permanently tuned to Radio Scotland. The lead item on the news was the sensational revelation that the person who had been murdered in Hyndland on Saturday evening had been identified as John Preston, previously known as John Murdoch, the man who had been on trial in the High Court a year ago on a charge of child molestation. The report concluded with the statement that Preston had been acquitted on a not proven verdict.

'Here we go!' Charlie sighed to himself as he switched off the radio.

Sue woke with a start when she heard the sound of the toilet being flushed. Staring through the gloom at her bedside clock, she saw it was twenty-five past seven. Grabbing Tony by the shoulder, she tugged him over onto his back to still his heavy snoring.

'What's happening?' the bleary voice protested. 'What are you doing?'

'Keep quiet!' Sue whispered forcibly, placing her index finger firmly across Tony's lips.

'What's going on?'

'I completely forgot that Jamie was getting up early this morning because my Dad's coming across to play football with him.' Scrambling out of bed, she hurried to the window and peered round the corner of the curtain. 'He'll be here any minute. It's high time you were out of here.'

Tony levered himself up into a sitting position and ran the fingers of both hands through his tousled hair. 'You mean I'm not getting my breakfast in bed of smoked salmon and scrambled eggs?'

'Stop messing about. Get out of there and get dressed. As quickly as you can. Oh, bugger!' Sue exclaimed as she saw a car come round the corner and pull up outside her gate. 'Where are you parked?' she demanded.

'Down the street – about twenty yards away.'

'I hope to God Dad doesn't recognise your car.'

Charlie was taking his gardening shoes from the boot of his car and slipping them on when Jamie appeared at the front door, already kitted out in his yellow goalkeeper's jersey, white shorts and football boots. As Charlie was closing the boot, his eye caught the registration plate of the black Ford Focus parked a few yards further along the street. Glancing up at the front bedroom window, he thought he saw the curtains twitch.

Frowning, Charlie followed Jamie round to the back garden to play the familiar game, Charlie firing shot after shot at the makeshift goal while Jamie dived about, trying to save as many of them as he could. They had been playing for ten minutes when Charlie heard the sound of a car engine starting up.

Charlie was breathing hard by the time he got back to his car almost an hour later. As he was changing his shoes, he noticed that the black Ford Focus had gone.

The commuter traffic was heavy as Charlie was heading towards the city centre. When he arrived in his office, just before nine o'clock, he found Tony O'Sullivan waiting for him.

'Is Renton here yet?' Charlie asked as he took off his jacket and hung it on the hook on the back of the door.

'He got in about ten minutes ago, sir,' Tony said. 'I think he's gone to the loo.'

'Did you sleep well?' Charlie asked pointedly.

'Okay, sir,' Tony mumbled, feeling his freckles flare up as he avoided eye contact.

'Good morning one and all,' Renton announced as he breezed into the office.

There was a stack of newspapers lying on Charlie's desk. He picked up one of the tabloids from the top of the pile. "Murder Victim Had Been Accused Of Rape", the banner headline proclaimed. The secondary heading, in small, italic type, stating: "*He was acquitted on a verdict of not proven.*"

'Why can't they just say he was acquitted,' Charlie complained. 'Why do they always have to add that it was not proven?'

'The red-tops consider you're guilty unless you're proved innocent,' Renton said. 'As far as they're concerned, not proven doesn't cut it.'

'What's that lot?' Charlie asked, pointing towards the documents stacked on top of his filing cabinet.

'The reports on the Carter family from the Drumchapel social work department,' Tony said. 'And also the transcript of Murdoch's trial.'

'Have you had a chance to look at them?' Charlie asked.

'I had a quick look through the transcript,' Tony said.

'Did you find anything of interest?' Charlie asked.

'In essence, it confirms what you were told by Judge Ramsay and Mark Houston. There's not a lot by way of additional information.'

'Have you arranged for someone from forensics to go with you to Preston's flat this morning, Colin?' Charlie asked.

Renton nodded. 'I'm meeting Eddie McLaughlin there at ten o'clock. As soon as we wrap up here I'll go across to the mortuary and pick up the keys for Preston's apartment.'

'Tell Eddie to fingerprint the place and get him to check out Preston's computer. And while you're there, have a word with the neighbours,' Charlie added. 'Find out if any of them know who Preston hung out with.'

'Will do,' Renton said. 'Tom Freer managed to contact Preston's service provider yesterday,' he added. 'They sent us the data on all the calls, to and from his mobile, for the past twelve months. I haven't had a chance to study the information in any detail, but one thing I noticed straight away was that the last three communications Preston made, between nine-thirty and ten-thirty on the evening he was killed, were all texts to the same number.'

'Tell Freer to trawl through the reports and see what they throw up.' Charlie said.

'Okay,' Renton said. 'Do you need me for anything else here, sir?' he added.

'I don't think so,' Charlie said.

'In which case, I'll head over to the mortuary.'

'I don't know about you,' Charlie said, looking pointedly at Tony when Renton had left, 'but I didn't get much by way of breakfast this morning, so go and get the coffees and biscuits in while I have a look through the social work reports.'

Lifting the stack of documents from the top of his filing cabinet, Charlie carried them across to his desk. As he was working his way through the files, he noticed that most of the reports had been compiled by the same person – a social worker called Lesley Adams.

When Tony came back with two coffees and two packets of biscuits on a tray, Charlie put down his pen. 'Here's what I've got so far,' he said, referring to his notes as he stirred sugar into his coffee. 'Terry and Alice Carter had two sons – Gavin, who's now nineteen, and Tommy, who committed suicide a year ago. Terry Carter has been on the dole for most of his adult life – he claims he's unable to hold down a job because he suffers from chronic lower-back pains. He has an older brother, Andy, who has a criminal record as long as your arm, including convictions for drug-dealing, extortion and GBH. Six years ago, Alice Carter did a runner with a bookie from Paisley, a bloke called Mitch Weir. The social work department first got involved with the Carter family when Gavin started getting into trouble,' Charlie continued, 'which was round about the time his mother jumped ship. Mainly it was dogging school, petty theft and getting into fights. He was up in front of the Children's Panel on three separate occasions. That's as far as I've got,' Charlie said, blowing on the hot coffee before taking a sip.

'Do you want me to go through the rest of that stuff?' Tony asked.

'Most of these reports were compiled by the same person – someone called Lesley Adams,' Charlie said. 'Rather than plough our way through this lot,' he said, waving his hand in the direction of the stack of paper on his desk, 'it would make more sense if we had a word with her. As well as saving us time, social workers often have more information about a family than they're prepared to put on file. Give her a call and try to set something up.'

When Tony phoned the Drumchapel social work office he was told that Lesley Adams had transferred to the Anniesland branch. He called that number and asked to be put through to her.

'This is Sergeant O'Sullivan, Glasgow CID,' he said when his call was connected. 'DCI Anderson and I would like to have a word with you about the Carter family.'

'Would that be the Carters from Drumchapel?' Lesley queried.

'That's correct. I believe you had quite a lot of dealings with them?'

'I did.' Lesley hesitated. 'You'll find all the information about them on file in Drumchapel.'

'We have a copy of those files.'

'So why do you want to talk to me?'

'We'd like some background information.'

'When were you thinking of, Sergeant?'

'How are you fixed today?'

Lesley hesitated again. 'I've got a very busy schedule. I have three family visits lined up for this afternoon.'

'Would it be possible for us to come to see you this morning?'

'This morning? I.. I don't know if I could fit that in.'

'We wouldn't take a lot of your time, Ms Adams.' Tony covered the mouthpiece and addressed Charlie. 'How about right now, sir?' Charlie nodded. 'We could be across in your office in half an hour, if you could see us then?'

'I… I suppose so. Do you know where the office is?'

'It's the one on Great Western Road, isn't it? Near Anniesland Cross?'

'That's right. We're in the building opposite the Anniesland library. The best place to park is round the back,' Lesley added, 'in either Morrisons' or Mothercare's car park.'

Tony smiled. 'I'm not sure Inspector Anderson would want to run the risk of getting clamped.'

'Not only is it common practice, Sergeant, it's what's actually recommended on our website.'

'What do Morrisons and Mothercare have to say about that?'

'I don't imagine for one minute that they ever look at our website.'

When Colin Renton pulled up outside the block of flats in Oakfield Avenue, he saw Eddie McLaughlin waiting for him on the corner, two cameras slung around his neck and a large, black holdall lying at his feet.

'What's the score?' McLaughlin asked as Renton led the way up the path towards the building.

Producing a set of keys from his jacket pocket, Renton unlocked the entrance door. 'The dead guy's flat is on the second floor,' he explained as they were climbing the stairs. 'As far as we know, he lived on his own. Charlie Anderson wants you to fingerprint the place to see if we can identify anybody who's been here recently. He'd also like you to give Preston's computer the once over,' Renton added, 'to see if that casts any light on what he's been up to.'

'No problem.'

Renton unlocked the door to the flat and ushered McLaughlin inside. 'While you're doing that,' he said, 'I'll ring a few doorbells around here and try to find out how well the neighbours knew Preston – and if they saw anyone visiting him recently.'

'Okay.'

Renton turned round when he heard footsteps ringing out on the staircase behind him.

When she saw Renton standing in Preston's doorway, the middle-aged woman, dressed in a sari, stopped half way up the stairs and put down her two heavy bags of shopping.

'Who are you?' she asked.

'The police,' Renton said, showing his warrant card.

'You're here because of what happened to Mr Preston, I suppose,' she said, picking up her bags and trudging up to the landing.

'Yes.'

'Poor man.'

'Can I give you a hand with those?' Renton offered, nodding towards her bags.

'No thanks, I'm fine. I'm used to it,' she added.

'Do you live next door?' Renton asked.

She nodded, producing a set of keys.

'Would you mind answering a few questions?' Renton asked.

She put down her shopping bags again. 'Go ahead.'

'What is your name?'

'Indira Singh.'

'Do you live on your own?'

'Yes.'

'How well did you know Mr Preston?'

'I hardly knew him at all. I only moved in here a couple of months ago.'

'Did you ever talk to him?'

'Not as such. He kept himself very much to himself. He was perfectly polite. He would say good morning or good evening if we bumped into each other on the stairs, but nothing more than that.'

'Did you ever see anyone with him? Do you know if he had any visitors?'

She stopped to think. 'No,' she said, shaking her head. 'I don't remember ever seeing anyone with him.'

'Okay, thanks for that.'

*

Colin Renton didn't get any response when he rang the doorbells of the two flats on the ground floor. The first bell he tried on the first floor also went unanswered. When he tried the flat directly underneath Preston's, an elderly man shuffled to the door.

Renton showed him his warrant card.

'Not before time,' he grumbled. 'Come on in.'

'You were expecting me?' Renton queried.

'You've come about my complaint, I suppose? At least, I hope you have.'

'I don't know anything about a complaint, sir,' Renton said.

'Oh, bloody hell! I've reported them three times. What do I have to do to get something done about it?'

'Done about what, sir?'

'Those students in the flat downstairs. It's the same every Saturday night. Rowdy parties going on half the night with their so-called music belting out. I can't get a wink of sleep. I can see the wee hairies arriving from my kitchen window, you know. Shameless hussies, they are, with their make-up slapped on with a ladle and their skirts up around their bums. And when I see the amount of booze that's carried in there – and there are sure to be drugs involved – you can bet your boots on that. Where do they get the money from, that's what I want to know? It's just one long, drunken orgy after another – and your lot do bugger all about it. It's a bloody disgrace.'

'Who have you reported this to, sir?' Renton asked.

'I don't have a name. Every time I phone up and complain, somebody takes down the details and tells me they'll get back to me, but they never do.'

'What I recommend you do, sir, is go in person to Partick Police Station and ask to speak to Sergeant Sid Cummings. You'll definitely get a sympathetic hearing from him.'

'Right,' he said grudgingly. 'I'll do that. So if you're not here today about my complaints,' he added, 'what are you here for?'

'How well did you know your upstairs neighbour, Mr Preston?'

'I didn't even know the guy's name, but he's okay.'

'How is he okay?'

'He doesn't have rowdy parties.'

Eddie McLaughlin was huddled over Preston's desktop computer when Renton returned to the flat.

'Any joy with the neighbours, Colin?' McLaughlin asked without turning away from the screen.

'Not a lot. The lady in the flat across the hall told me that Preston kept very much to himself. The only exchanges she ever had with him were an occasional hello on the stairs. Apart from her, the only other person who answered his door was a surly old bugger in one of the flats on the first floor.'

'So what took you so long?'

'He did. As soon as I showed him my ID he launched into a tirade about the racket the students in the ground floor flat make every Saturday night. According to him, it's just one long, drunken, drug-fuelled orgy after another.'

'Any chance of an invite?'

'You wish! Old misery guts told me he's reported the problem to the police three times, but he claims that nobody does anything about it. It took me all my time to get away from him.'

'How did you manage to placate him?'

'I gave him Charlie Anderson's home number and told him to give him a call.'

'You must be joking!'

'Correct!' Renton said with a broad grin. 'I've every intention of reaching my retirement age with my head still attached to my shoulders. I actually gave him Sid Cummings' name and told him to drop into the Partick nick and discuss the matter with him face to face.'

'Sid's not going to thank you for that.'

'It'll serve him right for taking the piss out of me when Thistle lost at home last weekend.'

'You're a braver man than I am.'

'How are you getting on here?' Renton asked. 'Have you come across anything worthwhile?'

'I've taken a few sets of prints which I'll check against the central data base when I get back to the office to see if they match with anyone we know. I've been trawling through his computer. I haven't found anything of interest so far, but it'll take me another hour or so to check it out thoroughly.'

'While you're doing that,' Renton said, 'I'll have a look through his desk.'

'Did you manage to get parked all right?' Lesley Adams asked as she trotted down the flight of stairs to the reception desk to meet Charlie and Tony.

As he took her proffered hand, Charlie reckoned she was probably in her late twenties; tall, slim, athletic-looking, shoulder-length auburn hair, shapely figure, strong, angular features.

'I decided to leave my car in Morrison's car park on the basis that there's a sporting chance I might be taken for one of their customers,' Charlie said. 'I'm not sure I could say the same about Mothercare.'

Lesley smiled. 'Would it be all right if we go for a walk round the block while we talk?' she asked, taking a packet of cigarettes and a book of matches from her handbag and holding them aloft.

'No problem,' Charlie said, returning her smile. 'My wife's always on at me to take more exercise.'

'It's a disgusting habit, I know,' Lesley said, screwing up her face. 'But if I don't get my morning "c-o-u-g-h-i-e" break,' she said, spelling out the word, 'I'm like a bear with a sore head for the rest of the day. I can't get by without my five a day,' she added, her gravelly voice leading Charlie to conclude that it might be considerably more than five.

As soon as they were clear of the building, Lesley lit up.

'The reason we wanted to talk to you today,' Charlie said as they were heading along Great Western Road in the direction of the city centre, 'is that there was a murder in the West End on Saturday night.'

'I read about that in the papers,' Lesley said, 'but I thought you wanted to talk to me about the Carter family?' she added hesitantly.

'There is a connection,' Charlie said. 'Have you heard the news this morning?'

'No.'

'The man who was killed has been identified as John Preston, who was previously known as John Murdoch.'

'John Murdoch?' Lesley stopped dead in her tracks. '*The* John Murdoch? The John Murdoch who raped Tommy Carter?'

'The John Murdoch who was acquitted of assaulting Tommy Carter, Ms Adams,' Tony interjected.

Lesley looked askance at Tony as she resumed walking. 'Don't expect me to shed any tears over him,' she said, drawing hard on her cigarette.

'What can you tell us about the Carter family?' Charlie asked.

'You said you've seen the social work reports?'

'The Drumchapel office sent us copies,' Tony said.

'In which case, I'm not sure there's much I can add.'

'What was Terry Carter like?' Charlie asked.

'Is this off the record?' Lesley asked. Charlie nodded. Lesley thought for a moment before replying. 'I had him marked down as a skiver, Inspector. He claimed to have a bad back, which meant he wasn't able to hold down a job.'

'And you didn't believe that?'

'He didn't seem to have any problem moving when it was a matter of going to the pub or the bookies. But despite that,' Lesley said, 'he was a decent enough bloke, who was doing his level best to bring up his kids up in very difficult circumstances.'

'What about his other son, Gavin?' Tony asked.

'Gavin?' Lesley paused to flick the ash from her cigarette. 'Gavin was the reason the social work services got involved with the family in the first place. It was one of the first cases I was assigned to when I joined the department six years ago. Terry Carter's wife had walked out on him and moved in with a bloke in Paisley. Not long after that happened, Gavin started to go off the rails. He was about thirteen at the time. I asked the Paisley social work department to get in touch with the mother to find out if she'd be prepared to get involved in looking after her sons, but the feedback I got was that she'd made a new life for herself and she didn't want to know.'

Turning left before the railway bridge, Lesley led the way towards the car parks. 'With the enthusiasm of youth, I invested a lot of my personal time in trying to get Gavin straightened out. It takes a few months before the battle-hardened cynicism begins to set in,' she added with a wry smile. 'I really thought I was beginning to get somewhere with him. He was up in front of the Children's Panel three times in as many years. Nothing particularly serious – he was caught nicking cigarettes from a shop, he got involved in a couple of fights and once he stole a bicycle. On the third occasion – he was sixteen at the time – the panel members were minded to send him to a young offenders' institution, however, I intervened on his behalf and I managed to convince the chairman that it would be in everyone's best interests to give Gavin a final warning and allow him to stay at home. Splitting up a family really has to be the last resort, Inspector. At the end of the day, the thing that swung it for the Panel was that it was evident that Gavin's father was doing his level best to keep his boys on the straight and narrow and if Gavin had been sent to a remand home, there were serious concerns about the knock-on effect that might have had on Tommy.'

'Did Gavin get into any more trouble after that?' Tony asked as they were passing in front of Mothercare and heading towards Anniesland library.

'Not really. He channelled his energies into playing football. I'm no expert on the subject, but I'm told he was very good at it. In fact, not far off Scotland under-eighteen standard. He was interested in all kinds of sports. I introduced him to tennis. I consider myself to be not too bad, but within a few weeks he was hammering me consistently. Of course, these don't help,' Lesley added, holding up her cigarette.

'Five a day shouldn't cause you too much of a problem,' Charlie said.

'Some days, it's six – or seven,' Lesley said defensively. 'I said that Gavin didn't get into any more trouble,' she continued, 'however, there's a really bad influence in the Carter family – Terry's brother, Andy. He's been in and out of prison most of his adult life. I mentioned that Terry's a lazy sod – permanently on the dole. His brother's a completely different kettle of fish. He associates with some very unsavoury characters. He's done time for drug dealing and GBH. I think that was mentioned in one of the reports?' Charlie nodded. 'Something that isn't referred to in the reports, because there was never any proof of it, is that, a few years back, he was one of a group of thugs who called themselves the alternative LGBT – the Lesbian and Gay Bashers' Team. Wearing hoods and masks, they broke into several gay bars in the city centre and smashed up the premises with crowbars – while laying into anybody who got in their way.'

'I remember hearing about those attacks,' Tony said. 'I don't recall any arrests being made.'

'There weren't any,' Lesley said. 'The gang disbanded after a couple of months when the heat started to come on. At the time, it was common knowledge in Drumchapel who the ringleaders were – they even boasted about their activities in the local pubs. The story was that someone had threatened to talk to the police, which resulted in him getting both his kneecaps smashed in. After that, no one was prepared to speak up.'

'Was Gavin a member of that gang?' Tony asked.

'Definitely not,' Lesley said with a firm shake of the head.

'How about Terry?'

'He wasn't either. As far as I'm aware, Terry didn't get involved in anything illegal, apart from fiddling his benefits, that is. Terry and Andy didn't get on. I don't know a lot about the background, but what I do know is that they were barely on speaking terms. I think the fact that Andy was always flush and would buy the boys more or less anything they wanted – things Terry could never afford to get for them – had a lot to do with it. Gavin hero-worshipped his Uncle Andy, which was not a healthy state of affairs. The only reason Gavin nicked the cigarettes was to give them to his uncle to try to impress him. A couple of years ago Gavin told me he was going to leave his father and move in with his uncle – and that probably would have happened if Andy hadn't been sent down again for assault.'

'Does Gavin still stay with his father?' Charlie asked.

Lesley paused to draw hard on her cigarette. 'I don't have any dealings with the family now, Inspector. Not since I transferred to Anniesland.'

'How long ago was that?'

'About nine months.'

'Tell me about Tommy Carter,' Charlie said as they arrived back in front of the social services' building. 'What kind of boy was he?'

Lesley stopped beside a waste bin and nipped out her cigarette. 'Let's talk about that inside,' she said, dropping her cigarette butt into the bin. 'There's an office on the first floor we can use.'

Lesley led the way up the staircase. Having closed the office door behind them, she indicated chairs for Charlie and Tony as she took the seat behind the desk.

'Tommy was a vulnerable lad,' Lesley began. 'Totally different in character from his older brother. Where Gavin was an extrovert and interested in sports, Tommy was introverted and lacked self-confidence. He kept himself very much to himself. He was bright enough academically, but he was overweight to the point of being obese and he was subjected to a lot of cruel bullying at school. Gavin was protective towards his young brother, often getting into fights with the louts who were bullying him. Initially, I found Tommy very difficult to communicate with, but once I won his confidence, I got to know him quite well. A couple of years ago – he was thirteen at the time – he confided in me that he was struggling to come to terms with his sexuality. He had a crush on one of the older boys in his school – and he had no interest whatsoever in girls. His biggest problem at the time was that he had no one he felt he could talk to about it. Thinking you might be homosexual in a predominately heterosexual world is difficult enough to cope with when you're thirteen, but it's a lot worse when you don't know anyone who shares your feelings – and it's not at all helped by having an uncle who continually goes on about how much he enjoys duffing up queers.'

'Charming!' Tony interjected.

'When Tommy plucked up the courage to tell me how he felt, I suggested he talk things through with his guidance teacher, who happened to be John Murdoch.' Charlie could see moisture forming at the corners of Lesley's sky-blue eyes. She blinked away her tears as she took a tissue from her pocket to dab at her eyes. 'That didn't work out well,' she said quietly, blowing her nose hard into the tissue.

Charlie took out his notebook and pen. 'What can you tell us about Tommy's relationship with John Murdoch?' he asked.

'At first, everything seemed to be going well. Tommy was more upbeat than I'd seen him in a long time. He told me that Murdoch was prepared to discuss everything with him – and that he was sympathetic and understanding. I took a step back at that point because I considered Murdoch to be a lot better equipped to provide advice and guidance to Tommy on such matters than I was.' Lesley's fingers twitched across her mouth. 'I didn't do Tommy any favours,' she added.

'You couldn't possibly have known how it would turn out,' Charlie stated. 'You weren't in any way responsible for what happened.'

'I realise that. But it doesn't make it any easier.'

'Did Tommy tell you that Murdoch had assaulted him?' Tony asked.

'Not at first. Initially, he only told Gavin, who had left school by then – he'd got a job designing computer games.'

'So did Gavin tell you that Murdoch had assaulted Tommy?' Tony asked.

Lesley nodded. 'When he came to see me, he was spitting blood, ranting and raving about what he was going to do to Murdoch.

I'd never seen him so angry. When I eventually managed to calm him down, he told me what had happened. Do you know what that bastard did to Tommy, Inspector?' Lesley asked.

'We've seen the transcript of the trial,' Charlie said.

'How did you react when you heard what had happened?' Tony asked.

'When I got over the initial shock, I told Gavin that Tommy would have to tell his father what Murdoch had done to him, but Gavin said the very idea of his father and his uncle finding out what had happened freaked Tommy out completely – there was no way he was going to go down that route. Gavin told me he was going to 'sort Murdoch out' – his words, but I told him that under no circumstances was he to go anywhere near Murdoch. I told him I would speak to Tommy.

'Gavin also let me know that this wasn't the first time Murdoch had been involved in something like that. There was a boy in Tommy's class, Ronnie Gilligan, who had a schoolboy crush on Gavin – hardly surprising, given that Gavin was good at sport and had the looks of a young George Clooney. Ronnie had tried to impress Gavin by telling him he was sleeping with Murdoch. Gavin thought that was probably just bravado on Ronnie's part, but Ronnie insisted it was true – he said he had the e-mails to prove it. There must have been something going on because not long after that Ronnie was withdrawn from the school in unexplained circumstances. There were rumours doing the rounds that Ronnie had been groomed by Murdoch, but that the affair had been swept under the carpet.

'When I saw Tommy, I did everything in my power to persuade him to tell his father what had happened, but he dug in his heels. There was no way he could do that. When I realised I wasn't going to get anywhere, I changed tack and insisted that his head teacher would have to be informed about what had happened. If Gavin's assertion was correct – and Tommy wasn't Murdoch's first victim – who was to say that there wouldn't be others if Murdoch was allowed to get away with it this time?'

'Did you at any time doubt that Tommy was telling the truth?' Charlie asked.

'Not for one minute.'

'Did he agree to tell his head teacher?' Tony asked.

'He said he couldn't do it face to face. He asked me to do it for him. It was during the school holidays, but I managed to get in touch with Mr Parker at home and I told him I needed to see him urgently. He invited me over to his house in Nitshill. That was a difficult meeting. When I told Parker about Tommy's accusations, his initial reaction was to go on the defensive, which was understandable. He was reluctant to involve the police just on Tommy's say-so because of the damage that might do to the school's reputation. However, he knew that his duty of care towards Tommy overrode any such concerns and he realised he was obliged to report Tommy's accusations to the police. I also made him aware that I'd heard about the rumours that were circulating with regard to Murdoch and Ronnie Gilligan.

'Parker mulled it over for a while, then he asked me to come back the following day and bring Tommy with me. After he'd listened to what Tommy had to say, he agreed to come with us to Drumry Road police station, where Tommy filed an official complaint.'

'That must have been difficult for Tommy,' Charlie said.

'Difficult?' Lesley shook her head slowly from side to side as the tears welled up in her eyes. 'If Tommy hadn't taken my advice, he'd still be alive today.' She cast her eyes down and stared at the floor, a lump forming in her throat.

'What happened after that, Ms Adams?' Tony prompted.

Lesley wiped away her tears with the back of her hand before looking up. 'The police initiated an enquiry and they interviewed Murdoch. Of course, he categorically denied that anything untoward had taken place. He claimed that Tommy had made the story up out of spite because he had rejected his advances. The investigation was hampered by the fact that Tommy had waited a fortnight before reporting the assault. The police doctor examined him, but after that lapse of time there was no physical proof of any sexual activity having taken place – and there was no DNA evidence available. Nevertheless, after the police had conducted their investigations, the Procurator Fiscal decided to proceed to trial and the case went to the High Court.'

'Where the verdict was not proven,' Tony stated.

'Not proven!' Lesley's voice was quivering with emotion as she fought to hold back her tears. 'Why on earth do we still have that stupid verdict?'

'It has stood us in good stead over the years,' Tony said.

'Do you really think so?' Lesley fixed Tony with a stare. 'It's not the first time I've been on the wrong end of one of those verdicts, Sergeant. If it ever happens to you, you won't be saying that.' Her voice was on the point of breaking. 'It's the great Scottish cop out – Not proven! Not guilty, but don't do it again!' Charlie allowed Lesley time to compose herself before continuing.

'With regard to Murdoch's trial,' Charlie said, 'I'm told there was no conclusive evidence on which he could have been convicted.'

Lesley took a deep breath. 'I have to accept that,' she said, exhaling slowly. 'I was in court throughout the proceedings. When it was Tommy's turn to give evidence he became flustered and he got confused about dates and times. My heart went out to him. I knew he was telling the truth, but I also knew the jury couldn't convict Murdoch on the evidence presented. When the verdict was announced, Tommy's parents and his uncle, especially his uncle, went ballistic. For the one and only time in my life I sympathised with the Carter family when they threatened Murdoch with retribution.'

'Was Gavin in court?' Tony asked.

Lesley nodded. 'He sat between his father and his uncle throughout the trial. I don't think he uttered a single word during the two days of the hearing, not even when the verdict was announced, but I could tell that he was simmering.'

'How did Tommy react to the verdict?' Charlie asked.

'I don't know. I never saw him again. I thought it would be a good idea to leave it for a couple of days before I spoke to him.' Lesley's voice dropped to little more than a whisper. 'But the following day he threw himself from a railway bridge in front of a train.' Tears again started threading down both of Lesley's cheeks. 'Can you even begin to imagine what it must have been like for him, Inspector?' she said, dabbing at her eyes with her tissue. 'To have to admit to his father and his uncle that he was gay was traumatic enough. But for him to accuse his guidance teacher of assaulting him – and then be told by a court of law that the man who had raped him had been acquitted. Is it any wonder he decided he couldn't go on?' Lesley's voice hardened. 'I can't pretend for one minute that I'm sorry that Murdoch – or Preston – or whatever the hell he called himself – is dead. People like that don't deserve to live.'

'Did that experience have anything to do with your decision to leave the Drumchapel social services?' Charlie asked.

'It did,' Lesley said. 'My first impulse was to get out of social work completely. It's a draining job at the best of times. You try to remain objective and you do your best to help the families you work with, but it's not possible to avoid getting personally involved, especially when you witness a blatant miscarriage of justice that led to a sensitive young boy taking his own life. But in the end,' she said with a sigh, 'I decided to carry on. It's a job I like – and I'm good at it. But I needed to make a clean break. I was carrying too much emotional baggage in Drumchapel, not only with the Carters, but with several other families I was involved with, so I applied for a transfer to Anniesland.'

'How's that working out?' Tony asked.

'It's a new set of families.' Lesley forced a rueful smile. 'With the same old problems. But despite everything I've been through, it is a worthwhile job – you really can make a difference to people's lives.'

'You mentioned earlier that Gavin had got a job designing computer games,' Charlie said. 'Do you know what company he works for?'

'As a matter of fact, I do. It's called SHERPA. I was actually instrumental in him getting the job. The company was set up a few years ago by a lady called Sheila McVey. Sheila and I used to hang out together at school. Her maiden name was Sheila Paterson and her middle initial is R, hence the company name. Gavin was into designing computer games so I gave Sheila a call to see if there was any possibility that she could put some work his way. She agreed to give him an interview, following which she offered him a job. I don't know much about that kind of stuff but, whatever Gavin was doing, he seemed to be doing it well. Sheila was apparently very impressed with the quality of his work, to the extent that he was often sent to represent the firm at computing conferences – which meant overnight stays in flash hotels with all expenses paid. I was really pleased for him that he seemed to be making a success of his life.'

'Okay, Ms Adams,' Charlie said, standing up stiffly and massaging the base of his spine. 'I think that's all we need for now – and thanks for fitting us in at such short notice. If you wouldn't mind letting me have your home address and your phone number,' Charlie added, 'in case we need to get in touch?'

'Of course.'

Charlie wrote down the information Lesley gave him in his notebook.

'I should mention that – ' Lesley broke off.

'Mention what?' Charlie queried.

'It's nothing,' Lesley muttered with a quick shake of the head as she got to her feet. 'It doesn't matter.'

'What doesn't matter?' Charlie probed.

'I was just – ' She took a deep breath. 'This is probably completely out of order, Inspector, but I was about to say that I would bet a lot of money that it was Andy Carter who murdered John Murdoch.'

'I can understand why you might think that,' Charlie said, taking a card from the breast pocket of his jacket and handing it to her. 'If you think of anything else that might be relevant,' he added, 'give me a call.'

CHAPTER 11

The rain was spitting down when Tony and Charlie came out of the building. They turned up their jacket collars as they hurried towards their car.

'What did you make of her?' Charlie said as he was clipping on his seatbelt.

'Actually, rather fanciable,' Tony said with a grin.

'One track mind, as usual.' Charlie shook his head as he fired the ignition.

'I'm a complete sucker for redheads.'

'Have you told Sue that?'

'I thought it politic not to mention it.'

'I could tell her for you, if you like?'

'Changing the subject quickly,' Tony said, feeling his freckles flare up. 'What did you make of her?'

'I had the distinct impression that our Ms Adams was holding back on something. Right at the end, there seemed to be something she wanted to get off her chest, but instead of going through with it she blurted out some nonsense about thinking that Andy Carter was the murderer. Considering her previous comments about him, that was hardly a world-shattering revelation.'

'What now?' Tony asked.

'It's time we found out what the Carter brothers have got to say for themselves,' Charlie said. Slipping the car into gear, he flicked on the windscreen wipers. 'They have to be prime candidates for Preston's murder.'

'What about Gavin?' Tony asked.

'He's in the frame as well.'

'Should we organise simultaneous visits to both Terry and Andy Carter?' Tony asked. 'So that they won't be able to tip each other off that we're coming?'

'There's not much point in that,' Charlie said as he indicated left at the Great Western Road traffic lights. 'If the Carter brothers are involved in Preston's murder, they'll have their story worked out by now.'

'Nothing much of interest, Colin,' Eddie McLaughlin said. 'Most of the stuff here is what you'd expect to find – music downloads, notes for lessons on computing science, various spreadsheets, bank statements et cetera. His Internet searches are also fairly typical. Various computing sites, sports news, BBC, Wikipedia, Google, as well as a few porn sites – predominately gay ones. However, there is one interesting thing,' he added. 'No e-mails – not even any e-mail software on the computer. That is unusual.' McLaughlin got to his feet and stretched his back as he powered off the computer. 'I'll head back to the office now and check if there are any matches on the database for the fingerprints.'

Colin Renton was perched on the arm of the settee in the middle of the room, looking through a sheaf of papers he'd come across in one of the drawers in Preston's desk. 'Hold on a minute, Eddie,' he said, holding up a single sheet of paper. 'Have a butcher's at this.'

'What is it?'

'A receipt for an iPad, purchased by John Murdoch from the Apple Store in Buchanan Street. It's dated three years ago, which was before he changed his name to Preston. Have you seen any sign of an iPad lying around?'

'No, but I suppose he might've bought it for somebody else – maybe as a present?'

'An expensive present. Maybe that's what he used for his e-mails – and possibly other activities he would prefer to remain secret?'

Renton suggested. 'If that was the case, where do you think he might've hidden it?' Renton stroked his chin reflectively. 'Probably not anywhere too difficult to find,' he surmised. 'After all, when he went out to the pub on Saturday night, he thought he'd be coming back here afterwards, in which case he might just have put it somewhere out of sight.'

'You check out the kitchen,' McLaughlin suggested, 'while I have a shuftie in the bedroom.'

Renton was working his way through the kitchen cupboards when he heard McLaughlin's cry of: 'Got it!' emanating from the bedroom. 'I found this under his pillow,' McLaughlin said, holding up a tablet as he walked into the kitchen. Flopping down on a chair, he flicked the cover open and powered it up. 'Password protected this time. That's a lot more like it,' he said, rubbing his hands together. 'Maybe I'll get somewhere with this. I'll take it back to the office and have a go at cracking the password.'

Just after half-past eleven, Charlie Anderson and Tony O'Sullivan pulled up opposite a high-rise tower block in Drumchapel and got out of the car. The rain had eased off, but the wind had picked up. Charlie leaned with both his elbows on the roof of the car as he studied the building.

'It's hard to believe that, in the nineteen-sixties, someone thought this would be the solution to Glasgow's housing problems. The architects who designed these monstrosities should've been made to live in them,' he said, craning his neck to look up.

'They're planning to demolish this one before too long,' Tony said.

'Not before time. Every time I see one of these tower blocks I'm reminded of the words of Adam McNaughton's song: '*The plans were well intentioned, but to say the least bizarre. Twenty thousan' drinkers, and no' a single bar*'.'

The rain started falling again, heavier this time, as they made their way towards the building. 'What floor is Carter on?' Charlie asked as he broke into a wheezing trot.

'The seventeenth.'

'I hope to God the lift's working.'

'I suffer from vertigo,' Tony said as the cramped, graffiti-covered lift groaned its way towards the seventeenth floor. 'It would kill me if I had to live in a place like this.'

'Living in places like this has killed a lot of people over the years,' Charlie said grimly as the lift shuddered to a halt. 'And they didn't have to suffer from vertigo.'

When the lift doors creaked open, they stepped out onto the landing. There were four doors leading off. Tony checked the name plates on each of the doors in turn, nodding to Charlie when he saw the name *Terry Carter* scrawled in pencil above a bell push. Tony depressed the bell. As the echo of the Westminster chimes was dying away, a stocky figure, dressed in a faded, Paisley-pattern dressing gown, came to the door.

'Terry Carter?' Charlie asked, showing his warrant card. Carter narrowed his eyes. 'We'd like a word with you,' Charlie said.

'What about?' Carter asked, sucking hard on his teeth.

'Can we come in?' Charlie asked.

'What if I say 'no'?'

'Then we'll do it down the station.'

Muttering a curse, Carter re-tied the belt of his dressing gown and took a step back. 'Close the door behind you,' he said, turning round and leading the way along the narrow hallway to the kitchen. Unwashed dishes were stacked high in the sink and several cardboard containers, the remnants of the previous night's Chinese take-away, were strewn across the kitchen table. Carter slumped down on an upright, wooden chair while Charlie and Tony remained standing.

'What's this all about?' Carter asked.

'Have you heard the news?' Tony asked.

'The news? I'm just out my pit, for fuck's sake.' Carter made no attempt to stifle a wide yawn. 'I haven't even had my breakfast yet.'

'Then you don't know that John Preston's dead?' Charlie said.

'Who the hell's John Preston?'

Charlie held eye contact with Carter. 'You knew him as John Murdoch.'

Carter's eyes widened. 'Murdoch's deid?' he said slowly. 'Is that right? How did that happen?'

'He was murdered on Saturday night,' Charlie said.

'You don't say?'

'Which happens to be a year to the day from when your son took his own life,' Tony said.

'Do you think I don't fucking-well know that?' Carter snapped. 'I spent half an hour at Tommy's grave on Saturday afternoon, in pissing down rain, cursing that pervert.'

'Do you know who killed Murdoch?' Charlie asked.

'I haven't a clue. But if you find out, be sure to let me know.' There was a glint in Carter's eye. 'I'd like to buy the guy a drink.'

'A man's been murdered,' Charlie said.

'A fucking pervert got what was coming to him!' Carter's fist came hammering down on the kitchen table. 'A pervert who raped my boy and was responsible for him taking his own life. Don't give me any of that 'a man's been murdered' crap. As far as I'm concerned, it's good fucking riddance!'

'A year ago, in the High Court, when Murdoch was acquitted, you threatened to take matters into your own hands,' Charlie stated.

'It's no secret that I've been looking for him.'

'Did you manage to catch up with him on Saturday night?' Tony asked.

Carter shook his head. 'If I'd got my hands on that bastard,' he growled, 'his death would've been very slow – and very painful. You can take my word for that.'

'Maybe you didn't have time for that?' Tony suggested. 'Maybe you spotted Murdoch in Cottiers and grabbed the opportunity while you had the chance?'

'Where?'

'In Cottiers. It's a pub in Hyndland,' Tony said.

'I don't hang out in that part of town.'

'Where were you between nine o'clock and eleven o'clock on Saturday night?' Tony asked.

'Here.'

'That was quick,' Tony said.

'We're not all as slow-witted as the polis,' Carter said with a smirk.

'Was anybody with you?' Charlie asked.

Carter's features broke into a slow, confident grin. 'This isn't your lucky day, pal. A few of my mates came round here on Saturday night for a game of poker. They got here the back of seven and stayed until well after midnight, so there's no way you're going to be able to pin this one on me.'

'How many of your mates were here?' Charlie asked.

Carter stopped to think. 'Five.'

Charlie took out his notebook and pen. 'I'll need their names and addresses.'

'How the hell would I know their addresses?'

'We'll start with their names.'

Carter counted off on his fingers as he recited five names, which Charlie noted down.

'And their phone numbers,' Charlie said, pointing to Carter's mobile phone, which was lying on the kitchen table.

Carter glowered, then picked up his phone and accessed his contacts' list. As he read out the numbers, Charlie wrote them down.

'Is there a Mrs Carter?' Tony asked.

'Not since she sloped off with a bookie from Paisley.'

'When was that?'

'About six years ago.'

'How about your son, Gavin?' Charlie asked. 'Does he live here?'

'He stays here off and on, if he doesn't get a better offer.'

'Where else does he hang out?'

'He hooked up with some posh bird a while back and he spends a lot of his time at her place. Apart from than that, he sometimes kips down in his mate's flat.'

'What's the posh bird's name?' Tony asked.

'I'm his faither, for Christ's sake! Do you think he tells me anything?'

'He must have told you something about her, for you to know that she's a posh bird,' Tony said.

'All I know is that when I asked him when he was going to bring her round here to meet me, he told me she had too much class to come to a dump like this.'

'Do you know where she lives?'

'I haven't a clue.'

'What about his mate?' Charlie asked. 'What's his name?'

'Stuart.'

'Is that his first name or his surname?'

'Search me.'

'Do you know where Stuart lives?'

'Nope.'

'When did you last see Gavin?' Charlie asked.

'About a week ago.'

'What about your brother?' Tony interjected. 'Do you know where he was on Saturday night?'

'I can't remember the last time I saw Andy. It must've been more than six months ago.' Carter spread his arms out wide. 'So what do you think the chances are that I know what he was up to on Saturday night?'

'We can do without the smart arse stuff,' Charlie said.

'And I can do without having to answer a load of damn fool questions,' Carter retorted. 'Where are you going with this?'

'A man has been murdered,' Tony said. 'A man you and your brother threatened to kill. Where do you think we're going with this?'

Carter snorted. 'Last week, down the pub, I told everybody who would listen that Partick Thistle were going to win the league this season. Unfortunately, not all my predictions come with a cast-iron guarantee. Now, if you don't have any more daft questions,' he said, yawning as he pulled himself to his feet, 'piss off and let me get my breakfast.' With a flamboyant gesture of his right arm, Carter indicated the door.

'Don't plan on going anywhere in the near future,' Charlie said. 'We'll be back to see you soon.'

'I can hardly wait.'

'What did you make of that?' Charlie asked as they were riding back down in the lift.

'I've never heard such a load of rubbish in all my life, sir,' Tony said. 'Partick Thistle to win the league? Totally ridiculous!'

Terry Carter watched from his bedroom window as Charlie and Tony were walking towards their car. Hurrying back to the kitchen, he snatched up his phone from the table and clicked onto his brother's number.

'What do you want?' Andy asked tetchily when he heard the familiar voice.

'Have you heard the news?'

'What are you on about? What news?'

'Murdoch's deid.'

Andy hesitated. 'How did that happen?'

'He was bumped off on Saturday night.'

'Where?'

'In Hyndland.'

'How did you find out?'

'I've just had the cops round. It's a fair bet you'll be getting a visit from them before too long.'

'Were they trying to pin it on you?'

'I'm sure there's nothing they'd like better, but there's no way they can. I had a poker school going at my place on Saturday night and I've got five witnesses who will swear on their mothers' graves that I never left the flat all night. How about you? What were you up to on Saturday?'

Andy hesitated again. 'We need to talk – but not on the phone. Get your arse round to my place.'

Charlie Anderson reversed into the parking place he'd spotted in Maryhill Road, not far from Andy Carter's tenement block.

'How do you want to handle this, sir?' Tony asked as they were trudging up the stone staircase to the third-floor landing.

'A pound to a pinch of shit he'll have had a call from his brother to let him know we're on our way, so we'll just play it by ear,' Charlie said as he depressed the bell push. When the bell didn't ring out, he hammered on the door with his closed fist.

After the third time of hammering, Andy Carter opened up.

'All right! All right! There's no need to knock the fuckin' door down.'

'Your bell isn't working,' Charlie said, flashing his warrant card.

Carter shrugged. 'I'm no' workin' either. My bell's probably come out in sympathy.'

'You were expecting us, I suppose?' Charlie said.

'Why would I be?'

'You mean to say your brother didn't give you a call to gloat over John Murdoch's murder?'

'My phone's not working either. I reckon it must've come out in sympathy with my bell.'

'A right wee comedian we have here,' Charlie said.

'Is it all right if we come in?' Tony asked, stepping across the threshold before Carter had time to object. 'Just a minute!' Tony stared at Carter, pointing at his face. 'Haven't we run into each other somewhere recently? Of course!' he said, snapping his fingers. 'In was in The Ettrick yesterday. Only it wasn't Andy Carter then,' Tony said, turning to Charlie. 'Let me introduce you to one of Jim Colvin's business associates, sir. He goes by the name of Andy Pandy.'

'You know why we're here, Andy whatever-your-name-happens-to-be-today,' Charlie said. 'So let's not waste any more time. Where were you between ten o'clock and eleven o'clock last Saturday evening?'

'Here,' Carter said, tugging a packet of cigarettes from his trouser pocket and tapping one out.

'On your own?' Tony asked.

'As it happens,' Carter said, lighting up and taking a long drag.

'What were you doing?' Charlie asked.

'Not a lot.'

'Did you watch any television?' Tony asked.

'No, I had a couple of cans of lager and I read the papers.'

'You didn't seem in the least bit surprised when I told you that John Murdoch had been murdered,' Charlie said.

'Didn't I? Oh, sorry about that, officer. Goodness gracious me! What was I thinking of?' Carter clasped his hands to the sides of his face. 'John Murdoch's been murdered, has he? Oh, dearie, dearie me! What a surprise!' Carter burst out laughing. 'Is that better?'

'A man's been killed,' Tony snapped.

'I'm fucking devastated.'

'A year ago in the High Court, you and your brother threatened to kill Murdoch if you ever managed to get your hands on him,' Tony said. 'And as it looks like Terry has a rock-solid alibi for his movements on Saturday night – that sort of leaves you out on a limb, wouldn't you say? I reckon the bookies will be laying heavy odds on you having killed Murdoch.'

'So it's no longer a case of trial by jury, is it? It's trial by William Hill now? That sounds like a watertight case you've got there, officer,' Andy sneered. 'I reckon you might have to gather a wee bit more evidence to be a hundred percent sure of securing a conviction, don't you think?' Carter sucked hard on his cigarette, letting the smoke drift out slowly from between his teeth. 'Unless, of course, you're just planning to stitch me up?'

'You're telling us you were here on your own between ten o'clock and eleven o'clock on Saturday evening,' Tony said with a dismissive shake of the head. 'Which means no one will be able to corroborate your story. That's what I call really unlucky.'

Carter grabbed O'Sullivan by his jacket lapels. 'I told you, pal. I was here on my own.'

O'Sullivan prised Carter's hands away. 'Back off, Carter.'

Charlie stepped in between them. 'That's enough of that.'

The colour flared up in Carter's cheeks. 'Are you going to charge me with something?'

'Not right now,' Charlie said.

'In which case, fuck off!'

94

*

When Charlie got back to his office he found a note from his secretary lying on his desk. The editor of the Daily Record had called and left a message, asking Charlie to phone him back as soon as he could.

'DCI Anderson here,' he said when the call was connected. 'I got a message asking me to give you a call.'

'A letter was delivered to our office this morning, Inspector. It was from the Avenging Angel.'

'Shite! Not him again? What did he say this time?'

'He's claiming responsibility for the murder in Hyndland on Saturday night.'

'I need that letter sent across to me – as soon as you can.'

'I'll see to that right away.'

CHAPTER 12

Gavin Carter was in the throes of a complicated dream when he was dragged back to consciousness by the shrill ringtone of his mobile. Fumbling on the bedside table for his phone, he saw the call was from Stuart.

'What time is it?' Gavin asked, yawning as he rubbed the sleep from his eyes.

'It's after twelve. Are you still in your pit?'

'Aye, I had a hard night last night.'

'So you haven't heard the news?' Stuart's voice was animated.

'What are you talking about? What news?'

'I've just seen it on the Internet, Gavin. The guy who was murdered in Hyndland on Saturday night has been identified as someone called John Preston.'

'So what?'

'The bastard had changed his name. It was John Murdoch.'

Gavin's features eased into a broad grin as he sat bolt upright in bed. He ran his fingers through his gelled hair. 'Thanks for letting me know, Stuart.' Cutting the call, Gavin clambered out of bed and got dressed as quickly as he could. Lighting a cigarette, he pulled on his coat, then yanked the apartment door closed behind him before trotting down the two flights of stairs to ground level. He ran along Dumbarton Road to the newsagent on the corner where he bought copies of the Daily Record, the Scottish Sun and The Herald. Flicking his cigarette butt into the middle of the road, he went into the café next door where he ordered a cappuccino and a bacon roll at the counter. Having carried his breakfast across, he flopped down on an upright chair at a table against the far wall. He scanned the front pages of the newspapers, all of them leading with the same story – that the murder victim, John Preston, was the same person who, as John Murdoch, had been on trial for molesting a young boy a year earlier.

Gavin squeezed a thick wedge of tomato ketchup into his bacon roll before taking a large bite and swilling it down with a slurp of hot coffee. Turning to the inside pages, he read every word of the report of the murder in all three newspapers.

As soon as he'd finished eating, Gavin scrambled to his feet. He ran along the road to the nearest bus stop. When a bus bound for Maryhill drew up, he clambered on board.

Sitting behind her desk, Lesley Adams unwrapped the tinfoil from the tuna sandwich she'd brought from home for her lunch. She took one unenthusiastic bite, then wrapped the rest of the sandwich back into the tinfoil and dropped it into the waste paper basket. She had no appetite – her mind was in turmoil. Why hadn't she told Inspector Anderson? She'd been about to tell him, just before he left, but she hadn't gone through with it. But why should she have to tell him? she asked herself. It was none of his business. It wasn't in any way relevant. But, of course, the police wouldn't see it like that. They were going to find out sooner or later, so it would've been a lot better coming from her. But if she contacted Anderson now to tell him, he'd want to know why she hadn't said anything about it earlier this morning. Cursing under her breath, Lesley rummaged in her handbag for her phone and clicked onto a number in her contacts' list.

'It's me,' Lesley said when Myra answered.

'How are things?'

'I had a visit from the cops this morning.'

Myra hesitated. 'What did they want?'

'They asked me a lot of questions. They'd identified the guy who was murdered in Hyndland on Saturday night as John Murdoch and they'd linked him to Tommy Carter's suicide. My name cropped up in the Drumchapel social work reports on the Carter family and they wanted to do some digging into the family background.'

'How did it go?' Myra asked.

'Okay – sort of. I told them what they wanted to know, but….' Lesley's voice tailed off.

'But what?' Myra demanded.

'Not the phone. What are you doing after work?'

DC Tom Freer rapped on Charlie Anderson's office door before walking in.

'I've been going through the data Preston's mobile phone company sent across, sir,' he said as he sat down. 'Renton asked me to give you an update.'

'Did you come across anything interesting?' Charlie asked, putting down his pen and sliding the memo he'd been replying to into his out-tray.

'The reports tell us all the numbers Preston called, or texted, over the past year, as well as the dates, times and durations of the transmissions, but, of course, not the contents of the messages.'

'Where is phone hacking when you need it?' Charlie grumbled.

'Preston's last three communications were all text messages to the same number – and they were all transmitted within the hour before he was murdered. None of them were replied to. Another curious thing,' Freer added. 'The number he was texting was one he had never previously phoned or texted.'

'Do we know anything about that number?' Charlie asked.

'The phone was purchased two months ago from the Carphone Warehouse in Braehead. I got in touch with them. Their records show that it was a cash transaction for a pay-as-you-go phone – so no contract – and no contact details for whoever bought it.'

'Just because Preston texted the same number three times shortly before he was killed,' Charlie said, 'that doesn't necessarily mean that the person he was trying to get in touch with is implicated in his murder. There might be a simple explanation, such as whoever he was trying to contact had his phone switched off at the time.'

'The reason it's significant, sir, is that that phone went off the radar at the same time as Preston's.'

'Meaning what, exactly?'

'According to Preston's service provider, his phone disappeared from their network at ten forty-two last Saturday evening, and within one minute of that happening, the same thing happened to the phone he'd been texting. Neither of those phones has been switched on since.'

'Is there any way the service providers can pinpoint the location of those phones?'

'Not unless they're switched on again,' Freer said.

'Not much chance of that happening,' Charlie said grimly. 'It's odds on that the killer disposed of both the phones as soon as he could.'

Harry Thompson was bored out of his skull. Turning up the volume of the CD player in the Volvo, he drummed his fingertips on the steering column in time to the music. He looked at his watch for the umpteenth time. Two o'clock. Time was dragging by. Another half hour before he'd be able to knock off. But at least the new girl looked promising. Harry ran his fingers round the inside of his shirt collar. He hated wearing a suit, never mind a shirt and tie, but Jim Colvin had insisted on it and, if you wanted to work for Colvin, you had to follow his instructions. This wasn't his idea of 'work' but his dad had told him that he had to serve his time, make a good impression. His father had worked for Colvin for more than twenty years. Colvin didn't normally take on nineteen year-olds, but Harry's father had pulled a few strings to get him on the payroll. You had to admire Colvin. He knew how to spot an opportunity and exploit it. Most people wouldn't look on a food-bank opening up on the south side of the city as a chance to make a killing, but Jim had spotted the potential straight away. That's why he was where he was today. Always one step ahead, always thinking outside the box. If people were in such a bad situation that they needed to use a foodbank, Colvin had told him, they had to be pretty desperate – and desperate people would clutch at any straw that was offered to them. That's where Harry came in. He didn't like this job – in fact, he hated it, but Colvin had assured him that it would only be for six months and if he did okay he would get more interesting work to do. That couldn't happen soon enough as far as Harry was concerned – four months down, two to go.

From where he was parked, Harry could observe everyone going in, and coming out, of the foodbank. Not for the first time he wondered who had named it Butterbiggins Road. Such a daft name for a street.

Having been here every Monday, Wednesday and Friday for the past four months, Harry recognised a lot of the regulars as they struggled along the road, carrying their laden carrier bags.

Harry picked up his packet of cigarettes from the passenger seat and tapped one out, cupping his lighter in both hands as he lit up. When he glanced up, he saw the girl he was waiting for. He'd never seen her before today, but he'd spotted her earlier on, pushing an infant in a buggy as she headed towards the foodbank. How long had she been inside? Harry checked his watch again. It would have been about twenty minutes – which was par for the course. He studied her as she walked past his car – oblivious to his presence. Black, attractive, with strong features – it looked like she was in her early twenties. Probably African, Harry surmised. What kind of hell hole must she have come from, he wondered, if Govanhill was an improvement? As she walked past his car, Harry saw several plastic carrier bags dangling from the handles of her push chair. It looked like she would be an ideal candidate.

Harry waited until the girl had turned into Cathcart Road before leaning over to the back seat and picking up his briefcase. Getting out of the car, he straightened his tie as walked briskly to the corner. He followed the girl down Calder Street until he saw her turn into a tenement close.

Wait at least ten minutes before approaching her to make sure she doesn't associate you with her visit to the foodbank, he reminded himself. Those were Jim Colvin's strict instructions.

Checking his watch as he walked up and down the street, Harry dropped his cigarette butt onto the pavement and crushed it under his heel before ambling down to the mouth of the close. There were six names on the bell pushes – not too bad – he'd seen a lot worse. He scanned the names. Probably not any of the four 'Macs', he thought. Jackson or Ikande? Ikande looked like a strong favourite. Deciding to try that one first, he pressed the bell.

'Who is it?' a female voice asked over the intercom.

'Could I speak to Mr Ikande, please?'

'There is no Mr Ikande.'

First hurdle overcome. 'Sorry, it's Mrs Ikande that I'm looking for.'

'Who are you?'

'I'm from the Home Office.'

'What do you want?' the voice said hesitantly.

'Would you let me in, please?' Harry said. 'There's something I need to discuss with you.'

There was a delay before the buzzer sounded to open the door.

When Harry climbed to the first floor she was waiting for him on the landing. He flashed an ID card in front of her eyes before following her into the one-room flat. Harry's gaze ran round the depressing room, the sum total of the furniture comprising a rickety kitchen table, two upright wooden chairs and a single bed with a torn sleeping bag draped across it. A child was asleep in a cot beneath the cracked window. The wallpaper was peeling off the walls and a stale smell of dampness permeated the entire room.

The food that she had collected from the foodbank had been ranged neatly on the draining board beside the sink. Various tins of soup, corned beef and vegetables, a packet of pasta, a jar of jam, a box of cereal, a jar of coffee, a bag of sugar and a carton of long life milk. Two packets of nappies were lying on the kitchen table. As far as Harry could see, the only other things in the flat were one plate, one mug, one knife and fork and a tin opener, which were lying on the ledge beside the sink.

Harry hated what he was about to do, but he justified it to himself on the basis that, if he wasn't doing this, Jim Colvin would have sent someone else to do it.

'What is your full name?' Harry asked, easing himself down gingerly onto one of the chairs beside the kitchen table, testing it to make sure that it would bear his weight.

'Chibundo Ikande.'

'Where do you come from?'

'Nigeria.'

Harry took a manila folder from his briefcase and placed it on the table. Removing a sheaf of paper, he started to thumb through the pages.

'What is your immigration status, Mrs Ikande?'

'I'm an asylum seeker.'

'Are you here on your own?'

'There's just me – and my daughter,' Chibundo said, nodding towards the infant in the cot.

Harry took a pen from his inside jacket pocket and ran it down a column on one of the pages. He let out a long, low sigh. 'I regret to have to inform you that your application for asylum has been turned down, Mrs Ikande. You and your daughter will have to return to Nigeria.'

The colour drained from Chibundo's face. 'But… I can't go back there,' she spluttered. 'They killed my mother and my father. They'll kill me. They'll kill my baby.'

'I only wish I had better news for you,' Harry said with a shake of the head as he got to his feet.

'There must be something that can be done,' Chibundo pleaded. Tears started to seep from her eyes. 'I can't go back there. I just can't.' Burying her face in her hands, she started to sob uncontrollably.

'You are entitled to lodge an appeal,' Harry said as he was putting the folder back into his briefcase. 'But in order to do that you would need to enlist the services of a lawyer – and they don't come cheap.'

Chibundo dropped her hands to her sides and shook her head slowly from side to side. 'I don't have any money – and I'm not allowed to work.'

'I'm very sorry.' Harry moved slowly towards the door, then turned back. 'Look, I really shouldn't be saying this, but – ' His voice tailed off.

'Saying what?

'I really shouldn't…'

'Tell me!' she pleaded.

'There might be a way. No.' He shook his head. 'I can't. It could cost me my job.'

'Please tell me!'

Harry hesitated. 'All right – but it would have to be just between the two of us.'

CHAPTER 13

Gavin Carter jumped off the bus in Maryhill Road and ran all the way to the entry to Andy Carter's close. Loping up the tenement stairs two at a time, he hammered on his uncle's door.

'Have you heard the news?' he blurted out as soon as Andy opened up.

'Aye,' Andy said. 'I had the cops round.'

'Was it you, Andy?' Gavin said excitedly. 'Did you get Murdoch?'

'I wish it had been me, son, but I'm sorry to say it wasn't.'

'Was it my Dad?'

'He's in the kitchen. Why don't you ask him?'

'Did you get Murdoch, Dad?' Gavin asked as he strode into the kitchen.

'It was nothing to do with me, Gavin. I was in a poker school on Saturday night.'

'Who could it have been, then?' Gavin asked.

'I've no idea,' Terry said. 'Talking about Saturday,' he added. 'What happened to you, Gavin? You were supposed to meet me in the cemetery at two o'clock. I stood waiting for you at Tommy's graveside for more than half an hour in the pissing rain.'

'I couldn't make it,' Gavin said. 'There were things I had to do.'

'What was more important than paying your respects to your wee brother on his anniversary?'

Ignoring the question, Gavin turned to Andy. 'If it wasn't you and it wasn't my Dad, who do you think could've bumped off Murdoch?'

'I haven't a clue,' Andy said. 'But it must've been somebody who knew his history. It can't be a coincidence that he was killed on Tommy's anniversary.'

'Apart from us, Andy, who else would've had a reason to do him in?' Terry asked.

'What about Alice's new bloke?' Andy suggested. 'Do you think your missus could have put him up to it?'

'I suppose she might have,' Terry said. 'I can't think of anybody else who would've had the bottle.'

'I can,' Gavin stated.

'Who?' Andy queried.

Gavin hesitated for maximum effect. 'I've been winding both of you up,' he said, his features breaking out in a broad grin. 'It was fucking-well me!' he exclaimed, puffing out his chest and punching the air.

'You?' Andy spluttered, staring open-mouthed.

'You better believe it!' Drumming his chest with his fists, Gavin marched up and down the kitchen. '*That's* how I paid my respects to Tommy, Dad. I didn't waste my time taking him a bunch of flowers. I fucking-well nailed the bastard who raped him!'

Andy snatched a cigarette from the packet lying on the table. 'For fuck's sake, Gavin,' he said, striking a match and lighting up. 'Why did you do it, son? I told you to let me know straight away if you ever managed to track Murdoch down.'

'Because I wanted to handle it on my own, Andy,' Gavin said, his eyes flashing. 'For Tommy's sake. I wanted to take care of Murdoch, all by myself. I found the bastard – I set him up – and I got him. And I did it on Tommy's anniversary. Did I do all right?' Gavin said, offering Andy a high five.

'Fucking hell! You did brilliant, son!' Andy said, reaching up to slap the palm of his nephew's hand. Throwing his arms around Gavin's shoulders, Andy held him in a tight bear hug.

'You shouldn't have done that on your own, Gavin,' Terry said, shaking his head. 'What if you get caught? I've already lost one son because of Murdoch, I don't want to lose you as well.'

'Don't you worry about that, Dad. You won't be losing me,' Gavin said as Andy released him slowly. 'I covered my tracks perfectly. There's no way the cops will be able to pin anything on me.'

'We need a plan,' Andy said. 'The first thing we have to do is sort out an alibi for you, Gavin,' he said, rubbing at the stubble on his chin. 'We'll need a watertight story about where you were, and who you were with, on Saturday night.'

'Could I say I was with you, Dad?' Gavin asked.

'I told you – I was in a poker school on Saturday night,' Terry said.

'I could say I was there.'

'That wouldn't work, Gavin,' Terry said with a shake of the head. 'I've already given the polis the names of everyone who was playing. It would look odd if I tried to add your name to the list now. Besides, I couldn't trust some of the blokes who were there to back up that version of events when they find out it's a murder enquiry. How about that bird of yours?' Terry suggested. 'Would she cover for you?'

Gavin's brow furrowed. 'I don't think so, Dad. She'd want to know why I needed an alibi. If she thought for one minute that I was in trouble with the polis, she'd go ballistic. Besides, I already told her I was in Edinburgh on Saturday night. Stuart was doing a gig and I told her I went through with him. I could stick with that story, Andy. Stuart's a good mate. If I ask him, he'll say I was with him in Edinburgh. That way, I couldn't have been in Glasgow when the murder took place. I covered up for Stuart last month when the polis were after him for flogging knocked-off fags. I'm sure he'd do the same for me.'

Andy shook his head. 'That won't work, Gavin.'

'Why not?' Gavin queried. 'Stuart's okay.'

'I'm not saying that he isn't,' Andy said. 'But this isn't in the same category as flogging dodgy fags, son. This is murder. If the cops suspect you were involved – and Stuart says you were with him in Edinburgh – they'll put him through the wringer. They'll threaten to charge him with perverting the course of justice. They'll threaten him with ten years in the Bar-L for being an accessory after the fact. They'll paint a picture of what life would be like for him on the inside – and it won't be pretty. There's too much of a risk that Stuart would crack – and then you'd be up shit creek without a paddle.'

'He wouldn't let me down, Andy,' Gavin protested. 'He knows what Murdoch did to Tommy – so even if he finds out why I need an alibi, he'll stick to the story.'

'It's not as straightforward as that, Gavin,' Andy said. 'If you tell the cops you were at a gig in Edinburgh with Stuart, they'll want to know where it was.'

'I can find that out.'

'That's not good enough. The cops will track down other people who were at the gig and ask them if they saw you there. They'll want to know how you travelled through to Edinburgh and they'll check the CCTV for the route you claimed to have taken.' Andy started pacing up and down the kitchen. 'Let me think this through,' he muttered to himself. 'I need to keep a clear head. Is there any possibility that somebody might've seen you doing in Murdoch?'

'No way!' Gavin said.

'Are you sure? Are you absolutely certain that there were no witnesses?'

'Of course I'm sure, Andy. No one saw me do it. I was dead careful.'

'Okay,' Andy said, sinking down onto a chair. 'Take your time, Gavin. Sit down, and tell us exactly what happened on Saturday night. I want to know every single detail.'

'It's what you might call a paedophile's paradise, sir,' Eddie McLaughlin announced as he walked into Charlie Anderson's office. Placing John Preston's iPad on the desk, McLaughlin took the chair opposite Charlie's desk. 'It didn't take me long to crack the password – and from there on it was one pornographic image after another – mostly of boys between the ages of ten and fifteen, I would guess.'

'Was there anything else on his iPad, apart from the indecent images?' Charlie asked.

'There were e-mail communications with several people – and from the tone of some of the messages, it looks like he was in contact with quite a few young boys. There was also a lot of correspondence with someone called Malcolm Steel, but that dried up about eighteen months ago. I gathered from the exchanges that Steel used to be Preston's partner – and from the content of the more recent e-mails, it doesn't look like it was an amicable break up.'

'Did you come across the names Tommy Carter or Ronnie Gilligan?' Charlie asked.

'Both of those names cropped up several times – and the more recent correspondence with Ronnie Gilligan is particularly interesting.'

'Print out all the relevant stuff for me, Eddie,' Charlie said.

'I need a fucking drink,' Terry Carter said, heaving himself to his feet as soon as Gavin had finished recounting what he'd done.

'There's whisky in the cupboard above the cooker,' Andy said.

Terry took the bottle of Bells from the top shelf and lifted three glasses from the draining board. Unscrewing the cap, he poured out three stiff measures.

'What are we going to do now?' Terry asked as he was adding a splash of water to his drink from the kitchen tap.

'For a start, Gavin will need to talk to the cops,' Andy said.

'Do I have to do that?' Gavin looked imploringly at his uncle. 'I don't want to go anywhere near the polis.'

'You have to talk to them, son.' Andy stood up and put a reassuring arm around Gavin's shoulders. 'They'll want to speak to you and it'll make them suspicious if they think you're trying to avoid them. It's much better to brazen it out and go and see them before they come looking for you. That way, you give the impression that you don't have anything to hide.'

'What'll I say to them?' Lifting his glass to his lips with a shaking hand, Gavin screwed up his face as he gulped down a mouthful of neat whisky.

'Before we talk about that,' Andy said, 'the first priority is to sort out an alibi for you for Saturday night.'

'Could I say I was with you, Andy?' Gavin asked.

Andy shook his head. 'I've already told the cops that I was here on my own.'

'That wasn't very clever,' Terry interjected. 'Could you not have come up something more original than that?'

Andy glowered at him. 'If you don't have an alibi, the worst thing you can do is tell the polis you were with somebody. When push comes to shove, you can't rely on anybody to back up your story. If you tell the cops you were on your own, the onus is on them to prove otherwise.'

'What were you up to?' Terry asked.

'I was doing a job for Jim Colvin in The Jaco – but it's not something I'd want to talk to the cops about.'

'Is there anyone who could vouch for that?' Terry asked.

Andy scratched at his chin. 'Aye, Jack Mulgrew. I nailed his hand to the bog door.'

Terry grinned. 'I suppose there's a reasonable chance that Mulgrew might remember you having done that.'

Charlie called Tony O'Sullivan to his office to show him the letter that had been sent across from the Daily Record office.

'Forensics gave it the once over before I handled it,' Charlie said. 'The stamp was the self-adhesive kind, so no possibility of a DNA match with the sender's saliva. They found several sets of prints on the envelope, which is what you would expect when it was collected from a post box somewhere in the city, then handled in the sorting office in Springburn as well as in the Daily Record mail room. There were only two sets of prints on the letter itself. The forensics guys are checking them out, but they're sure to belong to the girl at the Record who opened the envelope and the editor.'

'He's a fan of old technology, I see,' Tony said as he examined the single sheet of paper. 'Cutting and pasting words from newspaper articles.'

'Effective, nevertheless,' Charlie said.

Tony scanned the page:

ONE MORE PIECE OF VERMIN REMOVED FROM THE STREETS OF GLASGOW.

MAY THE LORD BE PRAISED! THE AVENGING ANGEL

'How many murders has he claimed now?' Tony asked.

'If you believe all the letters were sent by the same person, this is his fourth.'

'Do you not think they were?'

'How much do you know about him?' Charlie asked.

'Just what I read in the papers. I wasn't involved in any of those cases.'

'I was, for my sins. Up to my neck. It was the bane of my life. The first murder he claimed to have committed was in Aberdeen about eight years ago. The victim's name was Robertson, if I remember right. A man in his fifties. He was found bludgeoned to death with a hammer in a country lane on the outskirts of the city. Two weeks after he was killed a letter arrived at the office of the Press and Journal. In it, the self-designated Avenging Angel announced that he had been given a mission by God to rid the world of vermin. He said he'd killed Robertson because he had interfered with young boys in a school football team twenty years previously. Robertson had been charged with that offence at the time, and the verdict was not proven. But there was a lot about the Avenging Angel's claim that didn't ring true.'

'Such as?'

'Robertson hadn't tried to hide himself away. He'd been living in the same house for more than thirty years. If you're so enraged that you're contemplating murdering someone, why would you wait twenty years before doing it? Apart from that, the letter wasn't sent until the day after the Press and Journal ran a piece divulging Robertson's history and the not proven verdict. At the time I thought the murder had nothing to do with Robertson's past. I thought that whoever killed him was trying to muddy the waters. Either that, or a nutter was stirring things up.'

'When did the Avenging Angel next stick his head above the parapet?' Tony asked.

'About five years ago, in Edinburgh. This time the victim was a guy in his thirties who been charged with having sexual relations with a fourteen your-old girl. He had been acquitted with a not proven verdict on a technicality, something to do with the crown prosecution service not disclosing evidence to which the defence was entitled in a timely manner. Apart from the administrative cock-up, the case looked rock solid, so he probably got away with it – up to a point. A week later he opened his front door to someone who stabbed him several times in the guts.'

'Someone associated with his victim?'

'That's odds-on. The third murder the AA claimed responsibility for was a strange affair,' Charlie continued. 'A couple of years ago, late on a Saturday night, a car mounted the pavement in Castlemilk and side-swiped a man standing at a bus stop, then drove off without stopping. A few months previously, a charge against the victim for underage sexual activity had been found to be not proven.'

'So there is a pattern,' Tony said. 'All the victims had been charged with underage sex offences and all of them were acquitted on not proven verdicts.'

'That was Niggle's line of thinking,' Charlie nodded. 'He was convinced that the Avenging Angel was a serial killer and he was determined to demonstrate that the Glasgow CID could crack a case that had confounded both the Aberdeen and Edinburgh divisions. He lumbered me with the investigation – it was before I was bumped up to DCI. My team spent God only knows how many hours battering their heads against a brick wall. The Edinburgh boys had a field day. When they heard I'd been assigned to the case they sent me lots of useful advice, such as: 'you should pull in for questioning everyone in Scotland who owns a pair of scissors'; 'check out anyone who has bought a book of stamps within the past year'; 'focus on everyone who has bought a newspaper recently'. Unsurprisingly, the investigation went nowhere – it was needles and haystacks.'

'Do you think the same killer carried out all three murders?' Tony asked.

'I very much doubt it,' Charlie said with a shake of the head. 'For a start, there was no similarity in the way the murders were carried out. If the incident in Castlemilk was a premeditated murder, it's a weird way to go about it. You'd have to be certain that the person you were targeting would be standing at a particular bus stop at a particular time and, unless you had a total disregard for human life, you would have to be sure that no one else would be waiting at that stop. At the time I thought it had been a hit and run accident. My theory was that the driver was probably drunk and when he read in the newspapers the following day that the man he had killed had previously been acquitted of child sex offences on a not proven verdict, he jumped onto the Avenging Angel bandwagon in order to divert attention from himself. Besides,' Charlie added, 'I realise Scots are a multi-talented people, but being capable of bludgeoning someone to death with a hammer, stabbing someone in the guts with a knife and side-swiping a guy with a car would be a rare set of skills for any one individual to acquire – even in Glasgow.

'And I don't think our Avenging Angel friend had anything to do with the other two deaths either,' Charlie added. 'I reckon he's an attention-seeking saddo whose only interest is in trying to make our job even more difficult than it already is. Of course, the tabloids were in their element,' Charlie added. 'They lapped up the Avenging

Angel story and they published his letters. In his first missive the AA regaled us with the mission statement that had been sent to him by Almighty God, but the next two letters were more succinct.'

'What do you reckon in Preston's case?' Tony asked. 'Is this another instance of the saddo jumping onto the bandwagon?'

Charlie shook his head emphatically. 'That's not what we're dealing with here, Tony. This time it's kosher.'

'What makes you say that?'

'Take a look at the postmark on the envelope. It was time-stamped in the sorting office in Springburn at twenty-past ten on Sunday morning, which means it must have been put into a post box either late on Saturday night, or very early on Sunday morning, which was before the identity of the victim was known. This is the first time the Avenging Angel has had information that wasn't in the public domain at the time the letter was posted.'

When Tony left the office, Charlie turned his attention to the e-mails Eddie McLaughlin had printed out for him. As he worked his way through them, the pieces started to fall into place. Malcolm Steel was a teacher in the same school as John Murdoch and, from the tone of the communications, it was evident that they'd been in a relationship, up until about eighteen months previously when things had started to turn sour, with Steel accusing Murdoch of having tried to seduce Ronnie Gilligan, one of the second-year pupils in the school.

Charlie homed in on the correspondence between Murdoch and Ronnie Gilligan. The communications had started about two years ago, in December 2009, and from the content of the early exchanges it was apparent that Murdoch was trying to groom Ronnie. The dialogue had ended abruptly in February 2010 before starting up again in August 2011. Charlie noticed that both their e-mail addresses had changed in the intervening period; john.murdoch95 changing to john.preston73 and Ronnie Gilligan, while keeping the same name, switching from gmail to hotmail. The tone of the post-August 2011 correspondence was completely different, with Gilligan informing Murdoch he knew that he had changed his name to Preston and telling him that he knew where he was living now. He was threatening him with blackmail.

Leaning forward to depress the buzzer on his intercom, Charlie asked his secretary to set up a meeting for him as soon as she could with Donald Parker, the school's head teacher.

It was just after half-past seven when Lesley Adams arrived in The Rock. From the doorway of the lounge she did a double take when she saw Myra sitting on her own in a booth in the far corner.

Myra waved across when she saw Lesley come in. 'I started without you,' she called out, holding up her wine glass.

Lesley ordered a drink at the bar and carried it across to the booth.

'I didn't recognise you for a minute,' Lesley said as she flopped down.

'What do you think?' Myra asked, turning her head from side to side and patting her hair.

'I like the style, but the green streaks will take a bit of getting used to.'

'You should get something done with yours,' Myra said. 'Derek says auburn is so twentieth century.'

'Who is Derek?'

'My new stylist. Amanda in the office put me on to him. He's really hot,' Myra added with a sly grin.

'Is he available?' Lesley asked.

Myra shrugged. 'He's married.'

'I suppose that's not too bad – he could have been gay.'

'Amanda warned me off chatting him up in the salon,' Myra said. 'Apparently his wife works there too and she keeps a beady eye on him.'

'That's a bit of a bummer.'

'Derek told me that I'll need to get my roots done every four or five weeks. I can feel a heavy cold coming on in about a month's time,'

Myra added, 'so I'm planning to ask him if he'll come over to my place and touch me up.'

'You're incorrigible.'

'Just trying to lighten the mood,' Myra said, a serious tone creeping into her voice. 'You sounded a bit down in the dumps on the phone. Is there something wrong?'

Lesley gazed long and hard into her drink before replying. 'As I told you on the phone, I had a visit from the police this morning.'

'I thought you said that went okay?' Myra queried, raising an eyebrow.

'It did, up to a point. It was mostly routine stuff. They were looking for background information on the Carter family and my name happened to crop up in the social work reports. They asked me a lot of questions about Tommy and Gavin – as well as the father and the uncle.'

'So what did you mean by 'up to a point'?' Myra asked, picking up her wine glass and taking a slow sip.

'I didn't – ' Lesley let out a sigh. 'I didn't say anything to them about me and Gavin.'

'Jesus Christ, Lesley!' Myra spluttered. 'What in the name of God were you thinking about?'

'I don't know,' Lesley said, running her fingers through her hair. 'I panicked. I thought that if I didn't mention it, they might not find out about us.'

'Are you serious?'

'Keep your voice down!' Lesley said in a strangulated whisper. She glanced quickly round the bar, but no one appeared to be paying them any attention. 'I wasn't thinking straight.'

'Of course, they're going to find out about you and Gavin. That's a racing certainty. And that information had better come from you,' Myra added forcibly, 'otherwise they'll think you've got something to hide.'

'I realise that,' Lesley said, exhaling noisily. 'I'll call Inspector Anderson first thing in the morning and let him know.' Picking up her glass, she threw back the contents. 'I need another drink.'

CHAPTER 14

*I waited six months from the time I spotted Murdoch in Stravaigin
before getting in touch with him. Having set up a hotmail account
in the name of 'Ronnie Gilligan', I sent him an e-mail in which I
told him I'd seen him coming out of an office building in Bath Street
a few days earlier, but I'd decided not to approach him. I told him
that I'd followed him home to Oakfield Avenue and when I checked
his doorbell, I saw that he was using the name 'Preston'. I said that
I'd gone back to the office in Bath Street and when I saw there was a
firm in the building called 'Murdoch & Slater', I'd put two and two
together. I'd called the secretary in the office and she'd given me his
e-mail address.*

*I told him I had kept all the e-mails he had sent me while he was
my guidance teacher – and that the day of reckoning had arrived. If
he didn't want me to forward the e-mails to the police, it was going
to cost him a grand. I suggested that would be a lot cheaper – and
easier – for him, than having to change his name again, find another
job and move flat.*

*It was three days before he replied. When he did, it was the usual guff.
He said he would agree to pay what I was asking, on condition that I
would never come back looking for more money – and he wanted to
know how he could be sure the e-mails would be deleted.*

*I told him he'd have to trust me on that – just as I had to trust him
when he was trying to shag me. I suggested that we meet in Cottiers
in Hyndland Street for him to hand over the money because the pub*

had an outside garden area where children are allowed in. I told him I wanted the cash in used tens and twenties. I proposed that we meet the following Saturday night at eight o'clock. I told him we should exchange mobile numbers in case either of us needed to change the arrangements at short notice. He sent me his phone number and I sent him mine. I grinned when he e-mailed me to confirm the rendezvous.

CHAPTER 15

Jack Mulgrew was sitting on a bench seat at a table in the corner of the lounge bar in The Jacobite Arms, an untouched pint of heavy on the table in front of him. Chewing hard on the end of his pencil, he was engrossed in studying the midweek football fixed-odds coupon when Andy and Gavin Carter walked into the pub.

'I thought we might find him here,' Andy whispered to Gavin.

'I really don't like this, Andy,' Gavin said. 'I still think it would be better if I told the polis I was in Edinburgh with Stuart.'

'We've been through all that. The cops would tear a hole in that story in five minutes flat. Just do what I told you and everything will be fine. Come on.'

Striding across the bar, they sat down on the bench seat, one on either side of Mulgrew.

Mulgrew glanced in Gavin's direction. Turning round quickly, he stared at Andy.

'Do you remember me, Mulgrew?' Andy said quietly. 'We ran into each other last Saturday night downstairs in the bog.'

Mulgrew's jaw dropped and the pencil slipped from his grasp. He held both his hands up in front of his face, his left thumb gently massaging the tight bandage wrapped around the palm of his right hand. 'Aye,' he gulped. 'I remember you all right.'

'Have you told the cops what happened to you?' Andy asked.

'I didny say nothin' to the polis,' Mulgrew whimpered. 'Honest, mister – I didny say a fuckin' word.'

'Then it's about time you did.'

'What are you on about?' Mulgrew's voice was shaking. 'I willny say nothin.'

'Oh, yes, you will. You're going to tell the cops what happened to you – and who did it.'

'Are you aff your fuckin' heid? If I shop Jim Colvin, he'll kill me!'

'This has got nothing to do with Jim Colvin,' Andy stated. 'I'm not asking you to shop him. I'm *telling* you to shop me and the boy here. The boy's name's Gavin, by the way, he's my nephew. You happen to know his name because you heard me mention it on Saturday night when we claimed you. You're going to go to the polis right now and you're going to tell them that me and Gavin grabbed you downstairs in the bog on Saturday night and that we nailed your hand to the cubicle door.'

'But it was…… it was you and Jim Colvin,' Mulgrew stammered.

'Not at all! Your memory's playing tricks on you, Mulgrew. Jim Colvin wasn't anywhere near this place. It was me and Gavin who claimed you. And the reason we did it was because you owed me five hundred quid. Have you got that? You owed *me* five hundred quid – not Jim Colvin.'

'What are you guys playing at?' Mulgrew whimpered.

'We're not playing, pal.' Taking a firm grip of Mulgrew's bandaged hand, Andy started to squeeze it hard. 'You're going to go to the cops right now,' he whispered forcibly in Mulgrew's ear, 'and you're going to file an official complaint. You're going to make a statement, telling the polis that you know who nailed your hand to the bog door. Under no circumstances will you mention Jim Colvin's name. Do you understand what I'm saying?' Mulgrew nodded as he swallowed hard. 'And don't mess up,' Carter added, releasing Mulgrew's hand and reaching underneath the table to take a firm grip of his testicles. 'Because if you get this wrong, I'll be back. And it won't be your hand I'll be nailing to the bog door next time. It'll be these,' he said, gradually tightening his grip. Beads of perspiration broke out on Mulgrew's forehead and his eyes started to bulge. 'Have you got that?'

'Aye!' Mulgrew yelped.

Slowly relaxing his grip, Carter handed Mulgrew a slip of paper on which the names "Andy Carter" and "Gavin" were written. 'These are the names you're going to give to the polis. You're going to tell them that Gavin held your hand against the door while I hammered in the nail. Do you understand that?' Mulgrew nodded, wild-eyed. 'And one more thing,' Carter added, prodding his index finger hard into Mulgrew's chest. 'One very important thing. You're going to tell the cops at what time it happened – which was exactly half-past ten.'

Lesley Adams threw back the rest of her drink. 'Everything's a complete and utter mess!'

'Get a grip of yourself. You've got nothing to reproach yourself about,' Myra insisted.

'Try telling that to the police.'

'Is anyone saying you've done something wrong?'

'Not so far. But you can bet your boots the cops will as soon as they find out about me and Gavin.'

'You're beating yourself up about nothing, Lesley. Gavin was nineteen when the two of you got together.'

'The rules aren't the same when you've been his social worker.'

'He was nineteen, for God's sake. It's not as if he was a child. He was old enough to know his own mind.' Myra got to her feet. 'Same again?' she asked, pointing at Lesley's empty glass.

Lesley nodded.

Jack Mulgrew walked up slowly to the reception desk in London Road Police Station.

'What can I do for you, sir?' the duty officer enquired.

'I want to file a complaint,' he mumbled.

'What kind of complaint?'

'I want to report an assault.'

'Who was assaulted?'

'Me,' Mulgrew said, holding up his bandaged hand.

'When did that happen?'

'Last Saturday night.'

'Where?'

'In The Jacobite Arms.'

'Do you know who assaulted you?'

Mulgrew nodded. 'Two blokes. Andy Carter and a boy called Gavin. They grabbed me in the bog and they nailed my hand to a cubicle door. It happened at half-past ten,' he added quickly.

'That's a lot of detail, sir,' Sergeant Harding said folding his arms across his chest. 'Why did you not file a complaint before now?'

'I was... I was scared of them.'

'But you're not scared of them any longer?' Mulgrew lowered his eyes. 'How come?' Harding asked.

'Of course I'm still scared of them – shit scared,' Mulgrew said, looking up quickly. 'But I've had it up to here with them. That wasn't the first time they've given me a doing and if I don't do something about it now they're going to kick the fuck out of me again.' Mulgrew hesitated. 'Are you going to arrest them?'

'Before I decide about that, how about you tell me what *really* happened?'

'That's what really happened!' Mulgrew spluttered indignantly. 'Andy Carter and Gavin grabbed me in the pub on Saturday night, at half-past ten, and nailed my hand to the bog door. If you don't believe me, you can ask the landlord.'

'Did he see them do it?'

'No, they'd buggered off by the time he got there. But he found me nailed to the door all right. Just you ask him!'

Harding fixed Mulgrew with a stare. 'Are you quite sure you want to go through with this?'

Mulgrew gazed down at the floor. Without raising his head, he nodded slowly.

'Very good, sir,' Harding said, heaving a heavy sigh. Pulling open the top drawer in his desk, he took out a form. 'Let's get all this down in writing.'

Gavin Carter was lying stretched out on the settee, watching the football highlights programme on television, when his mobile phone rang. When he saw who was calling, he hit the mute button on the television and took the call.

'Can you talk?'

'Sure.'

'I think he suspects.'

'Christ! How can he? What did he say?'

'Nothing in particular, but he's been acting strangely. He asked to borrow my phone because he said the battery on his was flat, but when he went to the loo I checked his phone and the battery was fine.'

'Fucking hell! I hope there wasn't anything on your phone?'

'Of course not. I delete everything straight away.'

'Shit!' Gavin exclaimed. 'I can hear someone at the door. I have to go. I'll call you tomorrow morning.'

Cutting the call, he turned the sound back up on the television.

'Just me!' Lesley announced as she turned the key in the front door of the flat.

'You're late on the road tonight,' Gavin called out. 'What happened?' he asked as he used the remote control to switch off the television. 'I was starting to get worried about you.'

'I like it when you worry about me,' Lesley said, a silly grin plastered to her face as she stood in the doorway.

'It looks like you've had quite a session,' Gavin said, eyeing her up and down.

'I had a couple,' Lesley said defensively. 'I was celebrating with Myra.'

'Celebrating what?'

'Murdoch getting what was coming to him.'

'So you heard?'

'The police came to see me this morning.'

'The police?' Gavin hesitated. 'What did they want?' he asked, frowning.

'They asked me lots and lots of questions – about your Dad – and your uncle Andy – and Tommy.' Lesley weaved her way across the room. 'And they wanted to know all about you,' she added, running her fingers through Gavin's hair before planting a slobbery kiss on his lips.

'What sort of questions were they asking?' Gavin asked, easing Lesley away from him and holding her at arms' length.

'They'd seen the Drumchapel social work reports and they wanted to know if there was anything I could add.'

'What did you tell them?'

'Not a lot,' Lesley shrugged.

'Do they know who killed Murdoch?' Gavin asked.

'I don't think so. But if they do,' Lesley slurred, 'they weren't about to share the information with me.'

'Did you tell them about us?' Gavin asked.

'No.' Lesley let out a long, low sigh as she flopped down on the settee. 'But I wish I had.'

CHAPTER 16

Tuesday 6 September

When Charlie Anderson arrived a few minutes early for his nine-thirty meeting with Donald Parker, the school secretary ushered him into the head teacher's office.

Parker, a tall, slim man with rounded shoulders and a pronounced Adam's apple, got to his feet. Stretching across his desk, he took Charlie's hand in a limp grip, fingertips only.

'Thank you for agreeing to see me at short notice,' Charlie said as he settled down on the leather chair on the other side of the desk.

'What can I do for you, Inspector?'

'You know that we are investigating John Preston's death?' Charlie said. 'The man you knew as John Murdoch?'

'Yes.'

'I would appreciate some background information.'

'Such as?'

'Were you aware that, some time ago, Murdoch was in a relationship with a male member of your staff?'

'If you're referring to Malcolm Steel,' Parker said stiffly. 'The answer is yes.'

'How did you find out about that?'

'They told me.'

'On their own initiative?'

Parker nodded. 'They both came to see me. It must have been about three years ago. Malcolm was head of the maths department at the time and John was a member of his staff. They told me they were intending to move in together – and they realised

124

that could be perceived as causing a conflict of interest within the department.'

'How did you resolve that?'

'The month before, John had applied for a vacancy as a guidance teacher – and I knew he was going to be offered the position. He was qualified to teach both mathematics and computing science, so I adjusted the timetable in such a way that the only classes he would be taking from then on would be in computing science, which meant he would no longer be working in Malcolm's department.'

'Did the fact that they were going to be living together give you a problem?'

'Not as such. They assured me that they would be discreet about their relationship, which they were. The official line was that they were going to be flat-sharing, which is not at all uncommon – in fact, quite often necessary these days, considering the pitiful salaries teachers get paid. Of course, there were rumours. In such situations, there invariably are. But as long as it wasn't affecting the smooth running of the school, I had no reason to interfere. However,' Parker added, his brow wrinkling, 'things turned sour about eighteen months ago when their relationship came to an abrupt end.'

'Do you know what caused the break-up?'

'Round about that time,' Parker said, 'Martin Gilligan, the father of one of our second-year pupils, Ronnie Gilligan, came to see me. He told me he wanted to lodge a formal complaint about Murdoch's behaviour towards his son.'

'What was the nature of the complaint?' Charlie asked.

'That Murdoch had made – how can I put this?' Parker paused, his Adams' apple bulging as he swallowed. 'That Murdoch had made an improper suggestion to Ronnie in the school library.' Parker broke off to cough into his fist. 'I asked Mr Gilligan if he would be prepared to repeat his accusation in Murdoch's presence. He said he would, so I summoned John to my office. John denied everything. He told Mr Gilligan that his son had a crush on him and that it was Ronnie who had made the so-called improper suggestion.'

'How was the matter resolved?'

'The nature of the accusation was extremely serious so I had to report the matter to the police. I informed Murdoch that he would be suspended from all teaching duties, pending an inquiry. However, before the police had time to even initiate an investigation, Mr Gilligan phoned to tell me that, having spoken again to his son, it appeared that there had been some kind of misunderstanding and he informed me that he was withdrawing his complaint. I pressed him to explain the nature of this misunderstanding, but he wasn't prepared to discuss the matter any further. On that basis, Murdoch was re-instated.

'At the same time as he withdrew his complaint, Mr Gilligan informed me that he intended to take Ronnie out of the school. Things then went from bad to worse. Within a month, two more boys in Ronnie's class were withdrawn from the school in mid-term for what were, at best, spurious reasons. I assumed that Gilligan must have been stirring things up with some of the other parents. I was starting to have serious concerns about the damage this might do the school's reputation but, fortunately, things calmed down after that and there were no further withdrawals of pupils.'

'Was that the end of the matter as far as you were concerned?'

'A pupil has a crush on a teacher – the teacher doesn't reciprocate – the pupil turns spiteful and accuses the teacher of sexual harassment. It wouldn't be the first time that had happened, Inspector. I can't say with any degree of certainty that that's what happened in this case, but there are vindictive children around who would like nothing better than seeing their teacher get into trouble. Not long after that incident, I found out that Murdoch and Steel were no longer sharing a flat – in fact, it appeared that they were no longer even on speaking terms.'

'Do you know why?'

'No. But I suspected that Ronnie Gilligan's accusations might have had something to do with it.'

'Do you think there was any substance to those accusations?'

Parker shrugged his shoulders. 'I can't comment on that.'

'Would Tommy Carter have been aware of Ronnie Gilligan's accusations when he claimed that Murdoch had raped him?'

'I don't know. However, what I do know is that when Tommy's social worker got in touch with me – a lady called Lesley... something or other.'

'Lesley Adams,' Charlie offered.

'That's the name.' Parker nodded. 'When Lesley Adams contacted me to tell me that Tommy Carter had accused Murdoch of assaulting him, she also told me that she knew about the Gilligan affair. I can only assume that she must have heard about that from Tommy.'

'Would it be possible for me to speak to Mr Steel this morning?' Charlie asked.

Parker consulted the timetable on his desk. 'He's got a free period at ten o'clock.'

Charlie glanced at his watch. 'In which case, I'll wait.'

'You can use the deputy head's office,' Parker said. 'I'll let Malcolm know that you want to see him.'

Sergeant Harding called the Pitt Street switchboard and asked to be put through to Tony O'Sullivan.

'Harding from London Road,' he said when Tony took the call. 'I believe you were called out to an incident in The Jacobite Arms last Saturday night when a guy by the name of Jack Mulgrew had his hand nailed to a door in the toilets?'

'That's correct.'

'I thought you might be interested to know that Mulgrew came here last night. He wanted to file a formal complaint about the assault. He claims to know who attacked him.'

'It wouldn't happen to have been Jim Colvin, by any chance?'

'Apparently not. He says it was someone called Andy Carter and a boy called Gavin.'

'Really! That's very interesting. What did you make of his story?'

'More fishy than a barrel of kippers, if you ask me. After saying nothing for two days, all of a sudden, out of the blue, Mulgrew decides to file a complaint. And for some strange reason, he insisted that I record the fact that the assault took place at exactly ten-thirty.'

'How did you leave it with him?'

'I took down his statement and got him to sign it, then I told him I'd initiate enquiries and get back to him.'

'I know Andy Carter, Sergeant. Leave it with me and I'll get back to you when I get to the bottom of what's going on.'

'Very good.'

Charlie Anderson glanced up when he heard the sharp rap on the deputy head's door.

'Malcolm Steel,' the tall figure announced as he strode in, offering his hand. 'Mr Parker told me you wanted to see me, Inspector.'

Charlie did his best to hide his surprise as he took Steel's hand in a firm grip. Not at all what he'd been expecting. Mid to late-fifties, shoulders pulled back, ramrod straight back, narrow, pencil moustache – more of a military bearing than that of an academic – thick-rimmed, tortoiseshell spectacles, prematurely greying hair.

'Please accept my apology for interrupting your free period, Mr Steel,' Charlie said.

'That's not a problem.'

'The reason I wanted to talk to you today is that I'm investigating John Preston's murder.'

Steel nodded. 'Mr Parker told me that. It sounds strange when you refer to him as John Preston,' Steel said. 'To me, he'll always be John Murdoch.'

'I can understand that. How long had you known John?'

'For about six years. In fact, ever since he came to work in my department, which was in 2005. It was his first teaching position after he graduated from training college.' Steel hesitated. 'I assume you know that we were in a relationship?'

'Yes. I'm told your relationship broke up,' Charlie said.

'That is correct.'

'Would you mind telling me why?'

Steel's cheeks reddened. 'Do I have to?'

'No, you don't have to.'

Steel shook his head. 'I don't suppose there's any point in trying to cover anything up now,' he said with a quick shake of the head. 'There were problems, Inspector.'

'What kind of problems?'

'Other people. Young boys,' he added quietly.

'Did those young boys include Ronnie Gilligan?' Charlie asked. 'Yes.'

'And Tommy Carter?' Steel nodded. 'I'm trying to establish if there was any substance to the accusations those boys made against John,' Charlie said, 'in order to determine who might have had a reason, real or imagined, to want to harm him.'

Steel walked slowly across the room to the window and gazed down on the empty playground. 'I did everything I could to protect John, Inspector, even though I knew what he'd done.' His voice dropped to little more than a whisper. 'You see, I was in love with him.'

'There's nothing you can do to protect him now,' Charlie said.

Steel turned round to face Charlie.

'My job is to find out who killed John and bring them to justice,' Charlie said. 'It would assist me greatly in my enquiries if I could have your cooperation.' Steel nodded his assent. 'You mentioned just now that you knew what John had done.' Charlie took out his notebook and unscrewed the top from his pen. 'What did you mean by that?'

'The reason John and I split up was because I found out about his paedophile activities.'

'With Ronnie Gilligan?'

'I know he tried to groom Ronnie. I don't know if he managed to seduce him.'

'Did he assault Tommy Carter?'

'I'm sure he did. And there were others,' Steel added.

'Other pupils?'

'Other young boys – none of them pupils here, as far as I'm aware.'

'When did you find out about this?'

'About eighteen months ago.'

'How did you find out?'

'I was on my own one evening, in the flat I shared with John, when my laptop went on the blink. There was an e-mail I needed to send urgently, so I borrowed John's iPad – and I stumbled across images there I would have preferred not to have seen.'

'Was his iPad not password protected?' Charlie asked.

'It was, but I knew the password. John was blasé about such things. He used the same password for just about everything. When I stumbled across those images, I looked up the history of his online searches and I discovered that he had visited several paedophile websites the previous day – and that he'd downloaded dozens of intimate photographs of young boys. I then looked through his e-mails and found out that he had been grooming several young boys, in various chatrooms. It looked as if this had been going on for months.

'As soon as he got home, I had it out with him. At first he tried to make light of it. He said it was all just a bit of fun. He told me that he had only been amusing himself. He said that he liked looking at young boys' naked bodies. Then he started teasing me – or, to be more precise, taunting me. He reminded me how much I enjoyed looking at his naked body, which was twenty years younger than mine – so why shouldn't he enjoy the same kind of pleasure? I pointed out forcibly that grooming children wasn't at all the same thing. He then came over all apologetic, telling me that he would mend his ways – promising me that he would never again get involved with young boys.'

'Did you believe him?'

Steel shrugged his shoulders. 'I wanted to believe him, Inspector. Not long after that, Ronnie Gilligan's accusations came to light. At that point, I'd had enough. I told John I was leaving him. However, when Gilligan's accusations were withdrawn, John insisted they had been groundless and he pleaded with me to stay. I went along with it.' Steel gave a resigned shake of the head. 'Against my better judgement, I have to admit. Deep down, I knew I was deluding myself, but I so much wanted our relationship to work. But when the revelations about Tommy Carter came to light, that was it as far as I was concerned. I walked out on him.'

'Were you interviewed by the police at the time of John's trial?'

'I was. But I didn't say anything to them about John's paedophile activities. I told them that our split up had been amicable – that we had just decided to go our separate ways. Despite everything he might have done, Inspector,' Steel said quietly. 'I was still in love with him.'

'Were you in court during his trial?'

'I was in the public gallery throughout the proceedings – and there, my love for John dissipated like snow melting in the morning sun. For the first time in my life, I saw John in his true colours. Deceitful, manipulative and cunning. I realised then how much he had used me – how he used everyone he came into contact with. I felt bitter and resentful. I wanted him to pay dearly for what he had done. When the jury acquitted him, I felt physically ill.'

'Did you have any contact with John after the trial?'

'I tried to get in touch with him. I wanted to let him know in no uncertain terms what I thought of him, but he'd disappeared off the face of the earth. He'd moved out of his flat without leaving a forwarding address and both his mobile phone number and his e-mail address had been closed down. I never set eyes on him again.'

'I think that's all I need for now, Mr Steel,' Charlie said, getting to his feet. 'I appreciate you being so frank – and let me apologise again for interrupting your free period. If you wouldn't mind giving me your address and your phone number in case we need to get in touch?'

'Of course.'

When Charlie arrived back in Pitt Street, he found Tony O'Sullivan waiting for him at reception.

'We've got a visitor, sir.'

'Who's that?'

'Lesley Adams. She turned up ten minutes ago. She said she needed to talk to you urgently. I told her she could wait in your office.'

'Okay, let's see what she's got to say for herself.'

CHAPTER 17

When Charlie and Tony walked into the office together they found Lesley Adams sitting on a chair facing the desk.

'Are you not working today, Ms Adams?' Charlie asked as he was stripping off his jacket.

'I'm on my lunch break.'

Tony squatted with his buttocks on the edge of the desk while Charlie hung his jacket on the hook on the back of the door.

'What can we do for you?' Charlie asked, easing himself down onto his swivel chair.

'There's something I should have told you yesterday,' Lesley said hesitantly.

'What was that?'

Lesley gnawed at her lower lip. 'Gavin Carter and I are in a relationship,' she said in little more than a whisper.

'Really?'

Lesley straightened her back. 'I've done nothing wrong!'

'Nobody said that you had.'

'It's just that – well, I know how it looks.'

'How does it look?'

'I don't need to spell it out for you, Inspector. I was the family's social worker for six years. I've known Gavin since he was thirteen. I could tell from very early on that he fancied me, but I did nothing to encourage him. In fact, quite the reverse. I went out of my way to make sure I kept him at arms' length. When Gavin was seventeen, he plucked up the courage to ask me out for a drink. Of course, I refused. He was mature for his age – and I have to admit that I was attracted to him, but my duty of care as a social worker precludes me from having any kind of personal relationship with a client before they reach the age of eighteen. I was scrupulous about that. I even filled out a report stating that he had asked me out for a drink – and that I had refused. I brought the report to the attention of my manager. She gave me the third degree. Understandably. We take our safeguarding responsibilities very seriously. She wanted to know why he had asked me out. Had I ever flirted with him? Given him any indication whatsoever that I might be interested in him? I managed to convince her that I had done everything by the book. That was the real reason I put in for a transfer,' Lesley added, lowering her gaze. 'I was becoming more and more attracted to Gavin. I knew it would only be a matter of time before we got together – and tongues would begin to wag. A few months after his eighteenth birthday we met up for a drink – and things developed from there.'

'Is Gavin's father aware of your relationship?'

Lesley blushed furiously. 'Why should he be? It's none of his business. Gavin is nineteen – he's a grown man – and I'm twenty-eight. A nine year age difference isn't all *that* unusual, Inspector,' Lesley added defensively.

Charlie held up both hands in a conciliatory gesture. 'Nobody's saying you've done anything wrong, Ms Adams.' Charlie steepled his fingers and rested his chin on them. 'Do you mind telling me why you didn't say anything about this yesterday?'

'I was about to, but I knew you'd jump to conclusions – to the wrong conclusions. I gave Gavin no encouragement at all before he was eighteen, Inspector.'

'Okay, Ms Adams. Thank you for letting us know that.'

'While I'm in full confession mode,' Lesley said, turning to Tony, 'I should apologise for being tetchy about the not proven verdict yesterday, but Tommy Carter's case wasn't the first time I've been on the wrong side of that idiocy.'

'What else happened?' Charlie asked.

'Ten years ago, my sister was raped. She was only fifteen at the time.' A shiver ran down the length of Lesley's spine as she spoke. 'She was on her way home from school when she was jumped on from behind and dragged into the bushes. The attacker held a knife to her throat and threatened to kill her if she made a noise. He then proceeded to rape her before running off. She was traumatised beyond belief.'

'I'm very sorry to hear that,' Charlie said.

'She lay in the bushes for more than two hours,' Lesley continued, 'until she was found by a passer-by. She didn't want to go to the police – she just wanted to block everything out – pretend it hadn't happened. But our mother insisted that she had to report it. She eventually agreed to do that. She was examined by a police doctor. His report confirmed that her bruises were consistent with her having been raped, but there was no DNA evidence available because, apparently, her attacker had used a condom.'

'Was he ever caught?' Tony asked.

'Yes – and no.' Lesley shook her head. 'She agreed to look through a police file of mugshots and she picked out her assailant. She was a hundred per cent sure it was him. He was eventually arrested and the case went to trial. Having to take the witness stand and describe what had happened to her was a traumatic experience, especially as the bastard in the dock sat leering at her throughout the proceedings. The verdict was not proven – in the end, it came down to her word against his.'

'I can only imagine how difficult that must have been for her – and for you,' Charlie said. 'But if there was insufficient evidence to secure a conviction, the court would have had to find him not guilty, if there hadn't been a not proven verdict available.'

'Things didn't end there,' Lesley said, her voice hardening. 'Three years after that, a man was arrested in Birmingham and convicted of raping a German student – and it transpired that he had raped two other girls in Manchester during the intervening period. All the rapes had happened on the same date – his birthday. It was the same date my sister had been raped. There was a photo of him in the papers. It was the same guy. He was using a different name, but it was him all right. If he had been convicted in Glasgow, three girls would not have been raped.'

'I'm really sorry to hear that your sister was subjected to such a harrowing experience,' Charlie said. 'How is she now?'

'She's back to old bouncy self, but it took a long time for her to get over it. She was in counselling for the best part of four years. She was living in constant dread that he might come back and rape her again. It was a huge relief for her when he got sent down for life. That allowed her to have some kind of closure. It was only after he was convicted that she started to recover.'

'Is there anything else you would like to get of your chest?' Charlie asked.

Lesley gave a sheepish grin. 'I think that's it for today.'

'One more thing,' Charlie said. 'Do you happen to know where Gavin will be tomorrow morning?'

'Tomorrow's Wednesday, isn't it?' Lesley said. 'That's one of his days for working from home.'

'Where does he call 'home'?'

'My flat,' she said, blushing.

'Could you do me a favour?' Charlie asked.

'What's that?'

'Tell him I'd like to talk to him.'

'Why?' Lesley queried. 'You don't think he had anything to do with the murder, do you?'

'I didn't say that. I just want to have a word with him – nothing formal. Just find out what he was up to on Saturday night. Where he was – and who he was with. As a matter of procedure, we'll be talking to everyone who had any association with the deceased. The sooner we can eliminate people from our enquiries, the better. He wasn't with you, by any chance?'

'No, but, as it happens, I do know where he was.'

'Where was that?'

'He went through to Edinburgh with one of mates to go to a gig.'

'In which case, there's nothing for him to be concerned about. If he's going to be at your place tomorrow,' Charlie added, 'would it be all right if I drop round and have a chat with him?'

'No problem as far as I'm concerned,' Lesley said.

'Good. If you wouldn't mind letting let him know that I'll be at your flat at ten o'clock tomorrow morning.'

Having logged on to his internet banking, Malcolm Steel's heart sank when he checked his account. There was no way he could afford to go on like this. He scanned the most recent entries on his credit card statement. Over four hundred pounds charged to his card at the weekend, the most expensive items being nearly a hundred and fifty pounds in Rogano's last Friday and a similar amount in the Ubiquitous Chip on Saturday.

He would have to phone Gordon and have it out with him. There was no other way.

'Why the hell does Anderson want to talk to me?' Gavin complained, a sullen expression on his face. 'I haven't set eyes on Murdoch since the trial.'

'It's nothing for you to be concerned about, Gavin,' Lesley reassured him. 'It's just routine stuff. The police have to talk to everyone who knew him.'

'Routine, my arse! The cops need to convict somebody for his murder. My Uncle Andy told me that they don't give a shit who they pin it on – as long as they get a result. They're going to try to fit me up.'

'I wouldn't take your Uncle Andy's advice on the subject of the police – or on anything else for that matter. There's no reason to become paranoid, Gavin. The police are only doing their job. All Anderson will want to do is ask you a few questions. He'll want to know where you were, and who you were with, last Saturday night when the murder took place, so they can eliminate you from their enquiries.'

'You know where I was. I went through to Edinburgh with Stuart. *First Tiger's* drummer had called off sick and Stuart had agreed to stand in for him. They were doing a gig in Whistle Binkies, so I went through to see him perform.'

'That's fine. I've already told Anderson you were in Edinburgh. You don't have anything to worry about. Just confirm that to him and everything will be okay.'

Gavin waited until Lesley had gone for a shower before calling his uncle.

'The cops want to talk to me,' he blurted out as soon as Andy took the call. 'My bird gave me a message from Anderson. He's coming here at ten o'clock tomorrow morning. I'm shitting myself, Andy.'

'Pull yourself together, Gavin. We knew this would happen. Just do what we agreed and everything will be fine.'

'My bird has already told the polis that I was in Edinburgh.'

'That's okay. When you let Anderson wheedle out of you that you were with me, tell him that you lied to your bird. You were hardly going to let her know that you were helping me do a job in the Jaco.'

'Okay, okay… that'll work.' Gavin hesitated. 'I'm scared, Andy. Can you be here with me tomorrow when Anderson comes to see me?'

Andy hesitated. 'I'm not sure that's a good idea.'

'Oh, come on, Andy. Please! That way we can be sure we both stick to the same version of the story.'

'Okay, okay. If it'll make you feel better, I'll be there. What time did you say he's coming?'

'Ten o'clock.'

'Will your bird be there?'

'No. She leaves for her work at half-eight.'

'Give me the address,' Andy said. 'I'll be there at nine o'clock and we'll go over everything again to make sure we've got the story straight.'

As soon as Gavin disconnected the call, his phone rang. He shook his head when he saw who was calling. Cursing under his breath, he took the call.

'I was just about to call you,' he said quietly.

'You were supposed to phone me this morning.'

'I tried this morning,' he lied, 'but your number was busy.'

'Everything seems to be all right, Gavin. I think I might have over-reacted yesterday. He probably was checking up on me, but that's what he's like. It's his own guilty conscience that makes him suspicious.'

'Thank God for that.'

'He's going to be away overnight tonight. What time can you get here?'

'I'm sorry. I won't be able to make it tonight.'

Her tone changed abruptly. 'I hope you're not thinking of changing your mind, Gavin? It doesn't work like that. I've done a lot of favours for you in the past. I expect you to keep your side of the bargain.'

'I'm not changing my mind. It's nothing like that. It's just that there's a lot going on right now.'

'That's not what we agreed, Gavin,' she snapped.

'I know! But I can't get away tonight.'

'Why not?'

'The police are investigating a murder.'

'What's that got to do with you?'

'Nothing. But the victim was somebody I knew so the cops want to talk to me. They're coming to see me at ten o'clock tomorrow morning. It's just routine stuff, but I have to be here.'

There was an uncomfortable silence before she spoke. 'All right, this time,' she fumed. 'But in future, when I call, you come running. That's the deal.'

Gavin stared at the phone in his fist as the call was disconnected.

When Charlie got the message from his secretary, he called Tony O'Sullivan on his mobile phone.

'I appear to have a double booking for tomorrow morning, Tony,' Charlie explained. 'Pauline has arranged for me to see Martin Gilligan, Ronnie's father, at ten o'clock, which is the same time I'm supposed to be at Lesley Adams' flat to talk to Gavin Carter. I don't want to reschedule Gilligan. He wasn't at all keen to talk to me and I don't want to give him any excuse for opting out. Could you handle Gavin on your own?'

'No problem, sir.'

'After I've been to see Gilligan, we'll need a meeting with the team to bring everyone up to speed,' Charlie said. 'Schedule a briefing session in the incident room for eleven o'clock tomorrow morning. Tell Renton, Freer and McLaughlin to be there.'

Wednesday 7th September

Charlie Anderson drew up in the customers' car park behind the bank in Knightswood. When he went inside, he told a cashier that he had an appointment with the manager at ten o'clock. She showed him to Martin Gilligan's office at the rear of the building.

Gilligan walked across the office and closed the door behind Charlie before indicating a seat for him.

'Thank you for agreeing to see me, sir,' Charlie said as he settled down.

'I'd appreciate if we could do this as quickly as possible, Inspector. I have a busy schedule this morning.'

'In which case,' Charlie said, 'I'll come straight to the point. Why did you withdraw your son from his school?'

Gilligan's back stiffened. 'Ronnie had a problem with one of the teachers.'

'Which one?'

'John Murdoch.'

'You are aware that Mr Murdoch has been murdered?'

Gilligan nodded. 'I read about that the papers.'

'Mr Parker, the head teacher at the school, told me that you had filed a complaint against John Murdoch, but later withdrew it. Is that correct?'

'It is.'

'Why did you do that?'

Gilligan hesitated. 'Initially, Ronnie told me that Murdoch had made improper suggestions to him and that he had touched him intimately in the school library. It was on that basis that I made the

140

complaint. However, when I questioned Ronnie further, it transpired that he was the one who had instigated the intimacy.'

'Ronnie was thirteen, Mr Gilligan,' Charlie said incredulously. 'No matter if he had *instigated the intimacy*, as you put it, Murdoch was criminally responsible and he should have been held to account.'

'I didn't want to go down that route.'

'Why not?' Gilligan cast his eyes down. 'Because it might have created a bit of a scandal?' Charlie suggested. 'Because it might have shown your son up in a bad light?'

Gilligan's cheeks reddened. 'Something like that,' he mumbled.

'So, in order to avoid a minor scandal, you allowed a perverted teacher to carry on as if nothing had happened? You withdrew your son from his school with no thought as to who Murdoch might target next?'

'I informed some of the other parents of the situation,' Gilligan protested. 'They also withdrew their boys from the school.'

'You mean you told two of your friends? Isn't that what happened? And it was just hard luck on the sons of the parents you didn't happen to be friendly with?' Gilligan licked at his lips, but didn't respond. 'Was Ronnie still in touch with Murdoch after he left the school?' Charlie asked.

'Definitely not! I would never have allowed that to happen.'

'Are you sure about that?'

'Of course I'm sure,' Gilligan stated forcibly. 'I told Ronnie in no uncertain terms that he was never to have anything more to do with Murdoch.'

'I'll need to talk to your son,' Charlie stated.

'Is that absolutely necessary, Inspector? I don't want to have this sordid business dragged up all over again.'

'I'm afraid it is necessary,' Charlie said. 'And I would like to see him as soon as possible,' he added.

'I insist on being present when you talk to him.'

'Of course. Would tonight be convenient?'

'I have a dinner engagement this evening.'

'How about tomorrow?'

'I.. I suppose so.'

'I could come to your house after Ronnie gets home from school – at, say, six o'clock?'

'If you must.'

'Thank you,' Charlie said, pulling himself to his feet. 'If you could let me have your address?'

With bad grace, Gilligan wrote his address down on a slip of paper and handed it across.

CHAPTER 18

Andy Carter glanced at his watch. 'It's nearly ten o'clock. Anderson will be here any minute. Are you sure you've got the story straight?'

'I think so,' Gavin said nervously.

'Take your time – don't let him fluster you. I'll chip in if he throws anything unexpected at you.'

When the doorbell rang, Gavin went out to the hall and buzzed Tony in. He was waiting by the front door of the flat when Tony climbed to the second floor.

'You must be Gavin Carter?' Tony queried. Gavin nodded.

Tony produced his ID. 'Inspector Anderson couldn't make it this morning so he asked me to stand in for him. I'm DS O'Sullivan.' Gavin nodded again.

When they went into the lounge, Gavin jabbed his thumb in the direction of the figure slouched on the settee. 'This is my Uncle Andy.'

Tony stopped in his tracks. 'Our paths have crossed. You seem to turn up a lot these days,' Tony said, addressing Andy. 'Like the proverbial bad penny.'

Andy got to his feet. 'Better a bad penny than a bent copper,' he sneered.

'Ever the wee comedian. Have you been practising that one all morning?'

'Why are you here?' Andy demanded.

'To talk to Gavin,' Tony said. 'DCI Anderson couldn't make it.'

'Then get on with it,' Andy said, sitting back down.

'Were you about to leave?'

'Are you going to caution Gavin? Because, if so, he doesn't have to say anything without a lawyer present.'

'I've no intention of cautioning him. This is just an informal chat. There are a few things I want to clear up with him.'

'In that case,' Andy said, folding his arms across his chest. 'I'm going nowhere. I'm staying right here to make sure you don't harass the boy. Do you have a problem with that?'

Tony shook his head. 'No problem – as long as you leave *the boy* to answer my questions and don't interfere.' Placing the folder he was carrying on the coffee table, Tony sat down on an armchair. He indicated the armchair opposite for Gavin. Taking a sheet of paper from his folder, Tony smoothed it out on the table in front of him.

He addressed Gavin. 'Where were you last Saturday night between ten o'clock and eleven o'clock?'

'Me and my uncle went for a pint.'

'That's not what Lesley Adams told us. She said you went to Edinburgh with one of your mates.'

'That's what I told her,' Gavin said. 'She'd have had a hissy fit if I'd told her I was going out for a drink with Andy. She doesn't like me seeing him, so I made up a story about going through to Edinburgh with one of my mates.'

'Where did you go for a drink?' Tony asked.

'To a pub in the Calton. I don't remember the name of it.'

'It was The Jacobite Arms,' Andy chipped in.

'Why did you go there, Gavin?' Tony asked. 'You don't live any-where near the Calton.'

'I had a flat there a few years back,' Andy interjected. 'The Jaco used to be my local.'

Tony fixed Andy with a glare. 'When I want to hear from you, I'll be sure to let you know.' He turned his attention back to Gavin. 'Do you know a man called Jack Mulgrew?'

'Never heard of him,' Gavin said.

'Well it appears that he knows you. He lodged a formal com-plaint in which he stated that you and your uncle assaulted him in

The Jacobite Arms on Saturday night and that you nailed his hand to a cubicle door in the toilets. What do you have to say about that?'

Gavin shrugged his shoulders. 'That's a load of pish.'

Tony turned to face Andy. 'When DCI Anderson and I came to see you on Monday, you told us you were at home on your own on Saturday night, reading the newspapers. Are you now saying that wasn't the case?'

'No comment.'

'Oh, for Christ's sake, Carter!' O'Sullivan snapped. 'Don't give me any of that crap. Were you at home on your own on Saturday evening reading the papers? Or were you in The Jacobite Arms with your nephew? What's it to be?' Andy glared at Tony, but didn't respond. 'How about you, son?' Tony asked, turning back to Gavin. 'What were you *really* up to on Saturday night?'

'I was having a drink with my uncle, like I said.'

'Were you with him when he nailed Jack Mulgrew's hand to the bog door?'

'Don't answer that, Gavin,' Andy interjected.

'How about you answer it, then?' Tony said, swivelling round to face Andy. 'Were you in The Jacobite Arms on Saturday night assaulting Jack Mulgrew, or were you at home, on your own, reading the papers?'

'Okay, okay,' Andy said, exhaling noisily. 'I don't suppose there's any point in me trying to deny it. Me and Gavin nailed Mulgrew in the Jaco.'

'At what time did that happen?'

'Half-past ten.'

'Why did you do it?'

'Mulgrew had borrowed money and he'd got behind with his payments.'

'Borrowed money from Jim Colvin?'

'It had nothing to do with Colvin.'

'You don't say? Who did Mulgrew owe money to, then?'

Andy shifted on his chair. 'Me.'

'You? Are you telling me that you're into money lending?'

Andy hesitated. 'Aye.'

'And you're operating on Jim Colvin's patch? When Colvin finds out that you've been muscling in on his territory, do you think he'll be cool about that?'

'I don't know what you're talking about.'

'Come off it, Carter! Everyone and his uncle knows that the Calton is Jim Colvin's patch – and everyone knows that you're on his payroll.'

'This had nothing to do with Jim Colvin,' Andy insisted. 'It was a private matter between Mulgrew and me.'

'You and I both know that's a complete load of bollocks,' Tony said, clasping his hands behind his neck as he sat back in his chair. 'But let's assume I'm prepared to go along with that for the time being. How much did Mulgrew owe you?'

'Five hundred quid.'

'What about the yarn Colvin spun me in The Ettrick? He told me that he sent you to The Jacobite Arms on Saturday because he wanted you to pay back money he owed Mulgrew?'

'So he did. That was only a hundred quid. I hung onto that, which meant Mulgrew still owed me four hundred.'

'Give me a fucking break!' Tony said, unclasping his hands and slamming his fist down on the coffee table. 'Do you think I came up the Clyde in a banana boat?'

'If you're going to charge me with assaulting Mulgrew,' Andy said. 'I'm not saying anything else until I have a lawyer present.'

'Let me have a think about that.' Tony forced a thin smile.

'Is that it?' Andy said, getting to his feet.

'You can leave anytime you like, but I've got a few more questions for Gavin.'

Andy sat back down slowly.

Gavin stared anxiously at his uncle, who gave him a quick, reassuring nod.

Tony stared straight into Gavin's eyes. 'I want you to tell me exactly what happened in The Jacobite Arms on Saturday night.'

'Andy just told you.'

'I want to hear it from you.'

'We went to The Jaco to sort out Mulgrew because he owed my uncle money.'

'Describe Mulgrew.'

'What do you mean?'

'What was he wearing?'

'I don't remember.'

'What did you do to him?'

'We nailed his hand to the bog door.'

'At what time did that happen?'

'Half-past ten.'

'Who did the nailing?'

'Like Andy told you – me and him.'

'I mean, who did the actual nailing? Who hit the nail with the hammer? You or your uncle?'

'My uncle.'

'What did you do?'

'I held Mulgrew's hand against the door.'

'What did Mulgrew do?'

'What do you mean?'

'Did he try to keep his hand closed? Did you have to prise his fist open?'

'Aye. I had to do that. I had to force his fingers open.'

'How did he react?'

'React?'

'Did he scream? Did he whimper? Did he plead with you to stop?'

'Aye – all of that.' Gavin licked hard at his lips.

'Was there a lot of blood?'

'Quite a lot.'

'Did the blood spurt out?'

'A bit.'

'Did you get any blood on your jacket?'

'No.'

'How about your uncle? Did he get blood on his jacket?'

Gavin's gaze flicked to Andy, who shook his head quickly. 'I don't think so.'

'Have you ever done anything like that before?'

'No.'

'How did it feel, son? How did it feel to see a guy getting his hand nailed to the bog door? Did it make you feel sick? Did it make you want to throw up?'

'I don't remember.'

'How many times did Andy hit the nail with the hammer?'

'For fuck's sake! I don't know,' Gavin wailed.

'Think about it, son. Did the nail go through Mulgrew's flesh with the first hit? Did you hear any of his bones breaking? Surely you must remember if Andy had to use the hammer more than once to pin Mulgrew's hand to the door?'

'I don't fucking-well remember!'

'You don't seem to remember very much, son.'

Gavin gazed sullenly at the floor.

Getting to his feet, Tony picked up his sheet of paper from the coffee table. 'That's all for now,' he said. 'The only other thing I need, Gavin, is your mobile number.'

'Why do you need that?'

'Because I expect that DCI Anderson will want to have a word with you before too long.'

Having noted down Gavin's phone number on his sheet of paper, Tony slipped it back into his folder before turning to leave.

'Their story stinks to high heaven, sir,' Tony said.

Charlie Anderson rocked back in his swivel chair and swung his feet up onto his desk.

'Andy Carter might've nailed Mulgrew's hand to the bog door in the pub,' Tony said. 'In all probability, he did. But as sure as hell Gavin wasn't there.'

'What do you think they're playing at?' Charlie asked.

'Gavin was all over the place with his story, but one thing he was absolutely sure about was that the assault took place at half-past ten. And in Mulgrew's statement,' Tony added, 'he went out of his way to record the fact that he was attacked at ten-thirty – which just happens to be the time the murder in Lawrence Street took place.'

'How very convenient,' Charlie said.

'If we accept for now that Mulgrew *was* attacked at ten-thirty,' Tony said, 'and if Andy Carter was involved in the assault, then he couldn't have murdered Preston. Andy must realise he'll get a custodial sentence for attacking Mulgrew,' Tony continued, 'so why is he admitting it? Is he doing that to make sure we can't implicate him in Preston's murder?'

'That's a possibility,' Charlie said. 'But if you're convinced that Gavin wasn't present when Mulgrew was attacked, another possibility is that Andy is confessing to assaulting Mulgrew in order to give his nephew an alibi for his whereabouts at ten-thirty on the night in question.'

'Do you think Gavin could have murdered Preston?' Tony asked.

'I don't know. But I sure as hell want to talk to him.'

'How did it go with Martin Gilligan?' Tony asked.

Charlie glanced at his watch. 'The guys will be assembling now in the incident room for our eleven o'clock briefing session. I'll update you all at the same time, but my number one priority right now is taking a leak,' Charlie said, dropping his feet to the floor with a clang. 'While I'm doing that, tell Freer to bring the team up to speed with what he found out about the mobile phones. I'll join you in a couple of minutes.'

Coming out of Lesley Adams' flat, Andy Carter and Gavin walked briskly along Dumbarton Road to where Andy had parked his car. The mid-morning traffic was light as they crossed the city before heading out Great Western Road towards Drumchapel. Parking outside Terry's high-rise tower block, they took the lift to the seventeenth floor.

Terry hurried to the door when he heard the first note of the Westminster chimes. 'How did it go?' he asked anxiously as he was opening up.

'First things first,' Andy said as he walked in. 'I need a fucking drink.'

'I've poured them,' Terry said, leading the way to the kitchen where he indicated the three tumblers of whisky sitting on the table.

Andy lifted one of the glasses and threw the contents back in one gulp. 'I suppose it went as well as could be expected, under the circumstances,' he said, screwing up his face as the neat spirit hit the back of his throat. Picking up the whisky bottle from the table, he poured himself another stiff measure.

'Thanks for doing that for me, Andy,' Gavin said, holding up his glass and chinking it against his uncle's.

'You had to have an alibi, son.'

Gavin took a sip of his drink. 'It's a first offence for me, Andy. There's a good chance I'll get off with community service. But you're going to get sent down for assaulting Mulgrew.'

'I didn't do him a lot of damage.' Andy shrugged. 'I'll probably get six months, which means I'll be out in three, which is a hell of a lot better than you copping a life sentence for murder.'

'You really didn't need to do that for me,' Gavin said. 'Stuart would've covered for me if I'd asked him. I know he would.'

'We've been through all of that,' Andy said. 'There's too big a risk that the cops would be able to prove that you weren't with Stuart – or that he would've caved in under pressure. In a situation like this, the only people you can rely on are family.'

'I'm going to be in deep shit when my bird finds out that I told the cops I was with you,' Gavin said, dragging his fingers through his gelled hair. 'She'll go mental. I told her I was in Edinburgh with Stuart.'

'You're going to have to live with that,' Andy said. 'From now on, the only version of events you tell anybody is that you were with me in the Jaco.'

'She'll chuck me out the flat.'

'It's a lot better to be chucked out of a flat than chucked into the Bar-L,' Andy said.

'Did the cops buy the story about you and Gavin nailing Mulgrew?' Terry asked.

'I don't give a bugger whether or not they bought it,' Andy said. 'As long as they can't prove otherwise, that's all that matters.'

'I don't like it,' Terry said, shaking his head. 'I don't like it one little bit. The next twenty years of Gavin's life is on the line and we're depending on a deadbeat like Mulgrew to keep him out of jail.'

'For fuck's sake, Terry,' Andy snapped. 'I'm going to be doing a stretch for helping your boy out – and this is the thanks I get? And by the way, I didn't notice you coming up with a better idea.'

'I'm just saying. How can we be sure that Mulgrew will stick to the story?'

'Leave that to me,' Andy growled, lifting his whisky tumbler to his lips and taking a slow sip. 'I'll make fucking-well sure he does,' he said, throwing back the rest of his drink.

Charlie Anderson walked into the incident room and lobbed a felt-tip marker pen in Tom Freer's direction.

'You're the scribe today, Tom,' Charlie said as he slumped down on a chair. 'Nobody can read my writing.'

Freer turned over to a clean sheet of paper on the flipchart board.

'Have you updated the guys on what you found out about the mobile phones, Tom?' Charlie asked.

'Yes, sir.'

'In which case, let's start with the forensic report,' Charlie said. 'The floor's yours, Eddie.'

'DNA checks on the items collected by the SOC team in the immediate vicinity of the murder didn't throw up any matches with the central data base,' McLaughlin began. 'And the strands of fibre that were found adhering to the victim's neck are from a popular brand of clothes line.'

'What kind of strength would have been required to commit the murder?' Charlie asked.

'Nothing out of the ordinary,' McLaughlin stated. 'The victim's blood alcohol level was one point eight – more than twice the legal limit for driving, so he was probably a bit drunk. And it looks as if it was a surprise attack from behind, in which case anyone of average strength would've been capable of doing it.'

'Do you have anything else for us, Eddie?' Charlie asked.

'We didn't find a match on the database for any of the finger-prints we found in the victim's flat,' McLaughlin said. 'And apart from the child pornography and the e-mails on his iPad, which you know about, that's about it.'

'Okay, Eddie. Thanks,' Charlie said. 'What do you have for us, Tony?'

Tony recounted Andy and Gavin Carter's version of what had happened in The Jacobite Arms. 'I didn't believe a word of it,' Tony concluded. 'It's a fair bet that Andy Carter nailed Mulgrew's hand to the bog door, but I'd bet my pension that Gavin wasn't there when that happened.'

'If Gavin wasn't in The Jacobite Arms, where was he?' Charlie queried. 'Lesley Adams told us that Gavin had told her he was in Edinburgh with one of his mates. Was he lying to her? Or could that be the truth?'

'If he was in Edinburgh with one of his mates, that would rule him out of being involved in Preston's murder,' Tony said, 'so why wouldn't he tell us the truth? Why would he invent a cock and bull story about being in the Jaco with his uncle?'

'That's a good question,' Charlie said. 'Did you get Gavin's phone number?'

'Yes.'

'Let me have it. I want to have a go at him. On his own, without his uncle, or anyone else, present.'

Tony referred to his folder and copied the number onto a post-it, which he handed to Charlie. Having stuck the post-it inside his notebook, Charlie got to his feet stiffly.

'It's time for some blue sky thinking now, boys,' he said. 'We'll start by compiling a list of all possible suspects.' He nodded to Tom Freer to start writing on the flip chart. 'Let's have the names of anyone you can think of who could have had a reason to murder Preston – no matter how improbable – and state what you think their motivation might have been.'

As Freer held his marker pen poised, the suggestions came thick and fast.

'Terry and Andy Carter,' Tony offered. 'Even though they both appear to have alibis, at Murdoch's trial they threatened him with retribution if they ever managed to get their hands on him.'

'We have to include Gavin Carter on the list,' Freer suggested as he was writing the names on the chart. 'There's nothing he'd have liked better than getting revenge on Murdoch for what he did to his wee brother.'

'How about Mrs Carter and her new man, Mitch Weir?' Renton asked.

Charlie nodded to Freer to add those names.

'Malcolm Steel, the ex-boyfriend?' Charlie suggested. 'A disillusioned man who felt badly let down by Murdoch. He has to be a possibility.'

'Don't forget Lesley Adams,' Tony said. 'A social worker who saw an innocent boy take his own life because of what Murdoch had done to him.'

'You can add Martin Gilligan to the list,' Charlie said. 'An irate father who knew that Murdoch had been grooming – and perhaps seducing – his son.'

'What about Ronnie Gilligan himself?' Renton suggested. 'If, as Eddie said, no great strength was required to commit the murder, Ronnie could have wanted to get his revenge on the man who caused him to be removed from his school.'

'Fair point,' Charlie said. 'Add his name to the list. And to make things even more complicated,' he added, 'the editor at the Record received a letter from the Avenging Angel.'

Renton let out a groan.

'Who or what is he?' Freer asked.

'He's a nutter who gets his kicks from contacting the papers and telling them that he carried out a murder,' Renton explained. 'He claims that Almighty God has given him a mission to rid the city of vermin.'

'This is the fourth murder he's claimed responsibility for in the past eight years,' Charlie interjected. 'The first three letters could have been sent by a trouble-maker, but we have to take this one seriously. It was time-stamped in the main sorting office in Springburn at twenty-past ten on Sunday morning. The identity of the victim wasn't public knowledge at the time the letter was posted. The previous claims by the Avenging Angel received a lot of publicity in the press, so it's a fair bet that our killer knew about them. If so, he may well be jumping on the AA bandwagon in order to deflect attention from himself.

'Put the Avenging Angel down on the list, Tom. Though, if a random vigilante is responsible for Preston's murder,' he added, 'I don't rate our chances very highly of tracking him down.'

'Anyone else for the list?' Freer asked, looking round the room, marker pen poised.

'How about Judge Ramsay?' Tony suggested.

'What!' Charlie exclaimed.

'Why not?' Tony insisted. 'It's the judge's last case – his reputation's on the line – and he sees a man he knows to be guilty walk free? Stranger things have happened.'

'You can not be serious!' Charlie spluttered, exhaling noisily.

'It's blue sky thinking time, sir,' Tony said with a grin. 'Everyone we can possibly think of – no matter how improbable No line of enquiry is excluded. The judge knew Murdoch was planning to change his name and if anyone was in a position to find out what he'd changed it to, he was.'

'Okay, okay,' Charlie conceded grudgingly. 'But if word ever gets out that I allowed James Ramsay's name to be included in a list of murder suspects, I'll have whoever's responsible for breakfast.

'Any more names for the list?' Charlie asked. Everyone shook their heads. 'In that case, what we need now is an action plan. We'll interview everybody on the list and find out what they were up to at half-past ten last Saturday night – then we'll check out if what they tell us holds water. Let's divvy up the work.

'Colin, you've got contacts in the procurator fiscal's office,' Charlie said. 'Have a word with your mates and find out why they decided to put Murdoch on trial. If it was just Tommy Carter's word against his, they wouldn't have rated their chances very highly of securing a conviction, so they might have had something else on Murdoch. Try to find out if that was the case.

'Tony,' Charlie continued, 'a couple of things for you to follow up on. Do you know where Jim Colvin hangs out?'

'My snitch told me that he runs his operations out of an office on the south side, above the *Black Seven* snooker hall,' Tony said.

'Go across there and have a word with him. Bounce Andy Carter's version of events in The Jacobite Arms off him – see how he reacts. Try to find out if there's any truth in Andy's claim that he's been encroaching on Colvin's patch. Frankly, I very much doubt it,' Charlie added, 'otherwise Carter's voice would be several octaves higher by now.

'When you've done that,' Charlie said, 'we need to establish at what time Mulgrew was actually attacked in the pub. Everyone concerned seems awfully keen to let us know the assault took place at ten-thirty. There must be a reason for that. Check what time our switchboard received the call from the landlord reporting the attack – and find out what time Mulgrew was admitted to A&E. Have another word with the landlord to see if he can cast any more light on the situation.

'Tom,' Charlie said, turning to Freer. 'I'm told that Mrs C. and her new man live in Paisley. Find out their address and go across there this afternoon. See if they can account for their movements on Saturday evening. We also need to establish what Jack Mulgrew's role is in all of this. Why is he claiming that Gavin Carter was involved in the assault if he wasn't? He's almost certainly being leaned on. And why is he so keen to tell us the attack took place at ten-thirty? I'll take care of that myself.'

'How about the guys in Terry Carter's poker school?' Renton asked. 'Should we check out Terry's alibi for Saturday night?'

'It's worth a shot, Colin,' Charlie said. 'Though Terry was pretty relaxed about it when he told us he was in a poker school, so his alibi's probably kosher. But it wouldn't do any harm to have a word with the guys who were at his place on Saturday night. I've got their phone numbers. Find out where they live and speak to each of them individually to see if their versions of events match up. Find out if Terry went out of the flat at any point in the evening – perhaps on the pretext of going to get more food or booze? If so, could he have been away long enough to commit the murder, and then come back and re-join the poker school?'

'The e-mails on Preston's iPad tell us he was in contact with Ronnie Gilligan shortly before he was murdered,' McLaughlin said. 'Shouldn't we be questioning him?'

'I'm going to see Ronnie and his father tomorrow,' Charlie said. 'But don't jump to conclusions, Eddie. All the e-mails actually tell us is that Preston was in contact with someone – who might have been Ronnie Gilligan – or it could have been somebody purporting to be Ronnie. I'll dig into that when I talk to the boy – and I'll also question him and his father about their movements on Saturday night.

'Tom, you go and see Malcolm Steel and find out where he was and what he was doing at the time of the murder. I'll talk to Lesley Adams myself. Is there anyone else on the list?' Charlie asked.

'The Avenging Angel,' Freer said.

Charlie shook his head. 'We'll pursue that possibility, if and when we draw a blank elsewhere. Besides, I wouldn't know where to start trying to track him down,' Charlie added, running his fingers over his bald skull. 'I know there are vigilantes out there who think not proven equates to guilty,' he said, 'and who would have no compunction about evening up the score with the likes of Preston if an opportunity happened to present itself, but I'm not convinced that's what we're dealing with here.'

'Why not?' Tony asked.

'Think about the mobile phone situation. Preston makes three calls to the same number within the hour before he is killed. The murderer takes Preston's phone, then both the phones disappear from the network at the same time. As far as I'm concerned, that makes it a racing certainty that the killer is someone Preston knew.'

'Good point,' Tony nodded.

'Is that everyone?' Charlie asked.

'Apart from Judge Ramsay,' Tony said. 'Would you like me to check out his alibi?'

'Don't push your luck, Tony,' Charlie growled.

CHAPTER 19

Tony O'Sullivan pulled up in a parking bay a few yards from the *Black Seven* snooker hall. Getting out of his car, he walked up to the bouncer who was leaning against the open door.

'I don't think I know you, pal,' the bouncer said, eyeing O'Sullivan up and down.

'It's the first time I've been here.'

'Have you booked a table?' he asked, flicking the ash from his cigarette.

'I'm here to talk to Jim Colvin.'

The bouncer moved across to block the entrance. 'Is Jim expecting you?'

Pulling out his warrant card, O'Sullivan held it face up in the palm of his hand.

The bouncer kept his gaze fixed on O'Sullivan as he slid his mobile phone from his inside jacket pocket. He clicked onto a number. 'There's a guy at the front door, boss. He says he wants to talk to you.'

'What does he want?'

'I don't know – but he's got one of those nasty, shiny badges.'

'What's his name?'

The bouncer peered at the warrant card. 'DS Tony O'Sullivan.'

Colvin hesitated for a moment. 'Let him come up.'

Disconnecting the call, the bouncer slipped his phone back into his pocket. 'Straight across the room to the stairs at the far end,' he said, pointing. 'Jim's office is on the first floor.'

Blinking to accustom his eyes to the gloom, O'Sullivan walked the length of the low-ceilinged room, between two rows of snooker tables – all of them in darkness except for one table in the middle of the room where a youth was huddled over his cue, carefully lining up a shot.

As he was passing the table, O'Sullivan heard a sharp clack as the cue ball ricocheted off a red, followed by a muttered curse.

Climbing the stairs, O'Sullivan came to an open office door. Jim Colvin was seated behind the wide desk.

'On your own this afternoon?' O'Sullivan queried, looking all around as he walked in. 'Is your business partner not with you? Perhaps he's busy, checking the futures market for the best deal in rusty nails?'

'What the hell do you want, O'Sullivan?' Colvin snapped.

'I spoke to your pal, Andy Pandy Carter, this morning – along with his nephew.' Colvin's eyes narrowed. 'They told me they'd nailed Jack Mulgrew's hand to the bog door in The Jacobite Arms last Saturday.' Colvin stared in stony silence at O'Sullivan. 'Carter claimed that Mulgrew had borrowed money from him,' O'Sullivan continued, 'and he told me he'd nailed him to the door because he'd got behind with his payments.'

'What does any of that have to do with me?'

'When we bumped into each other in The Ettrick on Sunday, you told me Carter was your business partner. You told me you and him don't have any secrets. So I was wondering if you would be able to corroborate his story? Can you confirm that Carter does loan sharking in the Calton – and that, along with his nephew, he assaulted Jack Mulgrew in The Jacobite Arms last Saturday?'

'I don't know what your game is, O'Sullivan,' Colvin said, 'but whatever it is, I'm not playing.'

'I'm trying to establish if, when Carter nailed Mulgrew to the bog door, he was acting off his own bat – on your territory – or if he was taking his instructions from you?'

The colour rose in Colvin's cheeks. 'Stop wasting my time, O'Sullivan.'

'If you could just answer the question, I'll be on my way.'

'Fuck off!'

'It's a pity you're adopting that attitude,' O'Sullivan said, turning to leave. 'I was hoping we might have a game of snooker. It's a long time since I played.'

'Why don't you go and play with yourself?' Colvin sneered. 'I hear you're good at that.'

Tom Freer's sat nav directed him to Mitch Weir's block of flats near the bottom of Well Street in Paisley.

He checked the flat number and the name on the door before ringing the bell of the ground floor apartment. Alice Carter came to the door.

Freer introduced himself, showing his warrant card.

'What do you want?' Alice asked suspiciously.

'Is Mr Weir here?' Freer asked.

'Mitch!' she called over her shoulder. 'The polis are here. They want to talk to you.'

'I'd like to speak to both of you,' Freer said.

Mitch Weir pinged his red braces over his shoulders as he appeared by Alice's side. 'What's going on?' he demanded.

'We're investigating the circumstances leading to the death of John Preston,' Freer said. 'The man you knew as John Murdoch.'

'So what?' Weir said.

'Are you aware that he was murdered?' Freer asked.

'We read about it in the papers,' Alice said.

'His murder had nothing to do with us,' Weir interjected. 'If that's what you're thinking?'

'That's not what I'm thinking, Mr Weir,' Freer said. 'I'm merely collecting information. Can you tell me where both of you were on Saturday the third of September at half-past ten in the evening?'

'Didn't I tell you the cops would come sniffing round before long, Alice?' Weir said. He turned to Freer. 'I'm surprised it took you this long.'

'Would you please tell me where you were?'

'Nothing would give me greater pleasure,' Weir said with an expansive grin. 'We were at my boy's wedding in Carlisle. How many witnesses do you reckon we have, Alice?'

'Oh, about a hundred and fifty,' Alice said.

'About a hundred and fifty,' Weir repeated. 'The reception was in the Crown and Mitre,' he added. 'It's a real classy hotel in the centre of town. Would you like to see the wedding photos?'

'That won't be necessary.'

'Do you have any more questions?' Weir asked.

'Not for now.'

The door was shut in Tom Freer's face.

Tony O'Sullivan got to The Jacobite Arms shortly after four o'clock. There were only half a dozen customers in the pub; two youths playing darts at the far end of the bar and four men sitting at a table by the window, playing dominoes.

The landlord recognised Tony as he walked towards the bar. 'That's more like it,' he said, glancing up at the clock above the gantry. 'It's seven hours before we close. You've got plenty of time to sink a few.'

O'Sullivan took out his notebook. 'At what time did Jack Mulgrew get assaulted downstairs last Saturday?' he asked.

The landlord checked to make sure none of the customers were within earshot. 'Keep your voice down,' he said quietly.

'What time? Tony repeated quietly.

'Sometime the back of ten o'clock.'

'Can you be more precise?'

'Not really,' he said with a shrug.

'The phone call you made to the police was received at ten thirty-eight. How much earlier than that did you find Mulgrew?'

'Maybe ten minutes? Something like that. Like I told you on the phone, one of my customers came running up the stairs, shouting out that a bloke was nailed to the door of one of the cubicles in the bog. I ran down to find out what was going on. When I saw the state Mulgrew was in, I fetched a hammer from my flat upstairs and knocked the nail back through. Then I phoned my brother and got him to come across and take Mulgrew to A&E. It was only after that I called your lot. If you tell me I made the phone call at ten thirty-eight, Mulgrew must've got nailed round about half-past ten.'

'When we spoke on the phone, you told me that Jim Colvin was behind this,' O'Sullivan said.

'That was just between us girls,' the landlord said quietly, tapping the side of his nose.

'Okay, let me ask you another question, just between *us girls*. If one of Colvin's heavies was going to sort a client out, do you think Colvin would be present himself, or would he keep well out of the way?'

Before responding, the landlord glanced again in the direction of the darts' and the dominoes' players to make sure they were well out of earshot. 'Colvin's a fucking sadist,' he said, lowering his voice to little more than a whisper. 'He actually prefers it if his clients don't pay up on time so he can watch them squirm when they get claimed. He wouldn't miss a punishment being doled out for all the tea in China.'

'Thanks,' O'Sullivan said. Flipping his notebook closed, he slipped it back into his jacket pocket. He looked at his watch. 'I've probably got time for a quick one,' he said.

'What'll it be?'

'Make it a soda water and lime, with a lump of ice.'

'Last of the big spenders.'

Having phoned ahead and arranged to be at Malcolm Steel's house at half-past four, Tom Freer parked his car in the street and walked up the short drive to the semi-detached bungalow in Newton Mearns. When he rang the bell, Steel came to the door.

Freer introduced himself, showing his warrant card.

'This shouldn't take very long, Mr Steel,' Freer said as they sat down on chairs facing each other in the lounge. 'Inspector Anderson has asked me to follow up on his meeting with you yesterday, sir,' Freer said, taking out his notebook. 'There's just a couple of things we need to clear up so we can eliminate you from our enquiries into John Preston's murder.'

'Does that mean I'm a suspect?' Steel queried.

'Not at all.'

'That wouldn't be at all unreasonable, officer,' Steel said. 'After all, I had fallen out with John.'

'We'll be putting the same questions to everyone who knew the deceased, sir. Basically, all we need to know is where you were, and who you were with, at ten-thirty on the evening of Saturday the third of September.'

Steel looked perplexed. 'I…. I don't actually remember.'

'Have a think about it, sir. It was only last Saturday.'

Steel got to his feet and walked slowly across the room to the coffee table. Picking up his diary, he thumbed through the pages. 'Ah, yes,' he said. 'Of course. How silly of me.' Closing the diary he slipped it into his jacket pocket. 'I was in the Ubiquitous Chip in Ashton Lane, having dinner with a friend.'

'Could you give me the name and address of your friend?'

'I could.' Steel bristled. 'But I won't.'

Freer looked at him enquiringly. 'Can I ask why not?'

Steel sank back down onto his chair. 'If you must know, officer, he's a married man. I don't want the police bothering him.'

'We would be discreet, Mr Steel. We would only ask him to confirm that he was with you in the Ubiquitous Chip on Saturday night.'

'I said 'no', officer.'

'You do realise that it will make it more difficult for us to eliminate you from our enquiries if you're not prepared to cooperate, sir?'

'Then I'm afraid it's just going to have to be more difficult for you.' Steel got to his feet. 'Is that everything?' he asked.

'Yes.'

'In which case….' Turning round, Steel gestured towards the door.

Tom Freer drew up in a parking place in Byres Road, opposite Hillhead Subway station. From there, he walked the short distance up the cobbled lane to The Ubiquitous Chip. When he went into the restaurant he saw several members of staff were setting up for the evening meal. He showed his warrant card to one of the waiters and asked if he could speak to the manager.

She came through from the kitchen.

'What can I do for you, officer?' she asked.

'Would it be possible for you to check a dinner reservation for me?'

'For what date?'

'Last Saturday, the third of September.'

'Was the reservation in the main restaurant or the brasserie upstairs?'

'I don't actually know.'

'In which case, let's start with the main restaurant,' she said. 'That reservation book is here. What do you want to know?'

'Did you have a booking for two men, made in the name of Malcolm Steel?'

She flicked back through the pages. 'Yes, here it is. Mr Steel. A booking for two people at nine o'clock. They were allocated table C2.'

'Do you know Mr Steel?'

She shook her head. 'He's not one of our regulars.'

'Do you know at what time he left the restaurant?'

'I wasn't here on Saturday night,' she said. 'I was at my niece's birthday party in Perth. I could check with the staff who were on duty, but there's no guarantee they would be able to remember something like that. We're always very busy on Saturday nights.'

'Do your staff have a fixed set tables that they serve?'

'It's not as rigid as that. They have an area of the restaurant that they cover – and they interact with the customers as and when required.' She paused. 'However, there might be a way to find out the approximate time that Mr Steel left,' she said.

'How?' Freer asked.

'If he paid his bill with a credit card, the transaction would be dated and timed.'

'Would you still have the records for last Saturday?'

'We keep vouchers going back years – in case anything goes wrong with the banking system,' she added with a smile. 'Hold on and I'll fetch last week's.'

When she came back, she thumbed her way through a box of vouchers.

'Here we are,' she said, lifting a voucher out. 'A payment was made by credit card by Malcolm Steel on Saturday the third of September at twenty-two forty-three.'

'Could you let me have a copy of that voucher?'

'No problem.'

'Just one more question,' Freer said. 'This confirms that Mr Steel paid his bill at ten forty-three. Is there any possibility that he could have left the restaurant for quite a long time – say, thirty minutes – before coming back and paying his bill?'

'As I said, I wasn't here, but I'm sure the staff would remember if something like that had happened. The team who were working last Saturday will be on duty again on Friday night. If you could come back then, round about this time, they should be able to answer your questions.'

'Thanks.'

Thursday 8 September

Andy Carter checked his watch to make sure he wasn't late as he pulled up outside the *Black Seven* snooker hall. The text from Jim Colvin had been brief and to the point. 'My office – Thursday morning – ten o'clock.'

The bouncer standing by the door waved in recognition when he saw Andy approach. Hurrying across the empty snooker hall, Carter trotted up the flight of stairs to the first floor landing. He saw that Colvin's office door was closed. With a mounting sense of trepidation, he knocked on it tentatively.

'Come in!' Colvin barked.

Turning the handle slowly, Carter blinked his eyes to adjust to the glare as he walked into the brightly-lit office.

'I'll get back to you soon,' Colvin said into his mobile phone. 'I have a bit of urgent business I need to attend to.'

Disconnecting his call, Colvin placed his phone down on the desk in front of him before pulling himself to his feet. 'What the hell did you think you were playing at?' he demanded, gripping the sides of his desk as he leaned across, his face florid.

'Playing at?'

'Don't come the smart arse with me, Carter,' Colvin snapped. 'Why did you tell the cops that you and your nephew nailed Mulgrew in The Jaco?'

'Who told you that?'

'It doesn't matter a fuck who told me!'

'There's no need to get your knickers in a twist, Jim.' Beads of sweat were forming on Carter's brow. 'I didn't involve you.'

'Jesus Christ! Everybody knows you're on my payroll – and that includes the police. If you're involved, then I'm involved.'

'My brother's boy needed an alibi for Saturday night, Jim, so I told the cops he was with me when I sorted out Mulgrew. But I told them I was operating on my own. I told them Mulgrew owed me money.'

'And what happens when Mulgrew blabs his mouth off? What happens when he tells the polis I was there?'

'He won't do that. I'll make sure of it.'

'That's not the way I operate, Carter.'

When Colvin depressed a buzzer on the underside of his desk, the rear door of the office swung open. Two men were standing in the doorway.

'You don't ever do anything like that without clearing it with me first,' Colvin stated.

'Okay, Jim,' Carter stammered. 'I understand that. It won't happen again.'

'I'll make sure it doesn't.'

The two men approached the desk. On Colvin's nod, the taller of them grabbed Carter's arms and pinned them behind his back. Spinning Carter's body round, his stocky companion launched a vicious punch into the pit of Carter's stomach, causing him to retch.

'There's no need to overdo it, boys,' Colvin said with a sneer. 'Just give him enough to make sure he remembers the next time.'

Half a dozen punches rained into Carter's face, blackening both his eyes and splitting open his bottom lip.

'Is that okay, boss?' the man holding Carter's arms asked.

Colvin smiled cruelly. 'Och, how about one for the road?'

A sickening punch was thumped into Carter's midriff before his arms were released.

Sinking slowly to his knees, Carter cupped his face in his hands, blood seeping out from between his trembling fingers.

CHAPTER 20

Malcolm Steel came out of the school gates at lunch time and hurried a hundred yards along the road before pulling out his phone. He hesitated to collect his thoughts before clicking onto a number.

'It's me, Gordon,' he said when the phone was answered. 'Is it all right to talk?'

'As long as you're quick. Suzie's gone to the shops, but she could be back any minute.'

'It has to stop, Gordon,' Malcolm blurted out. 'I can't go on like this any longer.'

'What are you talking about? What has to stop?'

'My credit card,' Malcolm stammered. 'I need to have it back.'

'That's not what we agreed, Malcolm. Have you forgotten our deal? I keep quiet about your grubby little secret – and I get to spend five hundred quid a month on your credit card.'

'I can't afford for that to go on any longer.'

Gordon's voice hardened. 'Believe you me, Malcolm. You can't afford not to.'

'Are you threatening me?' Malcolm shouted into his phone.

'Threatening you?' Gordon chortled. 'I'm not *threatening* you, Malcolm. All I'm doing is reminding you that we have a deal. And if you try to welsh on it, there's a distinct possibility that the world and his wife will find out that John Murdoch, or Preston, or whatever the hell he called himself, wasn't the only teacher in the school who had something he wanted to keep hidden.'

'You've got to give me a break, Gordon! I had a visit from the police yesterday.'

'What did they want?'

'They wanted to know where I was – and who I was with – on Saturday night, when John was murdered.'

'Are you a suspect?'

'They said I wasn't – but until they find the killer, everyone who had anything to do with John is a suspect.'

'What did you tell them?'

'I almost panicked, then I remembered what I'd seen on my credit card statement. I told them I was in the Ubiquitous Chip with someone, but I didn't say who it was.'

'Why didn't you tell the cops where you really were?'

'I… I couldn't.'

'Why not?' Gordon laughed out loud. 'Were you with your special friend?'

'Shut the fuck up!' Malcolm snapped. 'It doesn't matter where I was or who I was with.'

'It doesn't matter to me, Malcolm. But apparently it matters a great deal to the cops.'

'What time did you leave the Chip on Saturday night?' Malcolm demanded.

'I don't remember. Round about eleven o'clock, I think. Why are you asking that?'

'I just want to know.'

Gordon paused. 'Oh, yes, I get it now,' he said slowly. 'You need an alibi for Saturday night, don't you? That's why you told the cops you were in the Chip. Is that your cunning plan?'

'No – it isn't.'

'I think it is, Malcolm. I think you're terrified that the cops will find out what you were up to on Saturday night, which can only mean one of two things. Either you were shagging your pal – or else you murdered Preston.'

'It was nothing like that!' Malcolm shouted.

'I don't believe you.'

'Why are you doing this to me?'

'Because I don't imagine for one minute that you would appreciate me contacting the cops and letting them know you weren't in the Chip on Saturday night, now would you?'

'You wouldn't do that!'

'Of course I wouldn't – not as long as my credit limit's extended to, say, six hundred quid a month?'

'For fuck's sake! You can't do that!'

'I'm sorry, Malcolm,' Gordon interjected. 'I have to go now. I hear Suzie's car in the drive.'

The line went dead as Gordon disconnected. Malcolm Steel's whole body was trembling as he stood staring at the phone clutched tightly in his white-knuckled fist.

Charlie Anderson called Jack Mulgrew's number from his mobile. 'This is Inspector Anderson, Glasgow CID, Mr Mulgrew,' Charlie stated when Mulgrew took the call. 'You and I need to talk.'

'What about?'

'I need some information from you regarding the complaint you filed about Andy and Gavin Carter assaulting you in The Jacobite Arms.'

'I told the sergeant in London Road what happened.'

'I realise that, but I still need to talk to you. I got your address and phone number from your complaint form, so how about I come round to your place? I could be there in fifteen minutes.'

'I... I won't be here. I'm on my way out.'

'When will you be back?'

'I'm not sure. Late – very late.'

'In that case, I'll come to see you first thing tomorrow morning. Would nine o'clock be all right?'

Mulgrew exhaled noisily. 'I suppose so,' he muttered.

Swearing under his breath, Mulgrew cut the connection.

Jack Mulgrew opened his front door in response to the persistent ringing on his doorbell. His jaw dropped when he saw who was standing there.

'What do you want?' he stammered.

'I need to talk to you,' slurred out from between Andy Carter's swollen lips.

Before Mulgrew had time to react, Carter had stepped across the threshold and closed the door behind him.

'What happened to your face?' Mulgrew said, narrowing his eyes.

'I got on the wrong side of Jim Colvin. And I don't even owe him any money,' Carter added. 'If you think this is bad,' he said, pointing to his bruised face, 'just imagine what will happen to you if you upset Colvin.'

'I willny upset him,' Mulgrew whimpered, backing off.

'If you say one word to the polis about Jim Colvin being in The Jaco when you got nailed, you're as good as dead. Do you understand that?'

'Aye – I understand!'

'Who attacked you in the pub?'

'Eh.. you.'

'And who else?'

'Your boy.'

'Not my boy, my brother's boy.'

'That's what I meant to say,' Mulgrew stammered. 'You and your brother's boy – Gavin.'

'Don't you ever say anything else to anybody,' Carter snarled.

'I willny, but....but the cops are coming here tomorrow,' Mulgrew whimpered.

'What the fuck!' Carter grabbed Mulgrew by the lapel of his jacket. 'Why are the polis coming here?'

'I don't know. An Inspector Anderson phoned me. He said he needed to talk to me. He told me he'll be here at nine o'clock tomorrow morning.'

'What does he want?'

'He said he wanted more information about the complaint I filed. I said I'd told the polis in London Road everything, but he still insisted on coming to see me. I tried to put him off. He wanted to come here tonight, but I said I was going out, so he told me he'd be round here tomorrow morning at nine o'clock. What am I going to do?' Mulgrew yelped.

Carter tightened his grip on Mulgrew's lapel. 'You're going to do exactly what I told you to do. You're going to stick to your story, no matter what. When Anderson asks you who nailed you to the bog door in the Jaco, it was me and Gavin. When he asks you why we nailed you, you're going to tell him it was because you owed me five hundred quid. Have you got that? You owed *me* five hundred quid. You do not, under any circumstances, mention Jim Colvin's name. Have you got that?' Carter repeated, releasing Mulgrew's lapel and prodding him hard on the chest.

'I'm shittin' myself,' Mulgrew whimpered.

'You'll be doing a lot more than shitting yourself if you mess this up,' Carter snapped. Turning on his heel, Carter let himself out.

Charlie Anderson drew up outside the Gilligan's end-terrace house in Verona Avenue in Scotstoun. Picking up his phone from the passenger seat, he checked the post-it in his notebook, then punched in Gavin Carter's mobile number.

'This is Inspector Anderson,' Charlie said when Gavin took the call. 'I need to talk to you.'

'I saw Sergeant O'Sullivan this morning,' Gavin protested.

'I know you did. That's why we need to talk. Where are you now?' Charlie asked.

'At Lesley Adams' place.'

'I have her address. I'll be across in about an hour's time,' Charlie said, checking his watch. 'Let's say, seven o'clock. Okay?' Gavin didn't respond. 'I said is seven o'clock okay?'

'I suppose so,' Gavin mumbled.

Disconnecting the call, Charlie got out of his car and used his remote control to lock up. When he looked towards the house, he saw the curtains in the lounge window twitch.

The front door was opened by Martin Gilligan as Charlie was walking up the path.

'I would prefer if my wife and my daughter didn't have to know the reason for your visit, Inspector,' Gilligan said quietly. 'It would only upset them unnecessarily.'

When Charlie nodded his concurrence, Gilligan ushered him into the front lounge where a young boy sat perched on the edge of the settee. Gilligan closed the door quietly behind them.

'You must be Ronnie,' Charlie said, smiling as walked across, proffering his hand.

Ronnie nodded nervously as he gave Charlie's hand a tentative shake.

Charlie sat down on the settee beside Ronnie while his father took the armchair opposite.

'This is Inspector Anderson, the policemen I told you about, Ronnie,' his father said. 'He just needs to ask you a few questions. There's nothing for you to be worried about.'

'That's right, Ronnie,' Charlie said reassuringly as he took out his notebook and pen. 'There's nothing at all for you to be concerned about. I just need to clear up a few details. Is that all right?'

Ronnie again nodded nervously.

'At your last school,' Charlie began, 'I believe you were friendly with your guidance teacher, Mr Murdoch. Is that correct?'

'We got on well at first.'

'And did that change?' Charlie asked.

'Yes.'

'Why was that?'

'There were problems,' Ronnie mumbled, his eyes cast down.

'What kind of problems?'

Ronnie looked up quickly at his father, who nodded his head.

'At first, Mr Murdoch was nice to me,' Ronnie said. 'He helped me with my homework. He was funny. I liked him a lot. In fact,

I liked him so much that…. that I told him I wanted to have a … a relationship with him.'

'What kind of relationship?'

'A physical relationship,' Ronnie said quietly.

'How did he react when you told him that?'

'He said that he would like that too. I wasn't expecting him to say that. I'd said it out of some kind of bravado. All I wanted to do was impress him. I wanted him to think that I was cool and grown up. I was sure he'd say no. But he told me that he would organise somewhere where we could meet in private. He suggested that I come round to his flat. He said we could tell my parents that I was going to his place for extra maths tuition. I was scared. I didn't want to go through with it. But Mr Murdoch was really insistent that I should come round to his flat. I didn't know what to do. I started to panic. I told my father that he had come on to me. That he was trying to groom me.' Tears were welling up in Ronnie's eyes.

'That's okay, Ronnie,' Charlie said reassuringly. 'You're doing fine. When your father found out what had happened, he decided to withdraw you from the school. Is that correct?'

Ronnie rubbed the tears from his eyes with his knuckles as he nodded his head.

'I've only got a few more questions, Ronnie,' Charlie said. 'Do you have an e-mail address?'

'Yes.'

'Who is your service provider?'

'Gmail.'

'Do you have a hotmail account?'

'No.'

'Have you ever had a hotmail account?'

'No.'

'Have you ever had any other e-mail accounts?'

'No.'

'Did you have any contact with Mr Murdoch after you left the school, Ronnie? Any phone calls, e-mails, letters, social media contacts, chat room conversations? Anything like that?'

'No, sir. Nothing. Nothing at all.'

'You realise that we can check that out, Ronnie,' Charlie said. 'We can analyse the hard drive on your computer and the memory on your phone, so think about this carefully before you answer. Are you sure that you didn't have any contact whatsoever with Mr Murdoch after you left the school?'

'I'm absolutely certain,' Ronnie stated emphatically, the colour rising in his cheeks. 'I'm not trying to hide anything, Inspector. I'm telling you the truth.'

'Okay, Ronnie,' Charlie said. 'I believe you.'

'Is that everything, Inspector?' Martin Gilligan interjected.

'I've only got one more question. Where were both of you on Saturday evening?'

'I was wondering how long it would take before you got round to asking that.' Gilligan gave a sardonic smile. 'Ronnie was performing at the Boys Brigade gymnastics display in Scotstoun Leisure Centre and I was there too, handing out the annual awards. There are a lot of people who will be able to confirm that.'

'Charlie put away his notebook and got to his feet.

'I've got a question for you, Inspector,' Ronnie said hesitantly.

'What's that?'

'Do you know who killed Mr Murdoch?'

'Not yet, son. But I intend to find out. Thanks for answering my questions, Ronnie,' Charlie added. 'You've been a big help.'

Martin Gilligan stood up and saw Charlie to the front door, closing it quietly behind him.

Charlie Anderson was breathing hard by the time he'd climbed the two flights of stairs to Lesley Adams' flat. When he rang the bell, Lesley came to the door.

'Good evening, Ms Adams. I've come to see Gavin.'

'I'm afraid he's not here, Inspector.'

Charlie looked puzzled. 'But I called him an hour ago and arranged to meet him here at seven o'clock.'

'He didn't say anything about that to me. He went out about twenty minutes ago.'

'Is it all right if I come in?' Charlie asked.

'Of course.'

'Do you know where Gavin was going tonight?' Charlie asked when they were both seated in the lounge.

'No.'

'Do you know when he'll be back?'

'He didn't say. What was it you wanted to talk to him about?' Lesley asked. 'Perhaps it's something I could help you with?'

'I need to establish where Gavin was, and who he was with, at half-past ten last Saturday night, when John Preston was murdered.'

'I've already told you that, Inspector. He was in Edinburgh with his friend, Stuart.'

'Unfortunately, that's not what he told Sergeant O'Sullivan yesterday. Gavin told him that he was with his uncle, Andy Carter, in a pub in the Calton on Saturday night – and that the two of them assaulted a man and nailed his hand to a cubicle door in the toilets.'

'What on earth are you talking about?' Lesley said, a stunned look on her face.

'Gavin's uncle was here when Gavin was interviewed by Sergeant O'Sullivan yesterday morning,' Charlie said. 'They both admitted to committing the assault at ten-thirty on Saturday evening.'

'That's… that's totally ridiculous!' Lesley spluttered. 'Gavin was in Edinburgh – at a gig – with his friend, Stuart. He told me all about it.'

'Then you will understand why I need to talk to him urgently – to get to the bottom of what's going on.'

'Of… of course. I'm totally confused about what's going on. He definitely told me he was through in Edinburgh.'

'Were you here on Saturday night when he got back?'

'I was in bed. He came in late.'

'How late is late?'

'I don't know. I was asleep. I put my light out after midnight and he wasn't back by then. In the morning, he told me that they had missed the last train so they'd caught a late-night bus back from Edinburgh.'

'Do you have any idea where he might have gone this evening?' Lesley shook her head. 'Do you know where he was earlier today?'

'As far as I know, he spent the day here, working. When I got back from work, which was around half-past six, he told me he was going out – but he didn't say where.'

'And he didn't say anything to you about having arranged to meet me here at seven o'clock?'

Lesley screwed up her face. 'Perhaps he forgot?'

'I very much doubt that.'

Would you like me to give him a call, Inspector?' Lesley said, picking up her phone from the coffee table. 'To find out where he is – and when he'll be back?'

'Yes. Please do that.'

When Lesley clicked onto Gavin's mobile number, the familiar ringtone emanated from the bedroom. 'He must have forgotten to take his phone with him,' Lesley said, a puzzled look on her face as she cut the connection. 'That's not at all like him. He never goes anywhere without his phone.'

'I need to talk to this friend of his – Stuart, you said his name was?' Lesley nodded. 'Do you know how to get in touch with him?'

'I'm afraid not. I met him a couple of times when he came here to see Gavin, but I don't know very much about him. Gavin met him at a computer forum a while back and they seemed to hit it off. They do the same kind of work and they have similar tastes in music. They swap ideas about computer games and they quite often go to gigs together, but I don't have his phone number and I've no idea where he lives.'

'Can I ask you what you were doing on Saturday evening, Ms Adams?'

'The same thing I do every Saturday, Inspector,' Lesley said with a resigned sigh. 'I was visiting my mother in a care home in Bearsden.'

'My father spent the last three years of his life in Abbotsford House in Bearsden,' Charlie said.

'My mother's in the Westerton. She's been suffering from dementia for quite some time, but her condition has got a lot worse recently. My sister goes to see her on Wednesdays, because that's her day off – and I do my duty on Saturdays.'

'When do you go to see her?'

'It depends. I prefer going in the morning so I can spend as much time as possible with her, but quite often I have to work on Saturdays and when I do, I go to see Mum in the evening. The care home is very flexible. There's an entry code at the door and, as long as you avoid meal times, you can visit the residents more or less any time you want.'

'When did you go to see her last Saturday?'

'I was working, so I went in the evening.'

'At what time?'

'I got there about eight o'clock.'

'How long did you stay?'

'I'm not sure – two or three of hours.' Lesley paused. 'Why are you asking me that?' She shrivelled her brow. 'You surely don't think that I had anything to do with – ?'

'I'm not thinking anything, Ms Adams,' Charlie interjected. 'All I'm doing is gathering information. Did you drive to the care home on Saturday?' Charlie asked.

'I never do. It's not worth the hassle of getting through Anniesland Cross when I can catch a train just along the road at Partick Station and be at Westerton in less than ten minutes. The care home is only a two minute walk from the station.'

'Thank you for your time, Ms Adams,' Charlie said, hauling himself to his feet. 'When Gavin gets back, please ask him to get in touch with me straight away.'

Gavin Carter sat at a table by the window in *The Three Judges*, nursing what was left of his drink. He badly wanted another one, but decided against it. Make this one last, he told himself. He needed to keep a clear head to decide what to do next. There was no way he could have talked to Anderson tonight. Anderson would have said something in front of Lesley about him being with Andy on Saturday night and all hell would have broken loose. It had been bad enough trying to stick to the party line about being in The Jaco when he'd been grilled by O'Sullivan yesterday. He could tell that O'Sullivan knew his story was riddled with holes. It would only be a matter of time before the cops blew his so-called alibi out of the water. Either that, or Mulgrew spilled the beans.

He was already regretting leaving his phone behind. He was lost without it. But he knew the police were able to trace phones. He reckoned there should be three or four hundred pounds in his bank account. He could withdraw up to three hundred at a time. He should do that straight away, he told himself, before the cops decided to track his bank card. Three hundred quid wasn't bad, but it wouldn't last him very long. He racked his brains about what to do next.

The immediate problem was where to spend the night. He couldn't risk going to his father's flat – or his uncle's. The cops would find him. Stuart would put him up, but he didn't know if he'd be at home – and he couldn't phone him to find out because the only place he had Stuart's number was on his phone – and going back to Lesley's place to retrieve his phone wasn't an option. The only thing he could think to do was catch a bus to Clydebank and hope to God Stuart was in. He didn't have anywhere else to go. He glanced at his watch. Anderson would be at Lesley's flat right now, talking to her, telling her about him claiming to have been in The Jaco with Andy on Saturday night. After he had told her he was in Edinburgh with Stuart, she wasn't going to be welcoming him back with open arms. But if he switched tack now – changed his story – told the cops he was in Edinburgh with Stuart, Andy would go ballistic. He was going to get sent down for trying to give him an alibi. How would he react if he found out he'd done that for bugger all, because Gavin had changed his story? That didn't even bear thinking about.

Throwing back the rest of his drink, he went up to the bar and ordered another one.

*

Driving out Great Western Road, Charlie Anderson turned right at Anniesland Cross and took the Switchback in the direction of Bearsden, turning left when he got to Maxwell Avenue. When he arrived at the Westerton care home he drove down the steep ramp to the underground car park. Getting out of his car, he walked back up the slope and round the corner to the main entrance at the front of the building. When he rang the bell he was buzzed in by a nurse.

Charlie showed her his warrant card. 'I believe you have a resident here called Mrs Adams?'

'Yes. Grace Adams,' the nurse said. 'Her room is on Skye. That's what we call the top floor,' she added by way of explanation.

'Sky sounds like an appropriate name for the top floor,' Charlie nodded.

The nurse smiled. 'It's Skye with an 'e', Inspector. Named after the the island. The other two floors are Iona and Argyll.'

'How long has Mrs Adams been with you?'

'Quite some time. I started working here two years ago and she was here when I arrived.'

'Do you keep a record of visitors to the home?' Charlie asked. 'Their names? The date they come? The time they arrive? How long they stay?'

'I wouldn't really call it a record. We have a register where we ask visitors to sign in when they arrive and sign out again when they leave. It's to do with fire regulations, so we know who is in the building in case of an emergency.'

'Would it be possible for me to see the register for last Saturday?'

'There are two registers. One here and one at the car park level. It depends which entrance the visitor uses.'

'The person I'm interested in comes here by train.'

'In which case, they'd probably use this entrance. The register is on the table over there,' she said, pointing.

'It's not very reliable, I'm afraid,' the nurse said as Charlie went across to pick up the book. 'Visitors are usually pretty good about signing in, but half the time they forget to sign out when they leave.'

Charlie turned back the pages until he came to the entries for the previous Saturday. He ran his finger down the column of names. On the second page for that date he came to the entry:

RESIDENT	VISITOR'S NAME	ARRIVAL TIME	DEPARTURE TIME
Grace Adams	Lesley Adams	2010	2245

Flicking back through the book to previous Saturdays, Charlie saw similar entries in the same, neat handwriting, the only difference being the arrival and departure times, sometimes in the morning, sometimes in the evening.

'Do you know Grace Adams' daughters?' Charlie asked.

'Of course. They're both regular visitors here.'

'Did you see Lesley Adams here last Saturday?'

'I wasn't on duty.'

'According to the register she arrived at ten past eight and left at quarter to eleven. Would there be anyone here tonight who was on duty last Saturday?'

'Hold on a minute. I'll check the rota.'

'Thanks.'

'Why are you interested in this?' she asked as she was flicking though the rota book.

'It's just boring, routine enquiries,' Charlie said with a fixed smile..

'Yes, here we are. Emily. She's the senior nurse on the Skye floor. She's on tonight.'

'Could I have a word with her?'

'I'll give her a call.'

When Emily came to the phone, Charlie introduced himself. 'Do you recall if Lesley Adams was here last Saturday evening to visit her mother?' he asked.

'My goodness, Inspector. It takes me all my time to remember what happened yesterday.'

'I know the feeling. Take your time.'

'I think she must have been,' Emily said hesitantly. 'Prior to Grace's dementia setting in, she suffered from mental health problems. She once told a nurse that one of her daughters had had a traumatic experience when she was young, but she clammed up when the nurse questioned her about what had happened. Grace gets easily muddled up. Whatever happened in the past, it seemed to have upset her a lot and I think she still carries that with her. Her world has to have structure, otherwise she gets agitated. An important part of that structure is her daughters' visits every Wednesday and Saturday. On the rare occasion that nobody comes to see her on one of those days, she gets very upset. That hasn't happened recently – at least, not when I've been on duty. But now I come to think of it, Inspector. Of course! Lesley was here. I remember now. I was walking past Grace's room and her door was open. Lesley was sitting on the chair beside her bed. She gave me a wave.'

'Do you know when she left the building?' Charlie asked.

'I've no idea. I didn't see her go.'

'Do you recall at what time you saw her?'

'I was going for my break, so it must've been round about half-past ten.'

Gavin Carter finished his drink quickly and hurried to the nearest cashpoint machine to check his bank balance. As he thought, he had three hundred and eighty pounds. He withdrew three hundred, then ran to the nearest bus stop in Dumbarton road. When a bus for Clydebank pulled up, he got on board.

Gavin's heart sank as he approached the block of flats. There were no lights on in the lounge in Stuart's ground floor flat. Could he have gone to bed early?

More in hope than expectation, Gavin pressed the doorbell and held his finger against it. There was no answer. Giving the door a kick in frustration, he turned round and trudged his way back to the bus stop.

While waiting for a bus to arrive, he remembered the Euro Hostel in Clyde Street. He'd stayed there for a couple of nights, about a year back, when he'd had a bust up with his father and stormed out of his flat.

He took the bus as far as Argyle Street, then cut through St Enoch's Square and headed down Dixon Street, turning right when he got to the river. When he got to the hostel he was relieved to find that there were beds available in one of the dormitories. That was what he needed. A cheap place to kip down, in a crowded environment, where no one would ask him any questions about what he was doing there.

More than anything else right now, he needed time to think.

CHAPTER 21

Friday 9 September

While waiting for his porridge to cool down, Charlie Anderson
phoned Tony O'Sullivan.

'There were some interesting developments yesterday, Tony,'
Charlie said when Tony took the call. 'I'm going across right now to
have another go at Jack Mulgrew, then I have to give a status report
to Niggle at ten o'clock. Round the team up for a briefing session at
eleven o'clock in the incident room.'

'Will do, sir.'

Disconnecting, Charlie called Lesley Adams on her mobile.

'Did Gavin come back to your flat last night, Ms Adams?' he
asked.

'No, Inspector.'

'Did he contact you?'

'He didn't,' Lesley said. 'I've no idea what's going on.'

'If you hear from him, please let me know straight away.'

When Charlie had cut the call, Lesley drummed her fingertips
on the kitchen table. She wasn't at all sure this was a good idea, but
she decided to go through with it.

Going through to the lounge, she switched on her laptop. As
soon as it had powered up she checked through her work files until
she found Andy Carter's telephone number. He answered on the
third ring.

'This is Lesley Adams, Mr Carter. I'm trying to get in touch with
Gavin. Is he with you, by any chance?'

'The last I heard he was kipping down at your place.'

'He has been staying here, but Inspector Anderson had arranged to come to see him here at seven o'clock last night and Gavin didn't show up.'

'Well he isn't here.'

Lesley hesitated. 'Why did Gavin tell the police he was with you on Saturday night?'

'Probably because it was truth.'

'He told me he was in Edinburgh.'

Andy chortled. 'He was hardly going to tell you he was helping his Uncle Andy claim a punter, now was he?'

'Do you have any idea where he is now?'

'I haven't a fucking clue. But even if I did,' Carter added with a sneer, 'there's no way I'd be letting on to Miss Goody Two Shoes.'

Lesley was left staring at her phone as Carter brusquely cut the connection.

Gavin Carter had spent a restless night in the dormitory in the Euro Hostel. The intermittent heavy snoring coming from three beds down hadn't helped, but even without that he doubted if he'd have been able to get much sleep. His mind was in turmoil.

Charlie Anderson recoiled from the strong stench of cheap booze coming off Jack Mulgrew's breath when he answered the ring on his door bell.

'DCI Anderson,' Charlie said, showing his warrant card as he stepped across the threshold. 'We spoke on the phone yesterday.'

'What do you want?'

'I want to know what really happened to you in The Jacobite Arms last Saturday night.'

'I told the polisman in London Road everything. It's all there in my statement.'

'I want to hear it from you,' Charlie said, taking his notebook and pen from his jacket pocket.

Mulgrew licked hard at his lips as Charlie prepared to take notes.

'I was in the The Jaco on Saturday, havin' a pint, mindin' my own business. I went downstairs for a crap and when I came out of the bog I got grabbed by two blokes who nailed my hand to the door.'

'Who were these two blokes?'

'Andy Carter – and a young guy called Gavin.'

'Why did they do that to you?'

'I owed Carter money.'

'How much?'

'Five hundred quid.'

'You owed *Carter* money? Or you owed Jim Colvin money?'

Mulgrew's eyes were dancing. 'I don't know anybody called Jim Colvin,' he said quickly.

'The landlord in The Jacobite Arms said that you told him you were attacked by two complete strangers.'

'I wisny goany tell him that I knew who had claimed me.'

'How do you know that the young guy's name was Gavin?'

'When Andy Carter grabbed me, he shouted: "Haud his hand against the door, Gavin".'

'So you didn't tell the landlord that you knew who'd attacked you,' Charlie said. 'You didn't tell anyone at the hospital, you didn't report it to the police at the time – then two days later you walked into London Road police station and filed a complaint against Andy Carter and Gavin. Is that right?'

'More or less,' Mulgrew mumbled.

'Well it doesn't sound right to me,' Charlie said with a quick shake of the head. 'In fact, to me, it sounds like a load of old cobblers.'

'I don't give a bugger what it sounds like to you, pal. That's what happened.'

'At what time did the assault take place?'

'Half-past ten.'

Charlie stared long and hard at Mulgrew as he slipped his note-book back into his pocket.

*

Charlie checked his watch as he climbed the stairs to the top floor in Pitt Street. At precisely ten o'clock, he knocked on Superintendent Nigel Hamilton's door and walked in.

Taking the chair opposite Hamilton's desk, Charlie referred to his notebook as he gave a summary of the status of the investigation.

'It's six days since the murder took place, Anderson.' Hamilton's piercing, high-pitched delivery grated in Charlie's ears. 'I have to brief the Chief this afternoon. He's holding a media conference at five o'clock – and, from what you're telling me, he's not going to have a lot to say to them.'

'We're gathering information and analysing it. We've drawn up a list of potential suspects and possible motives. We've put in place an action plan. I'm holding a briefing session at eleven o'clock this morning to review the status. What else do you suggest I do?'

'The press will want to know if an arrest is imminent.'

'I can't give a timeframe for that.'

'The Chief is looking for results, Anderson,' Hamilton snapped. '*I'm* looking for results, not some nebulous action plan. We need to be seen to be pulling out all the stops on this one. Inform everyone who is working on the case that all leave is cancelled until further notice.'

'Running the guys into the ground isn't going to do anything to improve the situation,' Charlie protested.

'Public perception is important, Anderson. I'll inform the Chief that he can let the media know that everyone on the team will be working twenty-four seven until we get a result.'

'In which case,' Charlie said, pulling himself stiffly to his feet. 'I'd be better employed managing the situation, rather than spending my time sitting here.'

Turning on his heel, Charlie strode out of the office.

Tony O'Sullivan was the last one to arrive in the incident room for the eleven o'clock briefing. Charlie signalled to him to close the door behind him.

'You go first, Tom,' Charlie said, turning to Freer. 'What have you got for us?'

'I went across to Paisley and I managed to speak to Alice Carter and her new man, Mitch Weir. They were as sympathetic with regard to Preston's death as the rest of the Carter clan – "good riddance to bad rubbish" would more or less sum up their attitude.'

'Can they account for their movements last Saturday night?' O'Sullivan asked.

'Not only can they account for them, they claim to have a hundred and fifty witnesses who will confirm that they were in Carlisle at the wedding of one of Mitch Weir's sons from a previous relationship. I haven't had a chance to check that out yet, but I don't imagine they would've come up with something as convoluted as that if it wasn't genuine.'

'How did you get on with Malcolm Steel?' Charlie asked.

'He wasn't at all cooperative, sir,' Freer said. 'He told me he was in the Ubiquitous Chip with a male friend at the time of the murder, but he wasn't prepared to divulge his friend's name because he's a married man and Steel doesn't want the police to give him any hassle. I checked with the Chip and Steel did have a reservation for two people at nine o'clock on Saturday night – and he paid the bill with his credit card at ten forty-three, so it looks like he's in the clear. However, I've arranged to go back to the Chip this evening to talk to the staff who were on duty on Saturday. It's a long shot, but the Chip is less than a ten minute walk away from where the murder took place. I'll find out if there's any possibility that Steel could have nipped out of the restaurant for half an hour to commit the murder and then be back in the restaurant in time to pay his bill.'

'Thanks, Tom,' Charlie said. He turned to Renton. 'Did you manage to find out anything from your mates in the Procurator Fiscal's office as to why they decided to prosecute Murdoch?'

'They told me they realised it would more or less come down to Tommy Carter's word against Murdoch's, but they concluded that the boy's evidence was credible and that he deserved his day in court.'

'Do you have anything else for us, Colin?' Charlie asked.

'I managed to track down three of the guys who were in Terry Carter's poker school last Saturday,' Renton said. 'They confirmed that Terry was in the flat all evening – and by all accounts he was well and truly pissed long before ten o'clock. When you consider that it would have taken him at least thirty minutes to get from his place to Cottiers and back – even if he'd gone by taxi, plus the time it would have taken him to bump Preston off, I reckon that's a non-starter. For my money, Terry's in the clear.'

'Cross him off the list, Colin. And Mrs C. and Mitch Weir as well, at least for now,' Charlie added, handing Renton a marker pen.

'Over to you, Tony,' Charlie said as Renton was drawing a line through the names.

Having reported back on his encounter with Jim Colvin in the *Black Seven* snooker hall, Tony gave a summary of his conversation in The Jacobite Arms.

'The landlord confirmed that Mulgrew got nailed round about half-past ten,' Tony concluded, 'which means that whoever assaulted him couldn't have got to Cottiers in time to strangle Preston.'

'But the fact that everyone involved in this affair is going out of their way to tell us that the assault in The Jacobite Arms took place at precisely ten-thirty,' Charlie said, 'leaves little room for doubt in my mind that the two events are connected. The question is – how?'

'From Andy Carter's description of the assault on Mulgrew, I'm certain he was involved,' Tony said, 'and, according to the landlord, it's a racing certainty that Jim Colvin would've been there to gloat at the time of the attack. However, I don't believe for one minute that Gavin was anywhere near The Jacobite Arms on Saturday night, so I reckon

Carter's claiming that Gavin was there in order to give his nephew an alibi.'

'That's a strong possibility,' Charlie said. 'I'd arranged to see Gavin at Lesley Adams' place last night but when I got there he'd done a runner. I checked with Ms Adams this morning. He didn't return to her flat last night. We know he has a mate called Stuart, so it's possible that Gavin might have gone to his place. Colin, as soon as we wrap up here, do some digging and see if you can track Stuart down.'

'What do we know about him?' Renton asked.

'Not a lot. Like Gavin, he designs computer games, so both of them might work for the same firm. Gavin is with a company called SHERPA, which is run by a lady called Sheila McVey,' Charlie said. 'See if you can find a phone number for her.'

'Will do.'

'Going back to the assault in the pub,' Charlie said, 'the one person who knows for certain who was present when the attack took place is Jack Mulgrew. You and I will pay him another visit first thing tomorrow, Tony. If we lean on him we might be able to find out whether – '

'I'm not working tomorrow, sir,' Tony interjected. 'I've got the weekend off.'

'Oh, that reminds me,' Charlie said with a grunt. 'I've got bad news for all of you. We're all working seven day weeks from now on until this case is put to bed.'

'But I've got tickets for Thistle's match at Dundee tomorrow, sir,' Renton protested.

'I hope you'll be able to find someone who can use them, Colin,' Charlie said.

'But, I've.... I've made plans for the weekend,' Tony stammered.

'Then I'm afraid you'll just have to un-plan them, Tony. I'm sorry about this, guys,' Charlie said, spreading his arms out wide. 'Orders from on high. It's a three-line whip – all leave cancelled until further notice.'

A stifled groan travelled round the room.

'I'll meet you here at half-past eight tomorrow morning, Tony,' Charlie said. 'Then we'll go across to Mulgrew's place and pay him a visit. Okay?'

Tony gave a resigned shrug.

CHAPTER 22

Charlie spent the next hour clearing his backlog of paper work. He was about to head off home when Colin Renton walked into his office.

'I've got a phone number for Mrs McVey, sir,' Renton said, handing across a slip of paper. 'There was a contact number on SHERPA's website. I spoke to one of their marketing guys and he gave me Mrs McVey's mobile number.'

'Thanks, Colin,' Charlie said, sitting back down on his swivel chair. Lifting the desk phone from its cradle, he punched in the number.

A female voice answered.

'Am I speaking to Mrs Sheila McVey?' Charlie asked.

'You are.'

'I'm Inspector Anderson – Glasgow CID,' Charlie stated.

'What can I do for you?'

'This is nothing for you to be concerned about, Mrs McVey. I'm just looking for some information.'

'What about?'

'I believe you run a company called SHERPA?'

"Running' SHERPA is a bit of an overstatement, Inspector. I'm more of a sleeping partner. I financed the initial set up and I handle the HR side of things – recruitment, commissions, stuff like that. I leave the day to day running of the business to the technocrats.'

'It's the recruitment side I'm interested in,' Charlie said. 'I believe you employ a young man called Gavin Carter?'

'I do.' Sheila hesitated. 'He's not in any kind of trouble, I hope?'

'It's actually one of Gavin's friends I'm trying to trace. A guy called Stuart. He does the same kind of work as Gavin and I wondered if you'd had any dealings with him?'

'Stuart, you said? I'm afraid not. We're a small company and I'm in charge of the hiring. I've never taken on anyone called Stuart.'

'Okay, thanks for that. It was bit of a long shot,' Charlie said.

'Is there anything else I can help you with?'

'What can you tell me about Gavin Carter?'

'Gavin? He's one of our stars, Inspector. I initially took him on as a favour for someone I knew from school, a lady called Lesley Adams. She's a social worker in Glasgow. She gave me a call a while back and told me that she was trying to help Gavin find a job. She hoped I might be able to put some work his way. As it turned out, it was Lesley who did me a favour. I've given Gavin several commissions now and he invariably produces innovative work, on schedule. That's why I was concerned when I thought he might be in trouble with the police. I would hate to lose him.'

'Thank you for your time, Mrs McVey.'

Tony's name was displayed on Sue's mobile as she took his call. Transferring the phone to her left hand, she swept her long hair behind her ear.

'I managed to dog off the last period at school,' she said excitedly before he could get a word in. 'I'm all packed. Have you finished at work?' she asked.

'It's bad news, I'm afraid, Sue,' Tony said disconsolately. 'All leave's been cancelled. I have to work this weekend.'

'Oh, shit! Is there no way that you could – '

'It's a three-line whip,' Tony interjected. 'No exceptions.'

Sue took a slow, deep breath. 'What are you going to do with the Radiohead tickets?' she asked.

'If you like, you could go to the gig with one of your girlfriends,' Tony suggested.

'Thanks for the offer, but it wouldn't be the same. Besides, the flights are booked in our names. Do you think you'll be able to get your money back?'

'I'll be able to cancel the hotel without any problem,' Tony said, 'and I'll probably make more than enough to cover the cost of the air fares by selling the Radiohead tickets on the Internet. But it's not the money that matters,' Tony added apologetically. 'It's your birthday that's been messed up.'

'That can't be helped,' Sue said. 'But, hey, don't worry about it. We'll find a way to celebrate my birthday tomorrow,' she stated emphatically, 'three-line whip or no three-line whip.'

'How about a three-line whip – with the bit between your teeth?' Tony suggested.

'Aye, right!' Sue said, laughing. 'Save your erotic fantasies for your own birthday. When is your birthday, by the way?'

'Would you believe – tonight?'

'No way!'

'It was worth a shot.'

'Do you know what time you'll be able to get off tomorrow?'

'It depends on what mood your old man's in.'

'Give me call when you know what you're doing.'

Charlie kicked off his shoes in the hall before pulling on his slippers and going through to the lounge. He settled down in his favourite armchair in front of the gas fire.

'Fancy a cup of tea?' Kay asked as she came through from the kitchen.

'No, thanks,' Charlie said, picking up the newspaper from the coffee table and turning to the sports' pages.

'You do well to take the opportunity to relax while you can,' Kay said, 'because you'll be getting plenty of exercise over the weekend.'

'What are you talking about?'

'We're going to have Jamie staying with us – and he's bringing across his football boots.'

Charlie folded his newspaper. 'I didn't know Jamie was going to be with us this weekend.'

Kay looked at her watch. 'Sue will be dropping him off any time now. Tony's taking her to London for the weekend for her birthday. He organised it as a surprise. He's got them tickets for a Radiohead gig.'

'Oh, bugger!' Charlie said, crumpling the newspaper in his fists.

'What's wrong?' Kay asked.

'Tony isn't going anywhere this weekend, love. I just broke the news to him and the rest of the guys. Instructions from on high. All leave has been cancelled until further notice for everybody working on the Preston case.'

'Oh, Charlie! Does that have to include Tony?'

Charlie heaved a heavy sigh. 'I can hardly make an exception for my daughter's birthday.'

The manager was on the phone, taking a booking, when Tom Freer arrived at the Ubiquitous Chip just before seven o'clock. She held up her hand to acknowledge his presence. He waited until she'd finished her call.

'Bruce,' she called across to a member of staff who was setting a table at the far end of the restaurant. 'Do you have a minute?'

'This is a police officer,' she said when Bruce ambled across. 'He's interested in two men who had a reservation at nine o'clock last Saturday. They were at table C2. Do you remember them?'

'Last Saturday? Two men? C2?' Bruce rubbed at his chin. 'Sure, I remember table C2 all right. But it wasn't two men. It was a man and a woman.'

'Are you sure?' Freer queried.

'Quite sure.'

'Was the man tall and slim? Fiftyish? With a pencil moustache?'

'Not at all.' Bruce shook his head. 'He was a fat slob. In his thirties, I would guess. Sorry!' Bruce broke off, his cheeks starting to redden. 'I hope he's not a friend of yours?'

'Not at all,' Freer said. 'Carry on.'

'He was an objectionable wee sod,' Bruce said. 'And his companion was as hard as nails. I remember them very well. The bloke acted as if he owned the place. He gave me the impression that he was more interested in finding something to complain about, rather than enjoying the meal.'

'Do you remember if he paid his bill with a credit card?' Freer asked.

'He did. I remember that very well because the tip he added on was stingy. You don't forget wankers like that in a hurry,' Bruce added with feeling.

As soon as he got back to his car, Tom Freer phoned Charlie's number.

'I'm sorry to disturb you at home, sir,' Freer said when Charlie took the call, 'but there's something I thought you'd want to know straight away.'

'What?' Charlie demanded.

'Malcolm Steel wasn't in the Ubiquitous Chip on the night Preston was murdered.'

Charlie sat bolt upright in his chair. 'Are you sure about that?'

'A hundred percent. There was a reservation in the Chip in Steel's name, but the staff told me that it was a couple in their thirties who turned up. The bloke was in possession of Steel's credit card and his PIN – and he used the card to pay his bill.'

'Good work, Tom,' Charlie said.

'How do you want to handle this?' Freer asked.

'We'll need to pay Mr Steel a visit to find out what this is all about,' Charlie said. 'I don't want to give him any warning that we're on our way. I don't want to give him time to fabricate another story. How about we meet outside his house at half-past seven tomorrow morning? That way, we should be able to catch him unawares.'

'Okay, sir. I'll see you there.'

'Did I hear you say you were going to meet someone at half-past seven tomorrow morning?' Kay asked as Charlie disconnected.

'Yes, love. Tom Freer's onto something important.'

'Well don't expect me to get up and make your breakfast.'

Gavin Carter had got up early on Friday morning and spent all day walking the streets, stopping off at various coffee shops and burger bars when he needed something to eat. Time had dragged by. He'd decided to stay close to the crowded city centre so he wouldn't stand out, but everywhere he went he had an uneasy feeling that people were looking at him – talking about him. It was as if everybody knew he had something to hide. He'd panicked when he saw two police officers on foot patrol coming towards him in the pedestrian precinct in Buchanan Street. Turning round, he'd hurried away, then sprinted along St Vincent Street in the direction of George Square, expecting the police to catch up with him at any minute. A flock of pigeons had scattered in a flurry of beating wings when he'd stopped in the middle of the square, his hands on his knees, panting for breath. When he'd looked over his shoulder, the police were nowhere to be seen.

By the time Gavin got back to the hostel his nerves were shot to hell. He'd booked a bed for another night, then turned in early, not wanting to get involved in conversation with anyone.

He knew he couldn't go on like this for much longer.

CHAPTER 23

Saturday 10 September

Tom Freer was waiting for Charlie when he arrived outside Malcolm Steel's house just before seven-thirty. They walked up to the front door and Charlie pressed the bell. There was no response.

'Maybe he went out early?' Freer suggested.

'With the bedroom curtains still closed – and two cars in the drive?' Charlie said. 'I very much doubt it.'

Charlie held his finger to the bell as he looked up at the bedroom window. He saw the curtains twitch.

Charlie opened the letter box and shouted through. 'We're not going anywhere, Mr Steel. You might as well come down now.'

A few minutes later a disgruntled Malcolm Steel came to the door in his slippers and dressing gown.

'What do you want at this time in the morning, Inspector?' he complained. 'The weekend is the only chance I get to have a lie-in.'

'If you'd told us fewer lies during the week, Mr Steel,' Charlie said, 'you might've been able to have a lie-in today.'

'What on earth are you talking about?' Steel demanded.

'I suggest that you invite us in,' Charlie said. 'And we'll tell you all about it.'

Without replying, Steel turned round and walked along the corridor. Charlie and Tom Freer stepped inside, Freer closing the door behind him before following Charlie and Steel to the lounge.

'We need to know the truth,' Charlie stated when they were all seated. 'You told Constable Freer that you were in the Ubiquitous Chip, with a male friend, on the night John Preston was murdered, but we have established that, while your credit card was in the Ubiquitous Chip, you were not. Would you care to tell us what's going on?'

Steel rubbed hard at his eyes. It was a few moments before he spoke.

'It was my nephew's birthday last Saturday. As a present, I let him have my credit card and I told him my PIN so he could treat his fiancée to a slap-up meal. That's not illegal, is it?'

'Your bank probably wouldn't be too happy about it, but we're not here to discuss that,' Charlie said. 'What I want to know is – why did you not tell us that before? Why did you say you went to the Chip with a friend?'

'I… I don't know,' Steel stammered.

'You'll have to do a lot better than that, Mr Steel,' Charlie insisted. 'As it stands right now, you have not provided us with a viable explanation as to where you were, and who you were with, at the time John Preston was murdered.'

'I didn't kill John,' Steel said quietly.

'Then where were you when he was killed?' Charlie asked

'I was with a male friend,' Steel insisted.

'You can't just keep repeating that, Mr Steel,' Charlie said, a note of exasperation creeping into his voice. 'You need to tell us your friend's name so we can confirm that what you're saying is the truth.'

'I won't give you his name.' Starting to sob, Steel buried his head in his hands. 'I can't do that!'

Charlie made eye contact with Freer and nodded towards the door. They both got to their feet.

'I'll give you some time to think this over, Mr Steel,' Charlie said. 'But not a lot. I want to see you in my office in Pitt Street at twelve o'clock today – and if you're still not prepared to divulge where you were and who you were with at the time of the murder, you will leave me with no option other than arrest you on suspicion of involvement in John Preston's death.'

Steel didn't look up as they both walked out.

'Do you think he'll turn up, sir?' Freer said as he closed the front door behind them. 'Are you not worried that he might do a runner?'

'He'll turn up all right, Tom. You have to trust your instincts in this business, son. The likes of Andy Carter or Jim Colvin might well do a runner, but Steel's not that type. And I'm sure there's someone with him in the house right now,' Charlie added as they were walking past the cars in the drive. Steel doesn't strike me as a two-car person.'

'Could one of those cars belong to his mysterious friend?' Freer asked.

'It could well do. Make a note of both the registration numbers and have them checked out as soon as you get back to the office.'

Gavin Carter had again slept badly, tossing and turning half the night, his brain churning with a nightmare of him standing in the dock, his legs trembling as he pleaded with the judge who had just condemned him to a life sentence in the Bar-L. The dormitory wasn't over-heated, but when he woke with a start, Gavin's underwear was soaked in sweat and clinging to his body. He turned onto his back and checked his watch for the umpteenth time. It was just after half-past seven. He got out of bed as quietly as he could and headed for the showers.

As the soothing, warm water cascaded down his body, Gavin's befuddled brain wrestled with his options. Going on the run didn't make any kind of sense. His money would run out soon and the cops would track him down before too long. Sticking to the story about nailing Mulgrew's hand to the bog door in The Jaco didn't make sense either. The police would keep probing away until they uncovered inconsistencies between his version of events and Andy's. And even if that didn't happen, it wouldn't be long before the cops applied sufficient pressure on Mulgrew to make him spill the beans.

The only practical solution was to switch his story. To admit that he hadn't been in The Jaco with Andy and tell the cops he'd gone to a gig in Edinburgh with Stuart. God only knows how Andy would react when he found out he'd done that. Kick the shit out him, probably – and who could blame him? Andy was going to get sent down for sod all – just for trying to give him an alibi. But what was the alternative? If he stuck to Andy's version of events, the cops would be able to prove that he wasn't in The Jaco at the time of the murder. From there, they would conclude that the only reason Andy was trying to give him an alibi was because Andy knew that he had killed Murdoch.

He was terrified at the thought of what Andy would do to him, but the prospect of a life sentence in the Bar-L chilled his blood.

Gavin turned on the cold tap and stuck his head under the shower, closing his eyes. He needed to talk to Stuart, as soon as possible, to let him know what he was planning to do. But to do that, he needed to get his phone back. He shook the water from his hair and rubbed at his eyes. As he stepped out of the shower and towelled himself down, he decided that the only thing he could do would be wait until Lesley had gone out, then go back to her flat and recover his phone.

After he'd sorted things out with Stuart, he realised he'd have to face Andy's wrath before talking to the police. The prospect sent a shiver running down the length of his spine.

'I'm led to believe I'm responsible for messing up your weekend,' Charlie said when Tony O'Sullivan walked into his office at half-past eight.

'Something like that, sir,' Tony muttered.

'Sorry about that.'

'It couldn't be helped,' Tony said with a shrug. 'Is there any chance I might be able to knock off at a reasonable time tonight?' he asked.

'I'll see what I can do,' Charlie said. 'A very interesting development this morning, by the way.'

'What was that?'

'Tom Freer found out that Malcolm Steel had given us a bum steer when he told us he was in the Ubiquitous Chip at the time Preston was killed.'

'Does that mean he's back in the frame?'

'In spades. Freer and I have just been across to his place where he flatly refused to tell us where he was, or who he was with, at the time of the murder.'

'Are you going to pull him in?'

'Not just yet. I've given him a bit of time to mull things over. I've told him to be here at twelve o'clock. If he hasn't come to his senses by then, I'm going to place him under arrest.'

Tom Freer stuck his head round Charlie's door. 'Are you interruptible, sir?'

'Sure,' Charlie said.

'I've got some interesting information regarding the car numbers,' Freer said.

'There were two cars in Steel's driveway when we went across to his place this morning, Tony,' Charlie said by way of explanation. 'I asked Tom to find out who owns them.'

'One of the cars is registered in Malcolm Steel's name, sir,' Freer said. 'But get this. The other vehicle is registered in the name of Mrs Sylvia Parker, the wife of Donald Parker, the head teacher at Steel's school.'

'You don't say!' Tony let out a long, low whistle. 'Indulging in a bit of hanky-panky with the headie's missus, was he? That's not going to do his promotion prospects much good if her old man ever finds out.'

'But Steel's gay,' Charlie said, frowning.

'Welcome to the twenty-first century, sir,' Tony said with a grin. 'Bisexual is all the rage these days.'

Charlie shook his head as he checked his watch. 'After we've been to see Mulgrew, Tony, we'll have time to pay Mrs Parker a visit before Steel comes to see me here at noon. Tom, find out Donald Parker's address and text it to me. Better still, text it to Tony. I might not be able to find the message on my phone.'

'How do you want to handle things with Mulgrew?' Tony asked as he and Charlie were driving across town.

'He's shit scared of someone,' Charlie said. 'And he's been well coached. We'll give him a grilling and see if we can get him to crack.'

It was just after nine o'clock when Gavin Carter got off the bus in Dumbarton Road at the nearest stop to Lesley Adams' flat. It being Saturday, he knew Lesley would either be working, or going to visit her mother. He checked his watch. If she was going to see her mother, she would be setting off around now. To be on the safe side, he went into the café on the corner and ordered a bacon roll and a cappuccino.

When he came out of the café, Gavin took the tenement steps two at a time. He turned his key in the Yale lock in the front door as quietly as he could and eased it open. There was no sign of life. He headed straight for the bedroom and was mightily relieved to see his phone was still where he'd left it, lying on the bedside table. As he picked up his phone, his eye was caught by Inspector Anderson's card which Lesley had left lying on the table. He hesitated for a moment, then lifted the card and stuffed it into the hip pocket of his jeans before paging through his contacts and clicking onto Stuart's number.

'It's Gavin,' he said when the call was answered.

'What time is it?' the bleary voice asked.

'Half-past nine.'

'Half-past nine doesn't exist on a Saturday. I don't take calls before eleven o'clock.'

'Stop messing about, Stuart. This is important. Are you at home?'

'No, I'm in Aberdeen.'

'What? What the hell are you doing there?'

'My mother fell and broke her arm last week. I came up here a couple of days ago to give her a hand.'

'When will you be back to Glasgow?'

'Tonight. I'm booked on the half-past six train. What's up, Gavin?' Stuart asked, yawning. 'You said it was something important?'

Gavin hesitated. 'The cops are trying to pin Murdoch's murder on me.'

'Fucking hell!'

'I have to talk to the police today. I'm going to tell them that we went to the *First Tiger* gig together on Saturday night, but my uncle is convinced they'll still try to stitch me up, so you're sure to get a visit from the cops before long.'

'That's not a problem.'

'If there's any difference in what we say to them, they won't let it go. My uncle says the bastards will stop at nothing in order to get a result. I'll give you call later on, when you're on the train, to make sure we both tell them the same story. Is that okay?'

'Sure.'

Disconnecting, Gavin steeled himself before clicking onto Andy Carter's number.

'Where are you?' Andy demanded as soon as he heard Gavin's voice.

'I'm at Lesley Adams' place.'

'What the hell's going on, Gavin? I tried calling you half a dozen times yesterday, but all I got was your bloody answering service.'

'I didn't have my phone with me yesterday.'

'That bird of yours phoned me. She told me that Anderson had arranged to come to see you on Thursday night, but you'd done a runner. She wanted to know if you were here.'

'It was nothing, Andy. I just made myself scarce. I didn't want to talk to Anderson.'

'For fuck's sake, Gavin! Don't do daft stuff like that. If Anderson wants to talk to you, you have to see him. All you need to do is stick to the story we agreed and everything will be fine.'

'I need to talk to you, Andy.'

'What about?'

'Not on the phone. Can I come across to your place just now?'

'All right.'

Jack Mulgrew was sitting at his kitchen table, munching a slice of toast, when Charlie Anderson rang his doorbell.

'What the hell do you want now?' Mulgrew whined when he opened the door of his flat and saw Charlie and Tony standing there.

'How about you tell us what really happened last Saturday?' Charlie said as he stepped inside.

'I'm sick and tired of telling you,' Mulgrew complained as Tony followed Charlie in, closing the door behind him. 'Andy Carter and a bloke called Gavin nailed me to the bog door in The Jacobite Arms.'

'We *know* that Andy Carter attacked you,' Tony said, 'but we also know that Gavin was nowhere near The Jacobite Arms last Saturday.'

'So maybe I misheard the lad's name? Maybe it wasn't Gavin? It could've been George, I suppose. My hearing's not all that great. Tall bloke, about twenty, spiky hair.'

'That doesn't sound like a very good description of Jim Colvin,' Tony said.

'Who's Jim Colvin?'

'Surely you remember him?' Tony said. 'He told me you lent him a hundred quid last month when he was skint.'

'Did I? My memory's not great either. If he says that's what happened, I suppose it must be right.'

'How come you had money like that to lend?' Tony asked.

'I remember now,' Mulgrew said, snapping his fingers. 'I had a good win on the gee-gees last month. I picked up a few hundred quid.'

'Cut the crap, Mulgrew,' Charlie interjected. 'We know who nailed you to the bog door in the pub, and it wasn't a bloke called Gavin.'

'Like I said, his name might've been George – or maybe it was Gerry? Come to think of it, Gerry sounds familiar. It might very well have been Gerry.'

'I'm beginning to get annoyed, Mulgrew,' Charlie growled. 'Very annoyed. We are conducting a murder investigation and if you persist with this half-baked story you're going to end up on a charge of perverting the course of justice. Now, for the last time, tell me what happened to you last Saturday. Who attacked you in The Jacobite Arms?'

'Andy Carter.'

'And who else?' Charlie demanded.

Mulgrew looked Charlie straight in the eye. He licked at his lips slowly before replying. 'A young bloke called Gavin, I think – or maybe it was Gerry.'

Tony glanced across at Charlie, who nodded. Opening the door of the flat, they let themselves out.

As she was standing on the platform at Partick Station, waiting for the train to Westerton to arrive, Lesley Adams tried to figure out what was going on. She was totally confused – and she was worried. What had happened to Gavin? Why had he made himself scarce when he knew Inspector Anderson was coming to see him? Where had he been for the last two nights? Were the police really trying to pin John Preston's murder on him? Gavin had told her that he'd gone to a gig in Edinburgh with his pal, Stuart – and she believed him. So what was all this about him claiming to have been in The Jacobite Arms with his uncle? Was Gavin trying to cover up for Andy, provide him with an alibi? Everything would get straightened out when the police got in touch with Stuart and he confirmed that Gavin was with him in Edinburgh. But if things were as straightforward as that, why had Gavin gone to such great lengths to avoid talking to Anderson?

When the train pulled up at the platform, Lesley got on board. She would have to put Gavin's problems to the back of her mind. She'd be spending time with her mother today and, as with every other visit for the past two years, she wondered if her mother would recognise her.

When she arrived at reception in the Westerton, Lesley bumped into the senior staff nurse.

'How is my mother today, Emily?' Lesley asked.

'She was very confused this morning. She's having a real problem with her short term memory these days.'

'Tell me about it!' Lesley said.

'By the way,' Emily said. 'We had a police officer round here a couple of days ago. He was asking about you.'

'Really? What did he want?'

'He wanted to know if you were here last Saturday. When I told him you were, he wanted to know what time you left the building. All very mysterious.'

'What did you say to him?'

'I told him I'd seen you with your mother around ten thirty, but I'd no idea what time you left.'

'I can't even remember that myself,' Lesley said, thumbing back through the pages of the visitors' book. 'Ah, here it is. Ten forty-five. Miracles will never cease. For once, I actually remembered to sign out.'

'What was that all about?' Emily asked. 'Why was he asking those questions?

''I've no idea,' Lesley said, glancing at her watch. 'I'm sorry, Emily. I don't have time to stand around and chat. I need to go up and see my mother,' she added, walking across and pressing the button to call the lift.

Harry Thompson liked to start his rounds early on Saturday mornings so he could get to the pub in time for a lunchtime game of darts with his mates. There were nine girls he had to collect from today, now that the Nigerian bird had decided to join the club. Harry had been confident that she would. The girls were always shocked at first by the suggestion that they should go on the game, but when they had time to think things through, they nearly always decided to go along with it, the alternative being so much worse. They had to hand over half their takings to pay for the lawyer, but they got to keep the other half for themselves. That wasn't a bad deal.

Jim Colvin was pleased with Harry for signing up the new girl. On top of his basic pay, Harry got ten percent commission on the girls' takings – which amounted to a lot more than he ever used to earn delivering pizzas.

*

Gavin Carter rehearsed over and over again what he was going to say to his uncle while he was on his way across to Maryhill on the bus. He knew Andy would be spitting blood when he told him he was going to change his story, but sticking to Andy's version of events wasn't going to work. The cops knew fine well he wasn't in The Jaco last Saturday and there was nothing he could say or do that would convince them otherwise. If he told them he was in Edinburgh – and Stuart backed that story up – that would work. But he had no idea how he would be able to convince Andy of that.

Getting off the bus, Gavin walked to the mouth of Andy's close, then slowly climbed the stairs to the third floor. He felt his heart rate quicken as he knocked on the door.

'What happened to you?' Gavin stammered, staring at Andy's bruised face when he opened the door.

'It's nothing,' Andy assured him. 'I'm okay.'

'Who did that to you?'

'A couple of Jim Colvin's goons.'

'Why?'

'Colvin wasn't at all happy when he found out I'd told the cops that it was you and me who had nailed Mulgrew in The Jaco. He was worried that it might come back and bite him, so I was taught a lesson for stepping out of line.'

'Fucking hell!'

'Don't worry about it, son. Making sure you have an alibi is a lot more important than a couple of black eyes. Come on in and tell me what it was that you didn't want to talk about on the phone.'

Gavin hesitated. 'It's about the alibi, Andy. I don't think it's going to work.'

'What the hell are you on about? Of course it's going to work. All you have to do is stick to the story we agreed and everything will be fine. Don't add any bells and whistles. Don't say anything to the cops that we haven't discussed.'

'Andy… I don't want to do that. The cops will trip me up – I know they will. Or else Mulgrew will crack. Then I'll really be in deep shit. The fuzz will know that I killed Murdoch.'

'Leave me to take care of Mulgrew. I'll make sure he doesn't crack. And anyway, you can't change your story now, Gavin. That's a sure-fire way for the cops to know that you did in Murdoch.'

'I want to tell the polis that I was in Edinburgh with Stuart, Andy,' Gavin pleaded. 'I can make that story stick. I know I can.'

'For fuck's sake, Gavin – don't even think about going there! Listen to me and listen good. I'm looking at a six month stretch inside because I told the cops I'd nailed Mulgrew – and the only reason I did that was to give you an alibi. Then I got this,' he added, pointing at his face, 'because I pissed Jim Colvin off by telling the cops that you were with me in The Jaco when Mulgrew got nailed, so don't give me any crap about changing your story now and saying you were in Edinburgh with your pal. It wouldn't take the cops five minutes to prove that was a load of old bollocks. You were with me in The Jaco on Saturday night. Full stop. Have you got that?'

'But, Andy..' Gavin sank his teeth into his quivering lower lip.

'No buts,' Andy snapped, grabbing Gavin by his shoulders and pulling him towards him, their foreheads touching. 'Have you fucking-well got that?' he mouthed in Gavin's face.

'Aye,' Gavin muttered.

'Now get your arse out of here and go and see Anderson straight away,' Andy said, slowly releasing his grip. 'Come up with a good excuse for why you weren't in your bird's flat on Thursday night when he came to see you. Then tell him exactly the same story we told O'Sullivan. Word for word. You were with me in The Jaco at half-past ten last Saturday night when we nailed Mulgrew's hand to the bog door. Right?'

'Okay, Andy,' Gavin mumbled. 'Okay.'

'And for God's sake, make it sound fucking convincing,' Andy growled.

CHAPTER 24

Grace Adams had good days and bad days. This was a particularly bad day.

'Who are you?' she asked, sitting on the edge of the upright chair in her room, wringing her skeletal hands together.

'I'm Lesley, Mum.'

'I don't know anyone called Lesley.'

'I'm your daughter.'

'I don't have a daughter.'

'Yes, you do, Mum. You have two daughters.'

Lesley sat down on the bed and took her mother's hands in hers.

Grace furrowed her brow. 'Why are you here?'

'I come to see you every week.'

'Do you?' Grace shook her head in confusion as she slumped back in her chair.

'I brought some photos to show you,' Lesley said, letting go of her mother's hands and producing a battered photograph album from her handbag. She opened it at the first page and handed it across. 'This is one of you and Dad on your honeymoon.'

Grace peered at the photograph over the top of her spectacles. 'That's me and Archie,' she said, her red-rimmed eyes lighting up as her finger slowly traced the two smiling figures, sitting hand-in-hand on a bench on a wide promenade. It was low tide and the sun was setting. In the background, the sandy beach at Scarborough stretched a long way out towards the sea. 'I've never seen this photo before,' Grace said.

'Yes you have, Mum,' Lesley said, doing her best to suppress a sigh.

'Last week,' she muttered under her breath, 'and the week before - and the bloody week before that, you – '

'Eh? What was that you said?'

'Nothing, Mum.'

'I got a text from Tom Freer with the Parkers' address, sir,' Tony said to Charlie.

'Where do they live?'

'In Nitshill.'

'Put their address into the sat nav and we'll swing by their place on the way back to the office,' Charlie said. 'With a bit of luck, Mrs Parker might be home by now.'

When they drew up outside the Parkers' residence, Charlie pointed to a vehicle parked a few yards further along the street. 'It looks like our luck is in. That's the car that was in Malcolm Steel's drive earlier this morning.'

When Charlie rang the bell, Donald Parker came to the door.

'I'm sorry to disturb you at home on a Saturday morning, Mr Parker,' Charlie said. 'Would it be possible for us to have a word with your wife?'

'I'm afraid not, Inspector. At least, not today. She's down in Derby, visiting her sister. She won't be back until tomorrow. Can I ask what it is you want to talk to her about?'

'How did she travel down to Derby?' Charlie asked.

'She drove.'

'Is that not her car parked outside?' Charlie asked.

'That is her car. But she took mine to go to Derby. It's more comfortable for a long journey.' Parker looked perplexed. 'Would you mind telling me what this is all about?'

'Maybe it's not your wife we want to talk to after all,' Charlie said. 'Maybe it's you. Were you visiting Malcolm Steel last night?'

Parker's face flushed.

'I paid Mr Steel a visit earlier this morning,' Charlie said, 'and your wife's car was parked in his drive. Were you in his house at the time?' Parker's Adam's apple bulged as he swallowed hard. 'Were you there?' Charlie repeated.

Parker nodded, his eyes cast down.

'Did you overhear the conversation I had with Mr Steel?'

'I did,' he said quietly.

'So is it you that Mr Steel is trying to protect?' Charlie asked. 'Are you the friend whose name he refused to give us?'

Parker nodded again.

'Were you also with Mr Steel last Saturday night?' Charlie asked. 'On the night John Preston was murdered?'

'I was. My wife's been down in Derby for the past fortnight, Inspector. Malcolm and I have been seeing quite a lot of each other while she's been away.'

'As you overheard what was said this morning, you will know that I told Mr Steel to be in my office at twelve o'clock today.'

'Malcolm and I talked things through after you left. He will be coming to see you later this morning. I told him that he had to tell the police about us, otherwise he's going to get implicated in John Preston's murder, but he's not prepared to do that. He doesn't want me – or the school – to have to face the adverse publicity that making our relationship public would attract.'

'In that case, I suggest that you be in my office at twelve o'clock as well, Mr Parker, so we can get this sorted out.'

Parker nodded his agreement.

'Happy birthday to you!' Tony chanted when Sue took his call.

'Thanks.'

'Did you get my card?'

'Yes, you cheeky bugger!'

Tony laughed. 'What are your plans for today?' he asked.

'I'm going to take Jamie to the Riverside Museum this afternoon. We went there just after it opened a few months ago and he's been nagging me ever since to take him back.'

'Would it be okay if I come round to your place this evening?' Tony asked.

'Will you be able to get away?'

212

'I hope I'll be able to knock off at a reasonable time. I think your Dad's feeling a bit guilty about your birthday arrangements getting messed up.'

'So he should.'

'Assuming I can get away, what do you fancy doing this evening?'

'Definitely *not* what you suggested in your birthday card!'

'Ah, well, nothing ventured – ,' Tony said with an exaggerated sigh. 'I suppose that means I'll have to settle for the bit between your teeth and a three-line whip.'

'It's either that, or eggs, beans and chips.'

'Tough call.'

Harry Thompson looked at his watch. He was making good progress this morning – might even get to the pub early for once. Only one more to collect from, the new Nigerian girl.

Harry straightened his tie as he rang Chibundo Ikande's doorbell. She pressed the buzzer to let him in.

'Do you have the money for the lawyer?' Harry asked.

'No.'

Harry shrivelled his brow. 'What do you mean by 'no'?'

'I didn't do it – I couldn't go through with it.'

'But I fixed you up with a good client.'

'I didn't go to see him.'

'What the hell do you think you're playing at? You do realise that if you don't have a lawyer to lodge an appeal on your behalf, you and your daughter will be deported?'

'I spoke to my social worker. She's going to help me. She thinks I might qualify for legal aid. She said she'd look into that for me. She thinks I've got a good case.'

Harry cursed under his breath as he trudged back down the stairs. Jim Colvin wasn't going to be happy. He didn't like complications.

*

Donald Parker arrived a few minutes early for the twelve o'clock meeting. He was sitting with Charlie in his office when Malcolm Steel walked in.

'What are you doing here, Donald?' Steel said, open-mouthed.

'The police know about us, Malcolm,' Parker said. 'We have to tell them everything.'

'But Donald….' Steel stammered.

'I explained to Inspector Anderson that we were in the Citizens Theatre on the night John was murdered – and I told him that the staff will be able to confirm that we stayed on in the bar in the foyer for a glass of wine after the performance.'

'You didn't have to tell them about us, Donald,' Steel blurted out.

'I couldn't remain silent, Malcolm,' Parker said. 'I could hardly stand by and say nothing when the police were about to arrest you on suspicion of being implicated in John's murder.'

Gavin pulled Charlie Anderson's card from his hip pocket. He turned it over several times in his hand as he tried to pluck up the courage to call. Steeling himself, he punched the number into his mobile, waiting nervously as the phone rang out.

'This is Gavin Carter,' he said when Charlie answered.

'You and I need to talk,' Charlie said

'I know.'

'Where are you?' Charlie demanded.

'In Lesley Adams' flat.'

'Is she there?'

'No.'

'Stay there,' Charlie said. 'I'll be across in twenty minutes.'

Charlie called Tony O'Sullivan's mobile.

'Meet me outside Lesley Adams' flat in twenty minutes,' he said when Tony answered. 'We're going to have a chat with Gavin.'

Tony O'Sullivan was waiting in the mouth of the tenement close when Charlie drew up outside. They walked up the two flights of stairs together. When Charlie rang the bell, Gavin came to the door to let them in.

'What happened to you on Thursday night?' Charlie asked when they were seated round the kitchen table.

'I went out.'

'I gathered that,' Charlie said. 'Why?'

'I needed time to think.'

'What was the result?' Charlie asked.

Gavin hesitated. 'I want to tell you what I was doing last Saturday.'

'When I spoke to you and your uncle on Wednesday,' Tony interjected, 'you told me you were in The Jacobite Arms, nailing Jack Mulgrew's hand to the bog door. Are you now saying that's no longer the case?'

Gavin lowered his eyes. 'Yes.'

When Tony glanced across, Charlie nodded imperceptibly – a signal that he should continue.

'So if you weren't in The Jacobite Arms,' Tony said. 'Where were you?'

'I went to a gig in Edinburgh.'

'What gig?'

'*First Tiger's*.'

'Who or what are *First Tiger*?'

'A new Glasgow group.'

'Did you go there on your own?'

'No. One of my mates was performing with the group, so I went through with him.'

'What's this mate's name?'

'Stuart Morrison.'

'Where does he live?' Tony asked.

'He has a flat in Clydebank.'

'I'll need his address and his phone number,' Charlie said.

'I can give you that,' Gavin said, checking his phone and reading out the information. 'But he's not there right now. He's up in Aberdeen, visiting his mother. She broke her arm last week so he went up to give her a hand.'

'When will he be back?' Tony asked.

'Tonight. He's catching the half-past six train.'

'Okay,' Tony said. 'I'll want to know all about this trip of yours to Edinburgh. But before we go into that,' he said, leaning back in his chair, 'let's start with The Jacobite Arms. If you weren't with your uncle when he attacked Jack Mulgrew, why did you waste our time with that cock and bull story?'

'That was my uncle's idea,' Gavin said. 'He was trying to help me out. My Dad was in a poker school, so he could account for his movements last Saturday night and, if push came to shove, Andy could prove that he was in The Jaco at the time of Murdoch's murder. But Andy told me that your lot had to pin the murder on somebody and he thought you'd pick on me, so he wanted to make sure that I had an alibi.'

'What was wrong with telling us the truth?' Charlie asked.

'Andy said you would stitch me up. He said you'd scare the shit out of Stuart by threatening to charge him with being an accessory to murder.'

'We may very well do that,' Tony said, 'if this story of yours turns out to be as full of holes at the last one.'

'It isn't.'

'I'm going to ask you a few questions,' Charlie said, 'and Sergeant O'Sullivan is going to note down your answers. Do you understand that?'

Gavin nodded.

Charlie waited until Tony had taken his notepad and pen from his folder.

'Where did you meet up with your friend, Stuart, last Saturday?'

'In Queen Street Station.'

'At what time?'

'Just after six o'clock. We were going to catch the seventeen minutes past six train to Edinburgh.'

'Who got there first?'

'Stuart. He was waiting for me when I arrived.'

'What station did you get off at?'

'Waverley.'

'At what time?'

'Round about half-past seven.'

'What was the weather like through there?'

'Drizzly.'

'What did you do then?'

'We split up. Stuart had arranged to go to somebody's flat – I don't know where – to do some last-minute rehearsing with the group. The gig was in Whistle Binkies and *First Tiger* were scheduled to be on at eleven o'clock, so I arranged to see him there.'

'What did you do between seven-thirty and eleven o'clock?' Charlie asked.

'I just wandered around.'

'Three and a half hours wandering around Edinburgh?' Tony interjected. 'In the drizzle? What was the attraction? Are you a big fan of Georgian period architecture?'

Gavin looked askance. 'I didn't walk about all the time. I went to a couple of pubs.'

'Where?' Charlie asked.

'In Rose Street.'

'Which pubs?'

'I started off in The Abbotsford to get something to eat, then I went to another pub along the road. I don't remember what it was called. I headed back to Whistle Binkies before eleven o'clock for the gig, but when I got there I found out that everything was running late. *First Tiger* didn't get on stage until almost midnight. By the time they'd finished their slot we'd missed the last train back to Glasgow, so Stuart and I went to the bus station and caught a late-night bus.'

'What time did you get back to Glasgow?' Charlie asked.

'We got to Buchanan Street about half-past two and we picked up a taxi. It dropped me off here before taking Stuart to Clydebank.'

'Okay, Gavin,' Charlie said, standing up and arching his back. 'I think that's all we need for now. Is there anything else you want to tell us?'

Gavin shook his head.

'What did you make of that?' Charlie asked as they were walking back down the tenement stairs.

'It was a big improvement on his last version of events,' Tony said, 'but it's by no means certain that he's telling us the truth now.'

'We'll head back to the office now and bring the guys up to speed,' Charlie said. 'I'll call Renton and Freer and tell them to meet us in the incident room at four o'clock.'

Charlie walked along Dumbarton Road to where he'd parked his car. When he got behind the wheel, he called Colin Renton. 'We need to get our hands on some CCTV footage, Colin,' Charlie said when Renton took the call. 'I want to see everything there is from Queen Street Station between six o'clock and seven o'clock on the night of the murder – as well as the footage from Waverley Station between seven-fifteen and seven forty-five. When you've organised that, find out what CCTV is available from Rose Street on that evening, as well as from The Abbotsford Bar. And if there are any street cameras in the vicinity of Whistle Binkies, try to get your hands on that footage as well. We'll meet in the incident room at four o'clock. Tell Tom Freer to be there.'

As soon as he'd disconnected, Charlie phoned home.

'How are things?' Kay asked.

'I'm going to have a briefing session with the guys at four o'clock, then I think I'll call it a day. What are you up to?'

'I'm going to go over to Sue's place this afternoon to give her her presents,' Kay said, 'then I'll be bringing Jamie back here. He was really disappointed when Sue told him he wouldn't be spending the weekend with us, so I thought the least I could do was offer him a sleepover and a game of football with you tomorrow morning.'

'Thanks a lot!'

'Will Tony be able to get off work after your briefing session?'

'I think so.'

'Good. He was hoping to go across to see Sue this evening. It would be nice if they could spend some time together on her birthday.'

Colin Renton was with Charlie in the incident room when Tony came along the corridor. They broke off abruptly from their conversation when he walked in.

'I'm sorry I'm late, sir,' Tony said. 'I got caught up in the traffic.'

'No problem,' Charlie said. 'Colin's just told me that Parker and Steel's story checked out. The staff at the Citz have confirmed that they are regular theatregoers and that both of them were in the bar in the foyer at the time of the murder.'

'Which puts the focus back on Gavin,' Renton said. 'I've submitted a request for the CCTV footage from both Queen Street and Waverley stations, as well as whatever's available from Rose Street and The Abbotsford – and also from any cameras there might be in the vicinity of Whistle Binkies.'

'Will Tom Freer be joining us?' Tony asked.

'He was called away to deal with a break-in at a jeweller's in Argyle Street,' Charlie said. 'While we were waiting for you,' Charlie added, 'I brought Colin up to speed with what we found out from our talk with Gavin.'

'What did you make of his story this time, Tony?' Renton asked.

'He was a lot more confident today than when I spoke to him and his uncle on Wednesday,' Tony said.

'I don't understand any of this,' Renton said with a puzzled shake of the head. 'Andy Carter might be a heidbanger, but he's not stupid. There's no way he would have deliberately set himself up for a stretch in Barlinnie in order to give Gavin an alibi, unless he knew that Gavin had murdered Preston.'

'Gavin's pal, Stuart Morrison, will be on his way back to Glasgow tonight,' Charlie said. 'He's catching the half-past six train from Aberdeen, so he should get to Central Station around nine-thirty, which means he'll be home in Clydebank round about ten o'clock.'

'You and I could go across to his place and wait for him, Tony,' Renton suggested. 'That way we'd be able to find out if he's able to corroborate Gavin's story.'

'That's a good idea, Colin,' Charlie interjected, winking at Renton on Tony's blind side. 'Tony took a note of everything Gavin told us, so it would make sense for the two of you to interrogate Stuart before Gavin has an opportunity to nobble him.'

Tony grimaced. 'Gavin will probably have been on the phone to his pal by now, sir,' he said. 'They'll have got their act together.'

'You never know,' Charlie said. 'Something might've slipped through the cracks. What do you think, Colin?'

'I'm a great believer in striking while the iron is hot, sir.'

'So am I,' Charlie said.

'But we don't know that Stuart will go straight home as soon as he gets back to Glasgow, sir,' Tony protested. 'We could end up spending half the night hanging around outside his flat in Clydebank – and achieve nothing. Would it not be better to leave questioning him until the morning?'

Charlie rubbed at his chin reflectively. 'What do you reckon, Colin?' he asked.

'Tony might have a point there, sir,' Renton said, doing his best to suppress a grin.

'Okay,' Charlie said. 'How about we all knock off now and have an early night? We can pick up the threads in the morning. I'll meet you at half-past eight outside Stuart Morrison's flat in Clydebank, Tony. That way we'll be able to catch him cold. How about that?'

Tony's 'okay' came out from between gritted teeth

Renton and O'Sullivan both got to their feet.

'Would you hold back for a minute, Colin,' Charlie said. 'There's something else I want to talk to you about.'

When Tony had left the office, Charlie and Renton burst out laughing.

'A nice bit of role playing there, Colin,' Charlie said. 'Well done.'

'For a minute there I thought you were going to send me to freeze to death all night outside a flat in Clydebank,' Renton said.

Charlie chortled. 'As I was saying to you just before Tony arrived, it's Sue's birthday today. Earlier on, Tony was angling for an early finish tonight so he could go across and see her. I couldn't resist winding him up.'

'But a half-eight start tomorrow morning, sir?' Renton said. 'Ouch! That's a bit rough. Did you have to do that?'

'I like to keep him on his toes,' Charlie said with a smile. 'But I'll do the decent thing. I wouldn't be able to get to Clydebank by half-past eight anyway, because Kay's got me lined me to play football with my grandson tomorrow morning. I'll give Tony a call later on this evening and change the rendezvous to half-past ten.'

CHAPTER 25

As he was walking down the corridor away from Charlie's office, Tony pulled out his phone and called Sue.

'I've managed to get away,' he said when she took the call. 'Is there any chance you could organise a baby sitter so we could go out for something to eat?'

'I can do better than that. My Mum's taking Jamie for a sleepover. So, as it happens, I'm footloose and fancy free.'

'Brilliant! I'll try to book us a table. How about I come across to your place at seven o'clock and we take it from there?'

'That sounds like a plan.'

Gavin Carter scrambled to his feet when he heard the front door of the flat being opened.

'How was your mother?' he asked tentatively when Lesley walked into the lounge.

'What the hell's going on, Gavin?' Lesley snapped. 'Where have you been?'

'I.. I haven't been anywhere,' he stammered. 'I've just been wandering the streets.'

'Why did you disappear like that? I was worried sick.'

Gavin sank back down onto the settee. 'I'm in deep shit, Lesley. I'm in trouble with the polis – and my uncle is going to kill me.' Lesley could see the tears welling up in Gavin's eyes.

'It's okay, Gavin.' Lesley felt her anger dissipating. 'Nobody's going to kill you,' she said, sitting down beside him on the settee and taking his hand in hers. 'Tell me what happened.'

'The cops think that I killed Murdoch,' Gavin blurted out. 'But I wasn't even in Glasgow when it happened. I was through in Edinburgh with Stuart.'

'Inspector Anderson told me that you had confessed to assaulting a man in a pub in the Calton at the time of the murder. What on earth was all that about?'

'It was Andy's idea. He was sure that the cops would try to stitch me up – that they would try to pin the murder on me – so he told me to tell the polis that I was with him when he attacked a man in a pub at the time of the murder so as to give me an alibi. I didn't want to go along with that, but Andy made me do it. He said the cops wouldn't believe me if I told them I was in Edinburgh with Stuart.'

'You have got to tell the police the truth, Gavin.'

'I did. Anderson came to see me this afternoon.'

'Did he believe you?'

'I don't know,' Gavin said, easing his hand from Lesley's grip. 'I gave him Stuart's address and his phone number. When the cops talk to him, he'll confirm that I was with him in Edinburgh.'

'Then everything's going to be all right,' Lesley said.

'No it's not, Lesley. Everything's not going to be all right. You don't know my uncle. When he finds out that I told the cops I was in Edinburgh last Saturday he'll…. he'll…. Oh, for fuck's sake, I have no idea what he'll do.' Gavin buried his head in his hands, tears seeping from his eyes.

Sue flopped down on the back seat of the taxi that the waiter in the Chardon d'Or had called for them.

'That was fantastic,' she said, patting her bulging stomach. 'That might've been the best meal I've ever had.'

'It wasn't at all bad,' Tony agreed, loosening his trouser belt buckle as he clambered in beside her. 'It was lucky that they'd had a late cancellation.'

'That must have set you back a bit.'

'No expense spared for your birthday. But don't worry about the cost. I got a lot more for the Radiohead tickets on the Internet than I thought I would.'

'One of the presents my Mum gave me,' Sue said as they were getting out of the taxi, 'was a twenty year-old bottle of McCallan. Do you fancy trying it?'

'Absolutely. But the bad news,' Tony said as Sue was turning the key in her front door, 'is that I have to be on the road before eight o'clock tomorrow morning.'

'On a Sunday? You have got to be kidding!'

'I'm afraid not. I have to meet your father in Clydebank at half-past eight.'

Sue pulled a face, then threw her arms around Tony's shoulders and pulled him towards her. 'In that case,' she whispered, nibbling gently at his earlobe. 'The whisky is on the table in the lounge. Why don't you put on some music and fix us a couple of drinks while I slip into something less comfortable?'

As Sue was disappearing up the stairs, the phone in Tony's jacket pocket started to vibrate. Checking it, he saw the call was from Charlie. He immediately cut the call and switched his phone off before stuffing it back into his pocket.

Sunday 11 September

Having set his sat nav, Tony O'Sullivan was breaking the speed limit as he drove across town. He arrived outside Stuart Morrison's flat in Clydebank just after eight-thirty. Sitting huddled in his car, he glanced continually in his rear-view mirror. There was no sign of Charlie. He checked his watch again. It wasn't like Charlie to be late. Switching on his phone, he saw that he had received a text message at ten-fifteen the previous evening:

> I tried calling you several times, but your phone was switched off. I don't think we need to go

to Stuart Morrison's place so early tomorrow morning. How about we meet outside his flat at half-past ten?

Tony thumped the steering column several times with his closed fist. Firing the ignition, he drove into the centre of Clydebank. When he spotted a café that was open, he pulled up. He went inside and ordered a fried egg roll, a roll with Lorne sausage and a coffee to take away. Having picked up a copy of the Sunday Herald from the newsagent's next door, he drove back and parked outside Stuart Morrison's flat.

Tony glanced in his rear-view mirror when he heard a car pull up behind him. He dropped his newspaper onto the passenger seat and got out of the car.

'On time for once, I'm pleased to see,' Charlie said, locking his car.

'I just got here, sir.'

'You got my text okay last night?'

'Of course.'

'Did you and Sue find somewhere to go?'

'I managed to get us a table at the Chardon d'Or. They'd had a cancellation.'

'I've never been there,' Charlie said. 'I hear it's good.'

Tony nodded.

'I changed our meeting time to half-past ten because I had to play football with Jamie this morning,' Charlie said, 'and also because I thought you might appreciate having a relaxed start to the day,' he added.

'Thanks.' Tony forced a wan smile.

Stuart Morrison was eating a bowl of cornflakes when he heard the ring on his bell. When he came to the door, Charlie introduced himself and Tony. They showed their warrant cards.

'Is it all right if we come in?' Tony asked. 'There are a few questions we'd like to ask you.'

'What about?'

'About what you were doing last Saturday night,' Tony said.

Stuart stood aside to let them in. 'Is it okay if I finish my breakfast while we talk?'

'Sure,' Tony said.

'I was playing at a gig in Edinburgh,' Stuart said when they were seated at the kitchen table. 'A mate of mine, Stevie McCormick, is the main man in a group called *First Tiger*. The group's drummer had called off sick and Stevie had asked me stand in for him because I'd played with the group a couple of time before. I jumped at the chance. I reckon *First Tiger* could be the next *Texas* and I was hoping that if I did well on the night, Stevie might take me on permanently.'

'How did it go?' Tony asked.

'Pretty well, I think.'

'Did you go through to Edinburgh on your own?' Charlie asked.

'No, I went with a mate.'

'What mate?' Tony asked.

'Gavin Carter. He and I often go to gigs together and when I told him I would be playing with *First Tiger* he decided to tag along.'

Charlie proceeded to go through the same list of questions he'd asked Gavin, with Tony noting down Stuart's answers.

'You said that you and Gavin split up round about seven-thirty when you got to Waverley Station,' Charlie said. 'Why was that?'

'I'd arranged to meet the *First Tiger* guys at eight o'clock to run over some of the stuff. Gavin wanted to get something to eat so he went to The Abbotsford. They do good fish and chips,' Stuart added.

'I'm told that your gig started late,' Charlie said.

Stuart shrugged. 'That's par for the course.'

'What time did you get on?'

'Just after midnight.'

'Did you see Gavin in Whistle Binkies before the gig started?'

'No. I was in the back room with the *First Tiger* guys up until the last minute before we went on stage. We needed all the time we could get to go over the music.'

'Do you know if Gavin was in the pub when you started your performance?'

'I think he was, but I couldn't swear to it. The lights shine straight into your face when you're on stage, so it's not easy to make out who is out front.'

'When did you actually see him?'

'After our session was over.'

'Which was?'

'Round about quarter to one.'

'Is there anything else we need to ask Stuart?' Charlie said, turning to Tony.

Tony shook his head.

'What did you make of that?' Charlie asked as they were walking back to their respective cars.

'I'm not sure,' Tony said. 'Stuart's version of events was the same as Gavin's, but it was all a bit too glib for my liking. If they were telling us the truth, I would've expected a few minor discrepancies along the way. Maybe I'm being over cynical, but the fact that every detail they gave us ties up leads me to think that they might have concocted the story together.'

'Okay,' Charlie said, getting into his car and winding down the driver's window. 'We'll take a checkpoint in the incident room at three o'clock. I'll round up the team. By that time, Renton should have got his hands on any relevant CCTV footage. On the way back to the office,' Charlie added, 'I'll stop off at Jack Mulgrew's place and see if he's in.'

Charlie spotted Jack Mulgrew coming out of his tenement close as he was driving along his street. Pulling up alongside him, Charlie flung open the passenger door.

'Where are you going?' Charlie asked.

Mulgrew bent down low to see who was in the car. 'Oh, for fuck's sake! You again? Do you lot never give up?'

'I said – where are you going?'

'If you must know, I'm going to The Jaco.'

'Get in – I'll give you a lift.'

'I can walk.'

'I said – get in,' Charlie repeated forcibly.

Reluctantly, Mulgrew slid himself onto the passenger seat. 'What do you want now?' he grumbled.

'I want to know who attacked you.'

'How often do I have to fucking-well tell you? It was Andy Carter and some young bloke – I'm not sure what his name was.'

'The time for playing games is over, Mulgrew,' Charlie said. 'I'm conducting a murder investigation and, if you don't tell me right now who attacked you, I'm going to charge you with perverting the course of justice. For that, you could get five years.'

The colour ebbed from Mulgrew's face. 'Andy Carter nailed my hand to the bog door,' he said. 'That's the God's honest truth.'

'I don't doubt that for one minute, but he didn't have a young bloke with him, did he?' Mulgrew didn't respond. 'There are no witnesses here,' Charlie said. 'Tell me who was with Carter when you got attacked last Saturday.'

Mulgrew's tongue flicked back and forth across his lips. 'I canny,' he stammered.

'Five years,' Charlie repeated slowly.

'He would fucking-well kill me,' Mulgrew muttered, shaking his head.

'Listen to me very carefully, Mulgrew. I need to know who was with Andy Carter when he attacked you. Whatever you tell me will remain confidential. It will never get back to whoever it was. If you don't want to press charges against him, I'm not going to pursue it. But it's critical to the murder investigation that I know who was there.'

Mulgrew hesitated. 'If he ever finds out that I told you, I'm as good as dead.'

'He won't. You have my word on that.'

Mulgrew gazed down at his feet. 'It was Jim Colvin,' he said quietly.

'Why did he nail you?'

'I owed him money. I borrowed fifty quid from him last month and he says I now owe him five hundred.'

'Are you going to pay him?'

'What do you think?' Mulgrew said, slowly massaging the palm of his right hand. 'I've been told to meet him in The Jaco at one o'clock today and if I don't pay up I'm going to get another doing – and next week I'll owe him six hundred.'

'Do you have the money?'

'Aye,' Mulgrew said, tapping his inside jacket pocket.

'How did you manage to get your hands on five hundred quid?'

'I pawned my mother's engagement ring and her wedding ring for four hundred – and I flogged my telly to one of my neighbours for the other hundred.'

Colin Renton and Tom Freer joined Charlie and Tony in the incident room at three o'clock.

'First, let me give you an update on my chat this afternoon with Jack Mulgrew,' Charlie said. 'To no one's great surprise, he told me that Gavin Carter wasn't anywhere near The Jacobite Arms on the night of the murder.'

Charlie turned to Renton. 'Do we have anything from the CCTV, Colin?'

'I've been through the footage,' Renton said. 'It looks like Gavin was telling us the truth this time around, at least, up to a point. Gavin met his pal, Stuart Morrison, at Queen Street Station just after six o'clock on the day in question. They were sighted getting on board the six seventeen train to Edinburgh – and they were picked up again on camera in Waverley Station when they got off the train. They split up at seven twenty-five and went their separate ways. The next images we have of them together is in Edinburgh bus station at quarter past one in the morning, and they were picked up again in Glasgow, getting off a bus in Buchanan Street bus station at two forty a.m. on Sunday morning.'

'What did you mean when you said Gavin was telling us the truth 'up to a point'?' Tony queried.

'There is no footage of Gavin being anywhere near Rose Street – and he certainly wasn't in The Abbotsford at any time on Saturday evening,' Renton said. 'However, there is one very interesting thing. I managed to get my hands on CCTV footage from the cameras on North Bridge, which is close to Whistle Binkies. They show Gavin walking towards the pub all right, but not before eleven o'clock as he told us. He crossed North Bridge at twenty-past twelve.'

CHAPTER 26

Charlie rested his chin on his fingers.

'Let's think this through,' he said. 'Gavin arrives in Edinburgh with his mate just before seven-thirty last Saturday, then they split up. Gavin gives us a fictitious account of his movements and the next known sighting of him is at twenty-past twelve on North Bridge, which leaves the best part of five hours unaccounted for. Who's to say he didn't nip back to Glasgow during that time and bump off Preston?'

'Do you want me to request the CCTV footage from Waverley Station and Edinburgh bus station throughout those five hours?' Renton asked.

'It's worth a shot, Colin. Check it out. However, if Gavin isn't picked up on camera in either of those locations, that won't necessarily prove anything. He wouldn't have to have returned to Glasgow from either Waverley Station or the bus station. He might have caught a train from the Haymarket, or he could've boarded a Glasgow-bound bus in Princes Street – or anywhere else along the route for that matter. CCTV is a useful tool when someone isn't trying to hide their movements,' Charlie added, 'but all it takes is a change of clothing and a hoodie for someone to disappear under the radar.

'Stuart Morrison said he was rehearsing with the *First Tiger* group before the gig started,' Charlie continued, 'and he told us that he didn't actually see Gavin until after the gig was over – which was around quarter to one in the morning. That means that Gavin had sufficient time to go back to Glasgow, murder Preston, then get back to Edinburgh and be in Whistle Binkies by half-past twelve. However,' Charlie reflected, 'if Stuart was trying to cover up for Gavin, it would've been the easiest thing in the world for him to tell us he'd seen his pal in Whistle Binkies before the gig started, which would've ruled Gavin out from being in Glasgow at the time of the murder.'

'What do you conclude from that, sir?' Tony asked.

'That there's a high probability that Stuart Morrison is telling us the truth. However, as far as Gavin's concerned,' Charlie mused, 'that's a completely different kettle of fish. We need to get to the bottom of what's going on. Give Gavin a call, Tony. Tell him that I want to see him here at ten o'clock sharp tomorrow morning – without his uncle!'

Tony O'Sullivan was standing in front of the vending machines, waiting for his coffee cup to fill, when his mobile rang. He recognised Bert Tollin's voice.

'I picked up a snippet that I thought might be of interest to you, Mr O'Sullivan,' Tollin said.

'I'm all ears, Bert,' Tony said, picking up his coffee cup and taking a sip.

'Are you still interested in Jim Colvin?'

'Very much so.'

'One of Colvin's more profitable sidelines is exploiting female asylum seekers. His guys hang around outside the foodbank in Govanhill and follow the girls when they come out to find out where they live. Colvin's main interest is in young, black girls. When one of his guys identifies a potential target, he rings the girl's doorbell and tells her he's from the Home Office. He tells the girl that her application for asylum has been turned down and threatens her with deportation. He says her only hope of staying in the country is to lodge an appeal and for that she'll need a lawyer. He tells her he can put her in touch with a good one who'll be prepared to fight her case, but he's expensive. The girls never have the kind of money Colvin's guy is talking about, so he helpfully suggests a way they can earn a lot of money quickly.'

'Not by going on the game, by any chance?' Tony chipped in.

'You're way ahead of me, Mr O'Sullivan. The girls are often desperate, so some of them agree to go along with it. Colvin's guy says he'll arrange with the lawyer to accept payments in instalments and that he'll come round on Saturday mornings to pick up the money. But, of course, the money the girls earn from prostitution never goes anywhere near a lawyer.'

'Colvin's a slippery customer, Bert,' Tony said. 'Is there any way he can he be linked to exploiting those girls?'

'I was coming to that, Mr O'Sullivan. One of the new girls – she's Nigerian – is rocking the boat. Initially, she agreed to go on the game, but she changed her mind. When Colvin's guy turned up to collect money from her yesterday, she told him she hadn't kept the rendezvous with the client that had been set up for her – which, by the way, was with one of the city councillors who is on Colvin's payroll. That totally pissed Colvin off, so the girl's going to be taught a lesson. And Colvin being Colvin, he's going to be there in person to oversee her punishment.'

'How did you find out all this?'

'I was out for a drink last night with a bloke called Harry Thompson. He's one of the guys Colvin hires to set up the girls and collect their money. Harry's got a loose tongue at the best of times, but he blabbers his mouth off when he's had a few. He's been told to meet Colvin outside the girl's flat at three o'clock tomorrow afternoon. His instructions are to carve up the girl's face – leave a few visible scars – so as to discourage any of the other girls from stepping out of line. Harry's not at all happy about it. He's never hurt a woman in his life, but he knows that if he refuses to do what Colvin tells him, he'll be the one who'll be needing stitches.'

'Do you know the girl's name and where she lives, Bert?'

'Not exactly. Her first name's Chibando, or Chibundo, or something like that. I'm not sure, exactly. Harry was slurring his words and I didn't want to appear too curious. I did manage to wheedle out of him that she lives in Calder Street but I didn't find out any more than that.'

'Okay, Bert. Thanks. I'll see what I can do with that information.'

When he disconnected, Tony called Charlie and relayed what Tollin had told him.

'Get on the blower to the Home Office in London straight away,' Charlie said. 'Use the hotline. An approximation of her first name and the street she lives in will probably be enough for them to iden-tify her. Try to find out her full name and address and get them to check her immigration status.'

When Tony got in touch with the Home Office he was given Chi-bundo Ikande's name and address. He was told that that her case was under review and that no decision would be made for another few months.

It was just after six o'clock when Tony and Charlie drew up outside the address in Calder Street. When they rang the doorbell, a female voice answered.

'Is that Chibundo Ikande?' Charlie asked.

'Yes.'

'This is the police. Would you let us in, please.'

When Chibundo opened the door of her flat, Charlie and Tony showed her their warrant cards.

'We'd like to talk to you, Ms Ikande,' Charlie said. 'Is it all right if we come in?'

Chibundo nodded nervously.

'We're here regarding your immigration status,' Tony said as he was closing the front door behind him.

Chibundo backed away, a look of panic in her eyes. 'I'm going to lodge an appeal against the decision. My social worker is looking into that for me.'

The sound of her mother's raised voice wakened Chibundo's daughter and she started to wail. Crossing quickly to the cot by the window, Chibundo picked up the infant and hugged her tightly to her chest, rocking her back and forth to try to still her crying.

'There's no need for you to lodge an appeal,' Tony said. 'Your case is still pending. No decision will be made for some time yet.'

Chibundo looked confused. 'But a man from the Home Office came to see me. He told me my application had been turned down. He said he could put me in touch with a lawyer who would fight the case on my behalf, but I couldn't afford him.'

'We're aware of that,' Tony said. 'That's why we're here. The man who came to see you wasn't from the Home Office. He works for a racketeer.'

Chibundo's jaw dropped.

'Did he suggest that you go on the game in order to raise money for the lawyer?' Charlie asked.

Chibundo blushed as she cuddled her daughter closer to her breast. 'He set up an appointment for me with a client, but I didn't go. I couldn't do it.'

'We have reason to believe that the man who claimed to be from the Home Office, and the person he works for, are going to come here tomorrow afternoon at three o'clock,' Tony said. 'They're not happy about the fact that you didn't go to meet the client and they intend to make an example of you – and they intend to resort to violence in order to make their point.'

'However, there is no need for you to be concerned about that,' Charlie interjected. 'We will not allow that to happen.'

'What do you normally do on Mondays?' Tony asked.

'Go to the foodbank,' Chibundo said. 'They're open on Mondays, Wednesdays and Fridays.'

'What time do you go there?' Tony asked.

'They open from half-past twelve to half-past two. I usually go round about two o'clock.'

'I want you to go there tomorrow as soon as they open,' Charlie said, 'and make sure you're back here by two o'clock.'

'All right.'

'How many rooms do you have here?' Tony asked.

'Just this one – and the bathroom.'

'Okay if I take a look?' Tony asked.

'Yes.'

Tony crossed to the bathroom and stuck his head round the door. 'It's a bit tight, sir, but it should be okay.'

'With your permission,' Charlie said. 'We'll be here tomorrow at two o'clock.'

Gently stroking her daughter's brow, Chibundo nodded.

Monday 12 September

When Gavin Carter arrived at CID headquarters in Pitt Street, just before ten o'clock, he was shown into an interview room. Charlie and Tony deliberately left him alone with his thoughts for fifteen minutes before going downstairs.

'Do you know why you're here Gavin?' Charlie asked as he lowered himself stiffly down onto the chair on the opposite side of the steel desk.

'All I know is that O'Sullivan told me I had to be here at ten o'clock.'

'Can you hazard a guess as to why?' Tony asked as he took the seat beside Charlie.

Gavin shook his head.

'Let's start with The Abbotsford,' Tony said. 'The CCTV cameras covering the entrance to the pub don't show you going in on the night in question. Why do you think that was?'

'The cameras must've missed me.'

'If that's the attitude you're going to take,' Charlie said with a slow shake of the head, 'it's going to be a very long day.'

Gavin sucked hard on his bottom lip.

'There are CCTV cameras the length of Rose Street,' Tony said. 'By some strange coincidence, all of those cameras seem to have missed you as well.' Gavin gazed sullenly at the floor. 'But on the other hand,' Tony continued, 'you were picked up on camera as you were crossing North Bridge on your way to Whistle Binkies, but not at eleven o'clock as you told us. You were seen there at twenty-past twelve. How do you account for that?'

Gavin didn't respond.

'We know you arrived at Waverley Station at twenty-five past seven,' Charlie said. 'And we know you were on North Bridge at twenty-past twelve. What I want to know is what you were doing during the intervening five hours.'

'Perhaps you came back to Glasgow?' Tony suggested. 'Perhaps you bumped off Preston, then went back through to Edinburgh in time to team up with your mate?'

'That's total crap!' Gavin's gaze flicked from Charlie to Tony and back again. 'I stayed in Edinburgh. I had nothing to do with Preston's murder. For God's sake, you've got to believe me!'

'You're not making that easy,' Charlie said. 'Let's start again. Did you or did you not go to The Abbotsford?' Gavin slowly shook his head. 'Were you ever in Rose Street?' He shook his head again. 'Where were you?'

'I.. I can't tell you.'

'You mean you won't tell us?' Tony said. 'In which case, a quick trip to Glasgow and back is beginning to look like favourite.'

'I told you!' Gavin shouted out. 'I had nothing to do with Preston's murder!'

'You've already given us two fictitious accounts of your movements on the night in question,' Charlie snapped. 'Either you provide us with evidence that you stayed in Edinburgh or else I'm going to charge you with the murder of John Preston.'

The colour drained from Gavin's complexion. He kept his gaze fixed firmly on the floor. 'I was with someone,' he said quietly.

'Who were you with?' Charlie demanded.

'A woman.'

'What were you doing?' Tony asked.

'For Christ's sake! What do you think?'

Tony and Charlie exchanged a quick glance.

'Where were you?' Tony demanded.

'At her place.'

'Where's that?'

'She has a flat near the Haymarket.'

'I need her name,' Tony said.

Gavin hesitated. 'It's Sheila.'

'I need her full name.'

Gavin hesitated again. 'She's married,' he muttered.

'It's not the first time that's happened,' Tony said. 'And I dare say it won't be the last. What's her full name?'

Gavin exhaled noisily. 'Sheila McVey.'

'Well, well, well,' Charlie said, smiling. 'That wouldn't be the Sheila McVey who owns SHERPA, by any chance?'

Gavin nodded nervously.

'Do you know her, sir?' Tony asked.

'I've spoken to the lady on the phone.'

'Where does she live?' Tony asked, turning to Gavin.

'She has a flat in Rothesay Terrace. I don't know the number. The first time I went through to Edinburgh for an interview she met me at Haymarket Station and she took me there.' Gavin paused. 'Will you have to involve her?' he asked.

'If you're going to be relying on her to corroborate your story and avoid a murder charge,' Charlie said. 'I think that would be a good idea. Don't you?'

'Fucking hell!' Gavin dragged his fingers through his gelled hair. 'Her old man's a jealous bastard. If he finds out about us, he'll kill us both.'

'We will be discreet,' Charlie said reassuringly. 'As far as we're concerned, there's no reason her husband should have to find out what the two of you were up to.'

'How long have you been seeing her?' Tony asked.

'On and off for the past couple of years. Lesley put me in touch with her. She handles the commissions for SHERPA. She told me that she liked what she'd seen of my stuff and she invited me back through to Edinburgh to discuss a possible contract.'

'I gather she had something else she wanted to discuss, apart from a contract?' Tony suggested.

'She's on her own a lot,' Gavin said. 'She's bored out of her skull. Her old man's got some high-powered job in an offshore oil company and he spends a lot of time away on business. At least, that's what he tells Sheila. She's convinced he's shagging his secretary. When Sheila knows he's going to be away overnight, she gets me to come through. She phoned me last Friday and told me to come through on Saturday evening because it was her birthday. She told me I couldn't stay over because her old man was going to a meeting in Perth and he'd be back at their place around eleven o'clock.'

'How do you explain your trips away to Lesley Adams?' Tony asked.

'I make up stories about going to computer conferences and having to stay over, but I didn't have to do that this time because I knew Stuart was going through to Edinburgh for a gig and I could tag along with him. And I knew I wouldn't be staying the night because Sheila's old man was coming home.'

'Does your friend, Stuart, know what you were up to?' Tony asked.

'No way! He's totally useless at keeping secrets. There's too much of a risk that he would let something slip in front of Lesley. To make sure he wouldn't suspect anything, I stayed on the train with him as far as Waverley. When we split up I told him I was going to The Abbotsford to get something to eat.'

'Did you go straight to Mrs McVey's flat when you got to Waverley?' Charlie asked.

'Yes.'

'How long did you stay there?'

'I was only planning to be there for a couple of hours, but her old man called her at nine o'clock to tell her that his business meeting in Perth had overrun and he would have to stay the night.'

'Saturday's an odd night to have a late-running business meeting,' Tony suggested.

'That's what Sheila said.'

'What time did you leave her place?'

'Just before twelve o'clock.'

'Was that not cutting it fine?' Tony asked. 'If your pal's gig had run to schedule it would've been over by midnight.'

'Gigs often run late. I phoned Whistle Binkies at half-past ten to find out what time *First Tiger* would be on. They told me there was no way their slot would start before midnight.'

'I've probably still got Mrs McVey's mobile number somewhere,' Charlie said to Gavin, 'but give it to me again, just in case I can't lay my hands on it.'

'Why do you need to talk to her?' Gavin protested.

'We could get in touch with her and arrange a suitable time to go and see her,' Tony said, 'or else we could drop in unannounced when her hubby might be at home. Which of those do you think she'd prefer?'

Muttering under his breath, Gavin checked his mobile and read out Sheila McVey's phone number.

'Of course,' Tony added, 'even if Mrs McVey confirms your story, this could turn out to be another red herring.'

'What are you on about?'

'You realised you were in deep shit, so perhaps you asked this woman to bail you out? Maybe you've got a hold over her?' Tony suggested. 'Perhaps you're blackmailing her? Threatening to spill the beans to her old man about what the two of you have been up to if she doesn't provide you with an alibi?'

'That's absolute pish!'

'Is it? If your lover is the only person who's in a position to corroborate your story,' Tony said, 'it's a flimsy alibi at best.'

Gavin gazed at the phone in his hand. 'There is something else,' he said hesitantly.

'What?' Tony asked.

'I took a – ' Looking up, he broke off.

'You took a what?'

'I took a selfie in her flat.'

'So what?'

'The photo will show the location and the time it was taken.'

'Let me see it,' Tony said.

Reluctantly, Gavin swiped to a photo in his phone and handed it across. Tony studied the image before handing the phone to Charlie. Two naked people; Gavin, grinning, lying on his back on a double bed, straddled by an attractive woman who looked to be about thirty. She was holding up a glass of champagne and smiling for the camera. The strapline at the top of the photo read: Edinburgh: 3 September : 22h46.

'So that's how you chose to mark the anniversary of your brother's death,' Charlie said, throwing the phone back to Gavin. 'Instead of taking a bunch of flowers to his grave like any normal brother would, you cooked up a tissue of lies so you could cheat on your girlfriend who, as far as I can see, is the only person who really cares about you.'

Gavin bit into his bottom lip as he stared at the floor. 'I loved my wee brother,' he muttered.

'Well all I can say,' Charlie said with a dismissive shake of the head, 'is that you've got a very funny way of showing it.'

CHAPTER 27

Harry Thompson had been parked in his usual spot for half an hour when he saw Chibundo Ikande coming out of the foodbank. Another new girl had come out ten minutes before her. Normally, Harry would have followed the new girl home, but his heart wasn't in it. He'd thought about calling in sick today, but Jim Colvin would have seen through that. He'd spent most of the morning trying to figure out if there was any way he could get out of doing what he'd been told to do this afternoon. Was there was some way he could warn Chibundo? She seemed like a nice enough girl. Was there any way he could get a message to her, telling her not to be in her flat at three o'clock? Harry shook his head in resignation. At best, all that would achieve would be to delay things until tomorrow – it wouldn't solve anything. And there was no point in him trying to talk Jim Colvin out of going through with it. When Colvin made up his mind about something, he never changed it.

When Tony O'Sullivan arrived outside Chibundo Ikande's flat at two o'clock he found Charlie waiting for him. Having dropped off the equipment, Tony drove round the corner and parked his car in a side street before hurrying back to the flat.

By half-past two, Charlie and Tony had completed the installation and tested the sound system. Two hidden microphones, one in the infant's cot, the other taped to the underside of the kitchen table, both linked to a recording device in the bathroom.

'As I told you yesterday, Chibundo,' Charlie said, 'we expect two men to come here at three o'clock. I want you to let them in. Try to act as naturally as possible – and leave the rest to us. Okay?'

Chibundo nodded nervously.

'How do you want to play things as far as Gavin's concerned?' Tony asked, shifting his position to try to relieve the numbness in his buttocks as he sat perched on the edge of the bath in Chibundo's cramped bathroom.

Squatting on the toilet seat, Charlie rubbed at his chin. 'We'll go through to Edinburgh and have a chat with Mrs McVey.'

'Do you want me to organise that?'

'Yes,' Charlie said. 'Give her a call this afternoon and, if possible, try to set something up for tomorrow morning. If she's available, we can go through to Edinburgh by train.'

Charlie checked his watch. 'It's quarter past three,' he complained. 'Are you sure Bert Tollin said three o'clock?'

'That's what he told me and – '

'Shush!' Charlie's command cut Tony off as they heard the ring of the doorbell. Leaning forward, Charlie activated the recording device as Chibundo buzzed to let them in.

'I wasn't expecting to see you,' Chibundo said, sounding puzzled as she opened her door and saw Harry. 'What do you want?'

'We need to have a word with you,' Harry stated.

'I don't have time. I'm just about to go out.'

'Good girl,' Charlie whispered.

'You're not going anywhere, dear.' Tony recognised Jim Colvin's voice. 'Explain to this daft, wee bitch why missing an appointment with one of our clients is a very bad idea, Harry,' Colvin said, producing a flick knife from his jacket pocket and handing it across.

Harry hesitated as he took the knife. 'Do we really have to do this, boss? Could we not just slap her around a bit?'

'For fuck's sake! Do I have to do everything myself?' Colvin shouted, his eyes blazing as he snatched the knife back and snapped open the blade. Placing the tip of the knife against Harry's temple, with one quick movement Colvin swept the blade down as far as his chin. 'There's nothing to it!' he yelled. 'It's as simple as that!'

To the accompaniment of Harry's agonised yelp as he sank to his knees, Colvin turned to face Chibundo.

'You or the wean?' he snarled, nodding in the direction of the cot. 'Who's it going to be first?' Twirling the bloodied blade, he jabbed at the air in front of Chibundo's face.

Colvin spun round when Charlie and Tony burst into the room.

The Jacobite Arms was quiet when Tony O'Sullivan walked into the pub at six o'clock.

Seeing Tony arrive, the landlord acknowledged his presence with a wave.

'I don't know how many times I've told my customers that your lot are a bunch of useless wankers,' he said, polishing a pint tumbler on a grubby tea towel as Tony walked up to the bar. 'But I take it all back,' he said, stretching up to put the tumbler into the overhead rack. 'It seems that, just occasionally, you can be useful wankers.'

'What brought about the sudden change of heart?'

'Good news travels fast. The word is that Jim Colvin's going to be out of circulation for quite some time, which means his dole-day lending customers are now dole-day spending customers.'

'We'll need all the help we can get in order to secure a conviction,' Tony said. 'Do you think some of your customers might be prepared to testify against him?'

The landlord chortled. 'Because they're willing to splash out a bit of cash, it doesn't mean they're prepared to commit suicide.'

'How about you?'

'You tried that one on before,' he said with a grin. 'The answer's the same. But I'm more than happy to show my gratitude. How about your usual – on the house? Which, if I remember correctly, is a soda water and lime?'

'Thanks,' Tony said. 'With a lump of ice.'

'We arrest Colvin at quarter past three,' Tony said, 'and by six o'clock everyone in The Jacobite Arms knows he's in custody. How do they do it?'

'They say that good news travels fast,' Charlie said, swinging his feet up onto his desk. 'Did you get anywhere with the landlord?'

'The good news is that I got a soda water and lime on the house,' Tony said.

'Don't forget to include that in your tax return.'

'But the bad news is that there's no way he, or anyone else, is prepared to testify against Colvin.'

'That's hardly a surprise,' Charlie said. 'Any news on the extent of Harry Thomson's injuries?'

'He needed twelve stitches, but nothing life threatening, apparently.'

'How is Chibundo Ikande bearing up?'

'She's a strong lady,' Tony said. 'She's prepared to take the stand and testify that Harry Thompson impersonated a Home Office official and that he and Jim Colvin incited her to prostitution – and she says she'll talk to some of the other girls who use the foodbank and try to get them to testify. What with that, and the GBH charge, it should be enough to get Colvin sent down for a long stretch.'

'Arrange for a message to be sent to the Home Office,' Charlie said. 'Let them know that Chibundo was instrumental in getting a particularly nasty customer put away. I don't know if that will cut any ice with the authorities as far as the lassie's asylum status is concerned, but it can't do any harm.'

'Will do.'

Having phoned ahead to let her know he would be across as soon as he could get away, it was after eight o'clock by the time Tony got to Sue's place.

'Is Jamie in bed?' he asked when she came to the door.

'Shhhh!' Sue said, placing her index finger across his lips. 'I've just got him settled down,' she said in a whisper.

Tony produced a chilled bottle of Prosecco from behind his back. 'I thought you might fancy a nightcap,' he said as he stepped across the threshold.

'You're incorrigible!' Sue raised her eyebrows. 'You do realise that I've got work to go to tomorrow?'

'So have I.'

'I've got a full timetable.'

'And I'm going to have to put up with your Dad all day, starting at nine o'clock. That means I need a drink.'

Sue smiled, stepping to one side to let him in. 'Okay, but just the one glass for me.'

'If you're only going to have one glass, that means I'll have to drink the rest of the bottle by myself,' Tony said as he was stripping the foil from the cork. 'Which means there's no way I'll be able to drive.'

'I very much doubt if you'll be able to do anything worth talking about if you drink the rest of the bottle.'

'That sounds like a challenge.'

'You wish!' Sue said. 'Go on through to the lounge and put on some music – and I mean quiet music – and I'll fetch the glasses.'

A Radiohead CD, with the volume turned right down, was playing when Sue came into the lounge with two wine glasses and a bowl of salted peanuts. Tony popped the cork on the Prosecco bottle and poured out their drinks.

'How did you manage to get the wine chilled?' Sue asked as she flopped down on the settee beside him.

'It's straight out of M&S's cold cabinet.'

'It's nice,' Sue said, taking a long, slow sip. 'Very more-ish.'

'Do I gather that madame might manage more than one glass?'

Sue took a handful of peanuts and washed them down with a slurp of wine. She put her glass down on the coffee table. 'Just to save you from yourself, madame might,' she said, snuggling in to Tony.

Tony wrapped his arm around Sue's shoulders and pulled her closer towards him. Their eyes met – and then their mouths – their tongues interlocking in a long, languorous kiss.

Easing Tony to one side, Sue stretched out to pick up her wine glass. Slowly draining the contents, she held it out for a refill. As Tony was topping up her glass, she leaned across and breathed into his ear. 'Would sir prefer the bridle, or the three-line whip, tonight?'

'You choose.'

Tuesday 13 September

Having parked his car in the underground car park in Pitt Street, Charlie glanced up at the sky as he walked back up the steep ramp. There were a few high clouds scudding across in the light breeze, but the weather forecast he'd heard on the car radio on the way into the office wasn't too bad. Checking his watch, he saw that he had time to walk to Queen Street station and meet Tony, as arranged, at nine o'clock.

When he got to George Square, Charlie saw Tony waiting for him outside the Millennium Hotel. Having purchased their train tickets at a booth, Tony headed over to the AMT caravan in the middle of the concourse to pick up two coffees while Charlie went to WH Smith's to get a copy of The Herald.

They boarded the nine-fifteen train to Edinburgh.

'How did Mrs McVey react when you phoned her?' Charlie asked as they were settling down in their seats.

'Her initial reaction was blind panic when she thought her hubby would find out about what she and Gavin had been up to,' Tony said, 'but she calmed down when I explained that all we wanted to do was talk to her on her own.'

'Where is old man today?'

'He's on an offshore oil rig, apparently. Somewhere off Orkney.'

'With his secretary?'

'I didn't ask.'

'Probably wise.'

Leaning back in his seat, Charlie sipped at his coffee and flicked through the newspaper. Tony drank his coffee quickly, then dozed in his seat all the way through to Edinburgh.

As the train was pulling into Haymarket Station, Charlie folded his paper and nudged Tony in the ribs.

'Are you sure you're getting enough sleep?' Charlie asked pointedly.

'I'm only knackered because I've been working too hard recently,' Tony said, interlocking his fingers. Yawning wide, he stretched both arms high above his head.

'Aye, right!' Charlie grunted.

The sun was filtering through the high clouds when Charlie and Tony emerged from the station. Crossing the main road at the traffic lights, they walked up Palmerston Place, as far as Rothesay Place, before turning into the classical Georgian terrace.

The entrance to the McVeys' apartment was half way along the terrace. When Tony rang the doorbell, Sheila McVey activated the intercom. He announced their presence.

'It's the second floor,' she said as she buzzed to let them in.

'Why does nobody live on the ground floor these days?' Charlie complained as they walked up the two flights of stairs. Sheila was waiting for them on the landing. They showed her their warrant cards.

Taking a seat beside Tony on the red-leather, Chesterfield settee, Charlie took out his notebook.

'Before we begin, would you like something to drink?' Sheila offered. 'A cup of tea – or coffee?'

'No, thanks,' Charlie said, 'we had coffee on the train.'

Twisting her long hair round her fingers, Sheila sat down on the armchair opposite them.

'I realise this is a delicate matter, Mrs McVey,' Charlie stated, 'but we do need to ask you a few questions.'

Sheila nodded nervously.

'When we spoke on the phone, you told me it was Lesley Adams who initially put you in touch with Gavin Carter.'

'That is correct.'

'Are you aware that Lesley and Gavin are an item?' Tony interjected. 'Have been for some time.'

Sheila caught her breath. 'That can't be right,' she stammered. 'Lesley told me she was his social worker.'

'That was the case at the time she contacted you,' Charlie said. 'The situation has developed since then.'

Sheila clenched both her fists until her knuckles turned white. 'Gavin forgot to mention that,' she said quietly.

Charlie paused for a moment to let the information sink in. 'A murder was committed in Glasgow at ten-thirty on the evening of Saturday, the third of September,' he said, 'for which Gavin Carter is a person of interest. When we interviewed him, he gave us what turned out to be a fictitious account of his movements at the time the murder was committed. However, he has since changed his story and he now claims to have been here with you, on the date and time in question.'

'To substantiate his claim,' Tony interjected, 'he showed us a selfie he had on his phone of the two of you together.'

'The bastard!' Sheila hissed. 'He promised me he'd deleted that photo.' She started to blush furiously. 'I don't know what I was thinking about. It was my birthday and I'd had far too much to drink. I should never have allowed him to take it.'

'Be that as it may,' Charlie said, 'can you confirm that Gavin Carter was here, with you, on Saturday the third of September at ten-thirty in the evening?'

'Yes,' Sheila said. She looked down at her feet. 'Will my husband have to find out about this?' she asked quietly.

'He won't find out about it from us,' Charlie said.

'Thank you.'

'Fancy a bite to eat before we head back to Glasgow?' Charlie asked as he and Tony were walking back down Palmerston Place.

'That sounds like a good idea,' Tony said. 'I've been to the Mercat a couple of times. It does decent pub food – and it's not far from the station.'

'Lead on.'

After a bowl of minestrone and a cheese and ham sandwich in the Mercat, Charlie and Tony headed back to Haymarket Station where they caught the five-past three train to Queen Street.

'I have to say that Gavin does not bad for himself,' Tony commented as the train was pulling out. 'Not only did he manage to get a job with Mrs McVey's company, he got to screw the boss.'

'When I spoke to Mrs McVey on the phone, she told me she was a sleeping partner in the business,' Charlie said. 'She gives a whole new meaning to the term.'

Tony smiled.

'I was just thinking,' Tony mused as the train was gathering speed. 'Is the photo evidence Gavin showed us definitely conclusive?'

'What are you getting at?'

'Gavin knows his way around computers and smartphones. Is it possible that he might have doctored the date and time of the selfie on his phone?'

Charlie narrowed his eyes. 'You are not seriously asking me a technical question about a smartphone, are you? As you are very well aware, Tony, it's only in the past couple of months that I've mastered the basics of texting.'

'Let's suppose, for the sake of argument, that Mrs McVey had agreed to provide Gavin with an alibi for the time of Preston's murder,' Tony surmised. 'It could be that the selfie he showed us was taken on some other occasion – and Gavin found a way to alter the date and time of the photo on his phone.'

Charlie shook his head emphatically. 'That's a complete non-starter,' he stated.

'How can you be sure?'

'Think it through, Tony. It's plausible that Gavin could have persuaded Mrs McVey to provide him with an alibi – and he could've told her that he knew how to alter the date and time of a selfie on his phone. Whether or not that is technically possible, I haven't the foggiest idea. For now, let's suppose it is. Mrs McVey would realise that Gavin would have to show the selfie to the police to substantiate his alibi, so what do you think the chances are that she would have agreed to pose for a photo of herself, tits out, straddling Gavin and swigging champagne?'

'When you put it like that….'

'Mrs McVey didn't strike me as stupid. She'd know that, if push came to shove, any selfie she agreed to pose for might end up being used as evidence in court – to say nothing of the possibility of it being brought to the attention of her old man. Trust me. If Mrs McVey had agreed to be in a photo with Gavin in order to provide him with an alibi, you can bet your bottom dollar that it would have been a demure shot of her and Gavin sitting at a table in her flat, discussing a contract for designing a computer game.'

'So do you reckon Gavin is in the clear as far as Preston's murder is concerned?'

'It very much looks like it.' Charlie scratched at his bald head. 'But if that is the case, why did his uncle go to such great lengths to incriminate himself in order to set Gavin up with a fictitious alibi when he already had a rock solid one?'

'Search me. Do you think it's time we had another chat with Andy Carter?'

'You're beginning to read my thoughts, Tony. Who knows? We might make a detective of you yet.'

It was after five o'clock by the time Charlie and Tony arrived back in Pitt Street. When he went into his office, Charlie found a note from his secretary lying on his desk, telling him that Superintendent Hamilton wanted to see him as soon as he got back.

'I'd better go and see what's biting his lordship's arse,' Charlie said. 'I'll be as quick as I can. Wait for me here.'

Muttering under his breath, Charlie trudged up the flight of stairs at the far end of the corridor.

'What is the latest status on the Preston case?' Hamilton demanded as soon as Charlie walked into his office.

'It would appear that one of our prime suspects, Gavin Carter, is able to prove that he was in Edinburgh at the time the murder took place,' Charlie said.

'Where does that leave us?'

'There are other lines of enquiry that we will continue to pursue,' Charlie said.

'I have a meeting with the Chief Constable at noon tomorrow,' Hamilton said, shuffling the papers on his desk as he got to his feet. 'I'll need an update on the status at ten o'clock.'

It was after six o'clock by the time Charlie and Tony left the building and went down the stairs together to the underground car park.

'I'll drive,' Charlie said, using his remote to unlock his car. 'You can pick your car up later.'

Getting behind the wheel, Charlie drove slowly, through the rush hour traffic, to Maryhill.

Having climbed the stairs to Andy Carter's flat, Tony hammered on the door with his closed fist.

It was a full minute before Carter came to the door.

'What the hell's going on?' he demanded as he opened up.

'We didn't bother trying to ring your bell,' Charlie said as he and Tony stepped across the threshold. 'We heard on the news on the way across that the national bell strike is still ongoing.'

'What the fuck do you want now?'

'Come on through and we'll tell you all about it,' Tony said, closing the door behind him and leading the way along the corridor to the kitchen.

'This is harassment – to say nothing of trespass,' Andy complained as he followed along behind them. 'You can't barge in here like that without a warrant.'

'What do you think this is?' Tony said, taking out his notebook and waving it aloft.

'I suggest you cooperate with us, Carter,' Charlie stated.

'Why the hell should I?'

'Sit down and we'll tell you.'

Glowering, Andy Carter slumped down on a kitchen chair.

'First, let me tell you something that will be of interest to you,' Tony said. 'There's no point in you ordering another consignment of rusty nails for the time being, because your erstwhile business associate is going to be out of circulation for quite a while.'

Carter's eyes narrowed.

'But that's not the reason we're here tonight,' Tony continued. 'We're here because we want to know where you were, who you were with, and what you were doing at ten-thirty on the night of Saturday the third of September.'

'For fuck's sake! I've told you that a dozen times. What more do you want me to say?'

'How about the truth, for a change?'

'The truth is that I was in The Jaco, nailing Jack Mulgrew's hand to the bog door.'

'So far, so good. Who was with you?'

'My nephew, Gavin.'

Tony shook his head slowly from side to side. 'That's the wrong answer. Gavin was in Edinburgh on the night in question – shagging some bird.'

'That's complete and utter shite!'

'Not according to Gavin,' Tony said. 'He even has a selfie to prove it.' Andy's eyes narrowed, but didn't react. 'Apparently, it was the bird's birthday,' Tony continued. 'And, as befits the occasion, Gavin took a photo of them in their birthday suits, swigging champagne while they were humping. A touch of class there, don't you think?'

'I'm not falling for any of this crap,' Andy snarled. 'Do you think I was born yesterday?'

'I think maybe it's time you had a wee chat with Gavin,' Tony said, a smile playing on his lips. 'It you ask him nicely, he might even show the selfie. It's well worth a look – nice pair of tits.'

Lesley and Gavin were sitting side by side on the settee, watching an old film on television, when the doorbell rang.

'Are you expecting someone?' Gavin asked as he hit the freeze button on the remote control.

'No.'

Gavin dragged himself to his feet and went to the front door.

'Who is it?' he asked over the intercom

'I've got a delivery for Lesley Adams.' The male voice was high-pitched.

'It's the second floor,' Gavin said, buzzing him in.

Gavin opened the door of the flat and waited on the landing, his brow furrowing when he heard the sound of rapid footsteps running up the stairs. His jaw dropped when he saw the figure, brandishing a crowbar, charging towards him. Stepping back inside quickly, he slammed the door shut.

Shards of splintered glass showered into Gavin's face as the crowbar came crashing through the opaque glass panel in the door. A gloved hand reached inside and opened the Yale lock, then pushed the door open. As Gavin turned to run back along the hall, the hook of the flailing crowbar caught him round the ankles, causing him to fall flat on his face.

'What the fuck are you playing at?' Andy Carter screamed, throwing down the crowbar. Grabbing Gavin by the shoulders, he turned him onto his back.

'Leave him alone!' Lesley shouted as she ran out from the lounge, her closed fists hammering on Andy's back.

Andy shrugged her off and threw her across the hall, her head thumping off the far wall. 'Stay out of this, you daft cow. This has got fuck all to do with you.'

Andy knelt astride Gavin. 'Answer my question! What the fuck are you playing at?' Andy's right fist thumped into Gavin's forehead, splitting open his eyebrow. His left fist followed in quick succession, crunching into Gavin's nose and causing blood to spurt all over the hall carpet.

'I'm about to get banged up in Barlinnie, just because I wanted to give you an alibi – and all the time you were through in Edinburgh, shagging the arse of some randy wee bitch!'

Andy picked up his crowbar and held the pointed end inches from Gavin's eyes. 'I swear to God,' he growled, 'if you weren't my brother's boy, you'd be blind by now.' He slowly lowered the crowbar. 'What the fuck is going on, Gavin?'

'I just wanted to impress you, Andy,' Gavin whimpered as he struggled to sit up straight. 'When Stuart phoned me to let me know that Murdoch had been murdered, I thought it had to be you who had got him. That's why I hurried straight over to your place – to congratulate you. But when I found out that it wasn't you – and it wasn't my Dad, I told you it was me. I'd read in the papers all about what had happened to him, so I said I'd done it. I just wanted you to be proud of me, Andy. That's the God's honest truth. I never wanted you to give me an alibi. All along, I wanted to tell the polis that I was in Edinburgh with Stuart, but you wouldn't let me do that. The cops knew fine well I wasn't in the Jaco with you when you attacked Mulgrew. They told me they were going to charge me with Murdoch's murder,' Gavin wailed. 'I couldn't do anything else. I had to tell them I was in Edinburgh.'

Andy got to his feet slowly. 'You're a complete and utter fucking waste of space, Gavin.' Turning round, he slung his crowbar over his shoulder and strode out of the flat.

Her head spinning, Lesley got to her feet slowly.

'What's going on, Gavin?' she asked, offering him a handful of tissues to stem the blood that was seeping from his eyebrow and his nose.

'Andy didn't think the cops would believe me if I told them I was in Edinburgh with Stuart, so he made me go along with the story that I was with him in The Jaco at the time of Murdoch's murder.'

'That's not what I'm talking about. What I want to know is – what's going on with the randy wee bitch you were shagging?'

Gavin blushed furiously. 'It was nothing, Lesley. Honest.'

'Shagging the arse of her doesn't sound like nothing to me.'

'It was just someone at work,' Gavin mumbled.

'Who?' Lesley demanded.

'Sheila…,' Gavin stammered. 'Sheila McVey.'

'Sheila! For fuck's sake, Gavin! I arranged with Sheila for you to get a job – and the way you thank me is by screwing her!'

'I didn't mean it to happen – it just did.'

'Really? How often have you shagged her?'

'Christ, I don't know,' Gavin said, stuffing a tissue up his nose.

'Well, have a think about it. Was it once? Was it twice? Ten times? Twenty times?'

'I don't know, Lesley. Four times, I think. Maybe five.'

Lesley fixed Gavin with a glare. 'Where are you planning on spending the night?'

'It was nothing, Lesley,' Gavin pleaded. 'She doesn't mean anything to me.'

'And you don't mean anything to me, Gavin. Get out of my fucking sight. And I mean – right now!'

CHAPTER 28

Wednesday 14 September

Having summoned O'Sullivan, Renton and Freer for a nine o'clock briefing session, Charlie went to the vending machines to pick up a coffee. When he got to the incident room, he found them all waiting for him.

Charlie took the chair in the middle of the room. 'Okay, guys, let's go through the names one more time,' he said, pointing towards the list of suspects on the flipchart board.

'Terry and Andy Carter both have rock solid alibis,' Tony said, 'and it now appears that Gavin Carter is in the clear.'

'Mrs C. and her new man's alibi checked out,' Freer chipped in. 'They were definitely at a wedding in Carlisle on the evening of the third of September.'

'What about Malcolm Steel?' Renton asked.

'He spun us a yarn about being in the Ubiquitous Chip at the time of the murder,' Freer said, 'but it turns out that he was in the bar at the Citizen's theatre with his head teacher.'

'Lesley Adams was visiting her mother in a care home in Bearsden,' Charlie said, 'and Martin and Ronnie Gilligan were at a Boys' Brigade gymnastic display in Scotstoun.'

'So, if we're ruling out the Avenging Angel,' Tony said, stroking his chin reflectively, 'that only leaves us with Judge Ramsay. Could it be him? In fact, might he be the Avenging Angel?'

'Don't flog it, Tony,' Charlie growled.

'Has anyone got any bright ideas?' Charlie asked, looking round the room.

They all shook their heads.

Charlie glanced at the clock on the wall. 'In which case, it's time I broke the good news to Niggle,' he said as he struggled to his feet.

Charlie gave Superintendent Hamilton a detailed report on the status of the investigation.

'Where does that leave us?' Hamilton asked when Charlie had concluded.

'Everyone we had identified as a potential suspect has been eliminated from our enquiries.'

'Which means the murderer was either someone we know nothing about, who happened to be bearing a grudge against Preston,' Hamilton stated, 'or else our friend the Avenging Angel, or some other vigilante who found out that Preston and Murdoch were one and the same person and decided to take matters into his own hands.'

Charlie shook his head. 'I'm convinced this wasn't the work of a vigilante.'

'Why not?'

'We have compelling evidence to support the fact that the murderer was someone Preston knew.'

'What action are you proposing to take now?' Hamilton demanded.

'I intend to organise a re-enactment of the crime scene in Cottiers next Saturday at half-past ten in the evening, in the hope that it might provoke a response from a member of the public,' Charlie said. 'It's possible that it might jog somebody's memory.'

'That's a long shot,' Hamilton said.

'I accept that, but apart from launching another investigation into trying to establish the identity of the Avenging Angel, we don't have any other viable lines of enquiry to pursue.'

'Would that be a sensible use of resources?' Hamilton queried. 'You don't need me to remind you that if a suspect hasn't been identified within a week of a murder being committed, the chances of him or her being caught are dramatically reduced.'

'I realise that, but we have to do everything we can to nail the person responsible.'

'This year's budget cuts were savage, Anderson,' Hamilton stated. 'We have to set priorities. You ran up a big overtime bill a couple of years back when trying to identify the Avenging Angel – with nothing to show for it. How would you rate your chances of success this time?'

Charlie shrugged. 'Somewhere between remote and non-existent.'

'We can't afford to spend time and effort pursuing enquiries that aren't going anywhere. Besides, the press aren't stupid. If we tell them we're planning to do a re-enactment of the crime scene, they'll know we've run into a brick wall.'

'What do you suggest we do?'

'The media aren't hung up about Preston's killer being found. The public aren't baying for blood. Nobody believes that an innocent man was murdered. The majority of people think Preston was a paedophile who managed to get off on a dodgy not proven verdict – and then got what was coming to him.'

'Are you instructing me to drop the enquiry?' Charlie queried.

'Not as such. We can't tell the media we're abandoning the investigation after less than a fortnight. That wouldn't go down well. However, what we can say to them is that, although we haven't identified the murderer yet, we are pursuing several lines of enquiry – and leave it at that. They won't push it – and the public's interest in the case will drop off before too long. On the other hand, the recent influx of crystal meth is getting a lot of media attention. BBC Scotland are going to transmit a special programme about it tomorrow night. I had a status meeting with DI Cunningham yesterday and he doesn't seem to be making much headway, so that's where we need to focus our resources.'

'What do you want me to say to the team?'

'Tell them that, if any new evidence comes to light, they should follow it up. Otherwise, they shouldn't spend any more time on the Preston case.'

*

Charlie summoned O'Sullivan, Renton and Freer to join him in the incident room.

'The good news,' he said when they were all assembled, 'is that we no longer have to work twenty-four seven on the Preston murder. The bad news is that, unless new evidence comes to light, we will no longer be working on the case.'

'Why not, sir?' Freer queried.

'Recent budget cutbacks mean that we can't afford to allocate resources to pursuing cases where there is a low probability of achieving a result.'

'Not even murder cases?' Tony asked incredulously.

'Apparently not,' Charlie said.

'What do we tell the people involved in the case?' Tony asked.

'Leave that with me,' Charlie said. 'I'll let them know the score.'

CHAPTER 29

As arranged, Lesley Adams met up with her sister in the lounge bar of The Rock at seven o'clock.

'How are things with Gavin?' Myra asked as they stood at the end of the bar, waiting to get served.

'Who?'

'As bad as that?'

'Yep!'

'Any news about – ' Myra looked all around before whispering in Lesley's ear. 'About – you know what?'

'It looks like the police are going to call it a day,' Lesley said quietly. 'Anderson called me this afternoon. He told me, in confidence, that due to budget cutbacks they're not in a position to allocate resources to pursuing cases that aren't going anywhere. Apparently Preston's murder falls into that category. Officially the case will remain open, but the police won't be taking it any further unless new evidence crops up.'

'So be it,' Myra said with a shrug.

'I checked the entry in the Westerton registration book,' Lesley said. 'You did a very good job of imitating my handwriting.'

'I should hope so – I'd been practising it all week. I meant to ask you,' Myra added, 'do you want the auburn wig back?'

'I've got the real thing,' Lesley said, tossing her hair. 'You can keep the wig as a souvenir. By the way, that was a nice touch of yours,' she added, 'writing to the Daily Record.'

'Thanks – I was rather pleased with it myself.'

'My round, I think?' Lesley said with a smile.

'This calls for a celebration,' Myra said. 'Let's make it large ones tonight.'

'I'm up for that.'

Lesley waved across until she caught the barman's eye.

'A large glass of New Zealand Sauvignon blanc for my friend, please,' she called out. 'And a large Captain Morgan's for me – splash of water – no ice.'

Raising their glasses, they chinked them together. 'To Tommy!' Lesley said.

'And,' Myra added, chinking their glasses again, 'to his Avenging Angels!'